Praise for Cheryl Eager's
A KISS TO WAKE ME

"I really enjoyed this book. The story was emotionally engaging. In fact, I was so into it, I kept having to go back and add comments since I was that much into finding out what happened next. I really liked Cara and Jamie. How they acted through what can only be considered enormous stress felt genuine and honest." –Starred Review 5/5

"I thoroughly enjoyed reading A Kiss to Wake Me. Cheryl did an amazing job creating characters that are likeable, relatable, and have you rooting for them the entire book. I would recommend this to anyone who loves romance and enjoys young love." –Julie Schrader, editor at Bookworm Yogi

"The first few paragraphs of this novel drew me in and would not let me go till I knew the outcome. From start to finish, it was engaging, romantic, and suspenseful. A story of young love, love at first sight, and a cautionary tale, this was indeed a great read." –Early Reader Review

About Cheryl Eager

Cheryl Eager is the author of *A Kiss to Wake Me* and *When Two Stars Collide.*

"A Kiss to Wake Me," a modern-day love story. When Jamie and Cara first lock eyes in the high school cafeteria, "love at first sight" is no longer just a cliché to either of them. Fans of romantic first love and those who desire to see first love withstand seemingly insurmountable obstacles will enjoy this sweet, yet intense novel.

"When Two Stars Collide," a young adult romance about Cin, a half-Japanese handsome misfit who doesn't care what others think of him, and Henri, a beautiful but sheltered, anxiety-ridden, people-pleaser superstar. They have nothing in common—but when a chance meeting brings them together, sparks fly, although she has no idea of his secrets and who he really is! An unlikely journey of love in this edgy and fractured romance.

A former English teacher and current high school librarian, Cheryl Eager lives with her family outside of the Dallas/Fort Worth area. A Texas native, she graduated from Hardin-Simmons University in West Texas and earned her master's degree in library science from Texas Woman's University, both summa cum laude. Her publishing history includes having an op-ed column in the Fort Worth Star-Telegram.

Cheryl Eager's books carry a theme of love, hope, optimism, and overcoming tough obstacles—things our world needs! With themes of love, hope, overcoming, and optimism, Cheryl has people from around the world that contact her after feeling touched by something she wrote and/or thanking her for giving them a fresh perspective with her books.

Follow @Ceager4Life on Instagram and Twitter!

A KISS
TO WAKE
ME

CHERYL
EAGER

5310
PUBLISHING

FOR MORE BOOKS, GO TO
5310PUBLISHING.COM

A KISS TO WAKE ME

CHERYL EAGER

5310 PUBLISHING

Published by
5310 Publishing Company
5310publishing.com

Our books may be purchased in bulk for promotional, educational, or business use. Please contact your local bookseller or 5310 Publishing at sales@5310publishing.com.

A KISS TO WAKE ME ISBNs:
Kindle & Ebook: 978-1-990158-75-9
Hardcover: 978-1-990158-74-2
Paperback: 978-1-990158-73-5

Author: Cheryl Eager
Editor: Alex Williams (5310 Publishing)
Cover design: Eric Williams (5310 Publishing)

First edition (this edition) released in July 2022.

SCAN ME

Themes explored:
Narrative Themes: Love and relationships; Interior life;
Coming of age; Identity / belonging;
Teenage fiction: Relationship stories – Romance, love or friendship;
Teenage personal & social issues: teenage pregnancy;
Teenage fiction: School stories;
Teenage personal and social topics: Life skills and choices; First experiences and growing up; Friends and friendships; Dating, relationships, romance and love;

Subjects:
YOUNG ADULT FICTION
Romance / Contemporary
Coming of Age
Social Themes / Dating & Sex

For Scott, my high school sweetheart, my husband, the father of my children, and the fulfillment of my dreams.

After all these years, you're still the one.

911 Transcript

Dispatcher: *911, what is your emergency?*

Me: *Please, please help me, help me! I just had a baby, and, and, and... I don't know! Oh my God... I don't (yelling) UNDERSTAND! (Shuffling, muffled) Help me! Please help me!*

Dispatcher: *Okay, ma'am, stay on the line, and please calm down. Is the baby breathing?*

Me: *Yes, yes, it's a boy; he's breathing. He—he's so tiny! What do I do? I wasn't even pregnant! This is crazy! I don't—*

Dispatcher: *Ma'am, you need to stay calm and answer my questions. What is your address so I can get someone there to help you?*

Me: *(Hysterical) 4227 East Conrad, please, please...*

Dispatcher: *Okay, stay on the line so I can help you until paramedics arrive.*

Me: *Please hurry, help us!*

Dispatcher: *Paramedics are on their way. I'm going to give you some instructions now. Listen, you need to wipe the baby's nose and mouth. Do that for me now.*

Me: *(Shuffling) Okay, I'm doing that. (More shuffling) I used a washcloth. There's nothing on his mouth or nose.*

Dispatcher: *Is there anyone else in the house with you?*

Me: *No, no, I'm alone. My dad is at work. Please...*

Dispatcher: *They're on their way, ma'am. Is the baby full-term? How many months pregnant were you?*

Me: *I—I don't know... I wasn't pregnant! I didn't know I was pregnant... I don't—don't know how I could have been... I... hurry, hurry!*

Dispatcher: *Help is on the way, ma'am. I am going to stay on the phone with you until they arrive, but you have to calm down, okay? Do I hear the baby crying? Is that what I hear?*

Me: *Yes, he is crying a little. He's trying to open his eyes...*

Dispatcher: *Listen to me, you need to wrap him up to keep him warm. Can you do that?*

Me: *Okay, yes, I'm wrapping him in a towel. He's wet. I'm going to dry him off... (crying hysterically) I—I had to take him out of the toilet... I—I—I thought I was sick... and he, he just came out... I don't understand... How did this happen?*

Dispatcher: *Okay, calm down now. What's your name?*

Me: *(Muffled) Cara... Cara Dawson, and I'm really bleeding. Oh, God, please!*

Dispatcher: How old are you, Cara?

Me: *I'm eighteen. Shhh—it's okay, baby, it's okay... Do I need to do something... do I need to cut the cord or anything? It's still in me. Ouch, it hurts...*

Dispatcher: *No, no, don't do anything with the cord. Wait for the paramedics. Until they get there, place a towel between your legs where you are bleeding, okay? Can you do that?*

Me: *Okay, I did that.*

Dispatcher: *You're doing great, Cara. Is the address you gave me your permanent residence?*

Me: *Yes, I'm at my house.*

Dispatcher: *Where is your location in the house now?*

Me: *I'm in the bathroom; I'm sitting on my bathroom floor.*

Dispatcher: *How is the baby doing? Is he still breathing?*

Me: *He's breathing. He's not crying now, but... Oh, oh, I hear sirens.*

Dispatcher: *Good, good. Is your front door locked?*

Me: *Yes, it... it probably is... My dad locks it when he leaves for work.*

Dispatcher: *All right, Cara, I don't want you to move. Stay right where you are, and I will advise Fire and EMS to go ahead and gain entry through the locked door. (Dispatches instructions to the fire department arriving on scene)*

Me: *Okay, thank you, oh, thank you...*

Dispatcher: *You're going to be just fine, Cara. As soon as you see the firefighters and paramedics, you can end this call, okay?*

(Loud noise of the front door being forced open and a shout, "Paramedics!")

End of call to Dispatch.

Cara

Seven months earlier

It's the end of lunch hour, and I'm sitting at a table with my friends in the noisy high school cafeteria, our usual midday milieu. I surreptitiously yawn behind my hand as Jessica tells yet another one of her stories—correction, snoozefests—and I dream of being anywhere else but here. This one is a whine about being forced to do the bulk of the work for her English class group project because no one wants to pull their own weight, blah, blah, blah.

My mind decides to rescue me and take me for a stroll across a thick forest floor at daybreak... *Yes, much better.* A cool mist burns off with the rising sun, and I mentally crunch soft pine needles under my feet.

As she drones on, I smile and nod my head while slipping easily back into my daydreams. This time, I trek across the sugary sands of the Texas Gulf Coast, each footstep feeling like warm fingers massaging my insteps. Large waves lap the shore like a famished mouth... and... oh... oh, wow, just... *wow!*

Who the heck is that?

A tall guy I've never seen before walks through the cafeteria entrance alone. I blink rapidly several times to make certain he isn't an apparition conjured by my daydreaming. No, I suppose not, because he is motioned over by one of my best friends, Eric Baines, to join us.

I assume he's a new student, but from a distance, this guy looks older, more mature than the usual fare at Oak Creek High School. *Maybe he's a plant sent by the feds to infiltrate the student body and break up a drug ring or something,* I half-seriously quip to myself. My throat instantly turns to sawdust as he approaches our table.

"Hey, guys, this is Jamie Gallagher, a senior, and it's his first day. He moved here from California. I helped him get checked in this morning during my office-help period," Eric introduces him.

With my first up-close glimpse of the new student, I am stunned and allow myself a two-second visual sweep to catalog his appearance. He is anything and everything my dream guy would be—tall, broad-shouldered and muscular, with dark, slightly unruly hair, a nice tan, and a bit of oh-so-attractive facial stubble. When it's too apparent I'm staring, mouth agape and all, I quickly close it and return my attention to my food.

"Hi, Jamie." Jessica bats her lash extensions like a gif character minus the hearts pulsing from the top of her head. "You can sit by me," she says too enthusiastically. She scoots over, practically crushing everyone else beside her to make room on the bench for Jamie's large frame.

That she finds him as hot as I do doesn't surprise me in the least, and I figure it will be only a matter of days before the pair is christened the best-looking couple in school. Jessica usually gets anything she wants, and the excitement on her face over the new guy is clear. Hell, both of their names even begin with J— how perfect is that?

I don't like the emotion of envy I feel toward Jessica and her carefree gregariousness. I stuff the feeling down into an emotional box labeled *To Throw Away* and close the lid tightly, waiting for her next flirtatious comment.

But I'm not at all expecting what Jamie does next and, frankly, it shocks the crap out of me. While I'm busy looking over at Jessica, inwardly rolling my eyes at her, I glance up to catch Jamie looking at me, watching *me* and no one else.

He looks into my eyes with a hint of something like surprised recognition. *Does he think he knows me?* He smiles broadly and speaks in a rich bass, "Thanks, but," still looking at me intently, he says just above a whisper, "I think I'll sit right here," and points toward me at the space beside me.

The sudden drop in the lowest part of my stomach when our eyes connect is a sensation completely new and foreign to me. It's as though our gazes—separate, stable elements in and of themselves—instantaneously fuse to create some type of combustion. The power of it is incredible and rattles me like window glass after an explosion. If I brought Jamie with me into AP Chemistry on our next lab day for show-and-tell, my teacher would be *very* impressed.

Of course, there have been guys I've found attractive before now, and I've had my share of boyfriends. However, none have come close to giving off the powerful vibe resulting from my first look into the disarming eyes of Jamie Gallagher.

As I mentally explore the fierce energy this total stranger is generating, he sits down right next to me. Right. Next. To. *Me*. The pulse in my neck is thump-thump-thumping in rapid succession, as it frantically taps out a message to Jamie in Morse code: *"WON'T LIKE CARA. TOO SHY."*

My outward response belies the intimidation I feel in Jamie's proximity. I have to be polite, right? So ignoring my usual taciturn nature, I turn to face him, smile tremulously, and say, "Welcome, Jamie, I'm Cara Dawson."

"Nice to meet you, Cara," he takes his time saying my name as though he is tasting it in his mouth... and savoring each syllable. The deep reverberation of Jamie's voice dispatches marching rows of goosebumps across my skin, invading every inch of my forearms. His smile, a beautiful set of white, even teeth, causes my stomach to do some kind of weird gymnastics again. He reaches for my hand, his light blue eyes never leaving mine as we shake. His touch emits sparks and should come with a high voltage warning. I have to look away. I can't handle the intensity of his gaze—the way he's making my insides melt like chewing gum on a hot Texas sidewalk.

He is *beautiful*.

Everyone else at the table makes introductions, and I've lost any urge to finish my lunch. While I push around the last of my green beans with my fork, I listen to the questions from the others and to Jamie's responses:

"Are you going to eat?" This question comes from Eric. "The food here sucks, but there's a snack line." Eric, with his long, almost flaxen hair, looks more the stereotypical surfer dude from California than Jamie.

There was a time when Eric would have jumped at the chance for me to be his girlfriend, but having grown up with him, he's more like a doting brother to me. Eric and I have only ever done things together in groups, like movies and watch parties or just hanging out at one of the gang members' houses. ("Gang" in the most non-L.A. sense of the word; think more a neighborhood treehouse gang.)

We have a lot of fun together, and I'm comfortable around Eric, yet there's not any kind of spark there with him. I've thought about what it would be like to kiss him as a sort of test of my feelings, but the thought leaves me with an awkward feeling rather than any excitement. I'm certain I was just a passing fancy for him when he entered puberty and I would catch him looking longingly at me. He's sweet to me, but there has never been anything more between us than friendship.

"Nah." Jamie shakes his head, biting his full lower lip in the most fascinating way. "I'm good. I don't think there's enough time now." He looks up at a clock on the cafeteria wall.

"What brought you to Texas from California? What part of California?" Mark Shelton asks, with his perfect bright smile against flawless skin of rich espresso.

"We moved from a suburb of L.A. for my father's business. He's expanding his company into more states, and Texas is one of them." Jamie then adds, "We've been here about a week."

He looks in turn at everyone while he speaks. His entire demeanor is so smooth, so cool, I feel as though he's hypnotizing me, placing me under some type of love spell.

Jessica bats her eyelashes again and leans forward toward Jamie, who now sits across the table from her. Arms squeezed together, she baits his gaze to move lower to her boobs, but he doesn't even nudge the hook, much less bite.

"How do you like it here so far?" Jessica's question is more like, *how do you like* me *so far?*

Pathetic.

I'm normally somewhat repelled by Jessica's type, but she, Eric, and I have been best friends since kindergarten, so I tolerate her more out of obligation than any deep camaraderie. She's the type of friend you outgrow but keep around anyway because of all the history. Beneath the superficiality, though, she's loyal, and that goes a long way these days. Our main conversations skim the surface of the latest Hollywood gossip, social media posts, popular songs and movies, or the latest fashions and makeup tips.

Not that I don't care about makeup and wearing fashionable clothes, or that I don't try to look good; I do. But I'd like to think I spend more time on my character than on my appearance or living up to Hollywood's standards. Come on, why would I spend fifty dollars to have someone blow-dry my hair for me or twice that amount for someone to glue eyelashes to lashes I already have?

Jamie looks at Jessica only briefly. "I like it. A lot of people are moving from California to Texas, and I can see why. The wide-open spaces here are incredible—very different from what I'm used to. Also, it's nice to drive to a busy store or restaurant and actually find somewhere to park." His laugh is a quiet, deep rumble, like distant thunder before a rain.

I grasp for more courage to speak up. "True, but California is so beautiful, and the beaches there are much better than the Texas coast."

Jamie turns his head slightly in my direction and being so close to him now, our gazes lock with no key to be found. My heart karate chops my rib cage.

After a beat, he blinks rapidly, as though he's thrown off as much as I am. "I hope to take a road trip this summer and check out the Gulf Coast. Until then, I can't wait to enjoy some cooler weather, to experience at least a little of all four seasons. I've had enough of the constant warm weather in SoCal, hardly any variety at all."

I envision Jamie walking across the sand with one of those beach pop songs playing in the background, him wearing only board shorts, headed out into the Pacific waves with a surfboard tucked under his arm. My own personal wave builds and breaks in my stomach.

"But our summers can get pretty stifling," I say, realizing people really do chat it up about the weather when they're not sure what else to talk about; or, in my present case, fear of embarrassing themselves. *How lame, Cara.*

"I can handle the heat," Jamie seems to intend the double entendre, eyes remaining tethered to mine, "and even though it doesn't get as cold as it does farther north, I look forward to a Christmas break that actually feels like, well, Christmas." There's that deep laugh again flowing so easily from him, buttery smooth.

Yeah, Jamie's definitely got it going on.

Mesmerized, all I can do is nod attentively as he speaks. I peel his words like a perfectly ripe banana and eat them for dessert. His eyes are clearly visible now that he's sitting so close to me. They're the lightest of blue with golden specks in the center, making them look ethereal, almost otherworldly—simply amazing. I have to swallow hard and look away, again.

Coward.

Eric asks another question, which, thankfully, shifts Jamie's attention away from me, "Where will you go to college after we break outta here?"

When Jamie shrugs, Eric channels his inner control-freak and advises Jamie as if he's the supreme authority on higher education, "You don't have long to decide with only a few months until graduation. Texas does have some of the best universities, though, and there are a lot of local community colleges around here to choose from."

"So I've heard, but when I'm not at school, I'm apprenticing with my dad to prepare to take over the family business... eventually anyway." Jamie then promptly adds, "Not that I won't go to college at all, ever, but I plan to take a gap year and work with him full time starting this summer. He can really use the help with his new start-up here in Texas."

His cool-as-the-California-surf presence is refreshing among our little group, and I allow it to splash all over me because Lord knows I could use a cool down about now.

Eric starts to ask Jamie what type of business his dad owns, but the bell rings, signaling the end of lunch. Jessica blurts, "We always sit right here at this table, so we'll see you again tomorrow?" She tosses her silky, raven hair over her right shoulder and flashes him one of her *aren't-I-beautiful* smiles.

Ugh.

However, when Jamie stands to leave the table, he looks at me, not Jessica; again, it's as if his gaze possesses some kind of curious ability to see past my flesh and bones straight into me. It's both unnerving and exciting.

I sense my cheeks flush with heat when he says directly to me, "I'll sit here again tomorrow, then. See you." He watches me. Waiting?

"Yeah, cool, see you," I stammer and can't contain a smile.

There's a flash of relief behind his eyes right before he winks at me. He then returns my smile as he moves to leave. God, his smile! There's another eruption inside of me turning my blood to molten lava. Exhilaration from his attentiveness rushes all the way to my toes, and I'm equal parts euphoric and confused.

What the hell just happened between the two of us?

As we move away from the table, Jessica sidles up to me with her bottom lip jutting out. "You made quite an impression on the new guy. Did you notice how he stared at you the entire time?" she whines with an edge of unmasked disdain.

She looks me up and down as if assessing what in the world I have that she doesn't, which causes me to consider the same. Why *did* Jamie seem to pay attention only to me? If animals, at some base level, truly imprint on other animals to be their mates, it's close to what Jamie was doing to me each time his eyes held mine. *Or, at least I hope he was.*

I rush to my sixth-period class and find myself thinking about Jamie for the rest of the afternoon. Not simply because he's beautiful, but because there is something that happened between us I can only describe as (yeah, sounds totally cliché) an instant connection, like the victorious final snap of my puzzle cube I've never been quite able to solve.

A couple of girls whisper together in class, "Did y'all see the new boy?" and "Omigosh, he's such a hottie!"

At this point, I have trouble thinking of Jamie as the new "boy" at school. He definitely looks like more of a man than most of the other guys do here. And he's a man I would love to get to know, a man I most certainly don't want to be interested in Jessica Ramos.

Did Jamie feel anything close to what I was? Maybe he's just your quintessential flirt and I'm making much more of it than what it is. Although I can't help replaying his eyes looking into mine—his smile, his wink. Has any guy *ever* winked at me?

I've seen—and had—my share of boys who pursue a girl based on some sort of "cuteness" quotient, which, sure, is instinctual and normal *initially*, but that's as far as it ever goes with some of them. They don't care if she's intelligent or independent or sharp-witted, don't care to truly know her. Their only concern is what she has to offer *them*, period—uh, no thanks.

I can already tell Jamie runs deeper than that. I could see it in his eyes and demeanor. If so, he would be the total package, might be exactly the kind of guy I've been holding out for. My gut assumption is that Jamie doesn't swim in the shallow end of the surf, and I would love the chance to dive in with him and explore just how deep he goes. If I were blowing out birthday candles today, that would be my one wish.

I find myself so curious about him, I can't stand it. Will he pursue the chance to get to know me? If he does, will he like the real Cara Dawson? Was it truly a real connection between us today, or simply my near-womanhood hormones going haywire... or my own wishful thinking?

My father has reminded me more than once of the adage, "If it seems too good to be true, Cara, it probably is."

Well, Jamie definitely seems too good to be true.

Jamie

t's Monday, and I haven't been looking forward to starting a new school, but knowing this is my final year of high school makes it bearable. I *am*, however, looking forward to remaining anonymous at a new school, to become lost in the crowd while biding my time until graduation. I've always loved to read anything I can get my hands on, and schoolwork comes fairly easy for me, especially math, so no worries there.

My plan is to go to all my classes, get my work done during class, and pretty much ignore everyone; because, number one, I don't really care to forge new friendships, and two, I don't have time to. Besides, many of the students have probably gone to school with one another since they started, with cliques as solid as granite. I'm sure they feel the same way I do about trying to make new friends at this point. My goal is to get through my senior year and move on to bigger and better things.

My morning classes go better than I expected. The teachers here so far are good, and the students seem to respect them more than the students did at my school back in Cali. It's time for lunch, and I plan to duck into the library every day until the lunch period is over. As long as I eat breakfast, I'll skip lunch and eat as soon as I leave school. I have an "off" period during the last period of the day and can leave after my last class.

But, while sitting in the library skimming through a copy of *White Fang* I retrieved from the classics shelf, the librarian strolls over smiling to introduce herself. "Hi, there, I'm Mrs. Easton. I don't believe I've met you. Are you new here?" She seems awfully young to be a librarian, but what do I know?

"Yes, ma'am," I say, "first day. I'm Jamie Gallagher."

When I tell her I'm here for my lunch period, she explains that students can't be in the library during lunch and must go to the cafeteria. "Sorry, it's a school rule, and I have to enforce it or else there would be a hundred or more students in the library every lunch period and no room for classes to conduct business," she explains in a cheerful tone.

It seems like a legit rule, so I thank her, return the book to the shelf, and make my way to the cafeteria to spend the remainder of the lunch period.

As I walk, I think about my school back in Cali. In addition to my best friend, Matt, I already miss the friends I left behind. I was well-liked and somewhat popular at school whether I cared to be or not—which I didn't—but I was still not as upset about leaving my school as my younger sister Amber was. Basically, school in California this year wasn't going that great for me, and

I knew in a few months when everyone began college, we would all be dispersed anyhow.

Last year, my junior year, was a good one, mainly because I love basketball and was a starter for our team. I spent most of my spare time shooting hoops in the driveway or playing with a group of kids on the basketball courts at a nearby park. At the time, playing ball was important to me.

Coach Maxwell affectionately gripped my shoulder and gave it a firm squeeze on the first day of school. "Jamie, looking forward to seeing what you're going to do for us out on that court again this year."

Guilt clamped my throat shut.

I'd already decided over the summer, while I worked the family industrial coatings business with my dad, that I wasn't going to play this year. It totally pissed off Coach Maxwell and Coach Simmons when I finally mustered the courage to tell them. I tried to explain to them that my dad was training me in the business and that he needed my help almost every day after school, yet they didn't listen or want to understand.

Simmons even called my dad and lectured, "What's this about Jamie not playing ball this year? He's got talent and has the rest of his life to work, but he doesn't have the rest of his life to be a kid. Please don't take that from him."

No amount of my dad's and my explaining that learning the business was what was more important for my future could convince them I was doing the right thing. Hell, it wasn't like I was going to go on to play ball nationally or even in college.

Helping my dad after school is what I *want* to be doing at this point in my life, more than playing ball or anything else. I got tired of seeing their disappointed looks every day. Seems to me they cared a lot more about winning than they cared about the players as actual people; however, losing a 6′3″ starter was a significant blow. Also, I was a big reason we won last season so there *is* that. Sure, I'll miss playing basketball, but it took up too much time—wouldn't be there to play with my old team now anyway.

When I enter the cafeteria, I'm relieved to see Eric, the kid who helped me with my schedule this morning and who showed me around the school, wave me over to sit at his table.

He introduces me, and I'm surprised he remembers both my first and last name. I look around enough to see five or six sitting at the table when I'm immediately asked by a cute, dark-haired girl to sit by her.

Before I can even think about it, my eyes fall on the most beautiful girl I've ever seen, no exaggeration. In all of two seconds, I take in her long, corn-silky hair and creamy skin, her large, dark eyes and full lips—simply a beautiful face from which I can't look away.

She must sense I'm staring at her because she looks at me then, and our eyes slam into each other—BAM! It's like the instant the ball connects with the bat, or the three-pointer swishes through the net. The very second she looks up and fixes her doe-eyes on me, instant and intense attraction steals my breath. All my senses are on red alert.

Remarkable.

It's as though I *feel* her!

Does she feel it too, this, this... whatever it is? Time pushes pause. I'm suspended in mid-air waiting to be dropped back into reality. I can't look away from her, afraid the spell will be broken. I don't want to lose this feeling because it feels crazy good.

All these emotions from looking into the eyes of a beautiful stranger? *What the literal hell here, Jamie?* I'm Odysseus, suddenly entranced by the call of a Siren.

I pull it together enough to awkwardly mumble something. Pointing to where I want to sit, I walk around the table and sit beside the beauty I have this instant crush on. I glance over and see the disappointment on the brunette girl's face, but I don't give her another thought because the one I now sit beside holds my full attention.

She smiles and speaks first, "Welcome, Jamie, I'm Cara Dawson." She shakes my hand, shyly lowering her gaze. Hearing my name on her lips feels shockingly intimate. There is that jolt again, threatening to undo me when our hands touch—an electrical charge zinging between us like a pinball bouncing from bumper to bumper. The lilt of her voice and the way she says "I'm" reveal her faint Texas accent.

Adorable.

Closer to her now, I'm captivated by the slight smile on her lips and inquisitive look in her more-brown-than-green hazel eyes. There's some type of question there. I'm instantly fascinated with her, intrigued by the effect she's having on me. Does she also feel whatever this current is flowing between us?

Damn, and there you have it, the best-laid plans and all that BS.

So much for ignoring everyone at school and showing up every day as a means to an end, ha! I'll look forward to coming to school every day if it means I get to see her. After making introductions and answering the questions of why I moved to Texas, I focus only on Cara and what she has to say to me. We are able to talk only briefly before the bell rings to return to class.

I'm tempted to pull a let's-get-out-of-here line from the movies, ask Cara to ditch school and go with me somewhere to talk to get to know one another. I would do it in a heartbeat... but wouldn't she think I was crazy? What if she has a boyfriend? My heart sinks at the thought and causes me all the more to want to see Cara again soon, to get to know her—hell, to steal her away from a guy if need be. That's how strongly I feel.

As I stand to leave, the dark-haired girl, Jessica, says, "We all sit at the same table every day."

I tell them I'll see them tomorrow, but I look solely at Cara. I only care whether or not I see *her* tomorrow.

"Yeah, cool, see you," Cara assures me while still holding my gaze and smiling.

Her smile is like a bright light shining directly into my heart. Within just a few minutes of meeting her, I am completely taken by this beautiful girl named Cara. Never have I felt so attracted to someone. I'm absolutely screwed.

But it feels so damn good, I'm rolling with it.

When my parents ask Amber and me at dinner how our first day of school went, I tell them it went really well, which it did. They see I'm smiling and seem satisfied, and I let Amber be the one to talk about her day in detail.

In truth, I want to get my dad alone and tell him about Cara, kind of try to get a sense of what he thinks about me being so radically drawn to a girl I've only just met and talked with for all of five minutes.

Maybe he can help me put my feelings into perspective. He might tell me to chalk it up to your average schoolboy crush, but it's more than that. If what I've felt upon meeting the few girlfriends I've had in the past was equivalent to a 3.2 California tremor on the Richter Scale, then this is a 9.9 that has totally rocked my world.

After we finish our dinner, Amber and I pitch in to load the dishwasher. My dad retreats to his office, so I give him a few minutes to work before I go in.

Since my older sister Megan, who is still in Cali attending college, wants no part of the "boring" business, as she calls it, this role falls to me. Over the last couple of years, my dad and I have become more like friends and partners in business than father and son, so this works for both of us. We do almost everything together, and now that we work together, we've gotten even closer.

We're able to talk about anything; nothing is off-limits. I don't understand the kids I've heard say they hate their parents, but then there really isn't anything to hate about either of mine.

I especially don't understand how a father could leave his family and make his kids grow up without him the way my best friend Matt's dad did. He came home when Matt was only a baby and told Matt's mom he was leaving. "I'm just not cut out to be a father," he had said according to Matt's mom, and then his dad just walked away from them, forever.

Asshole.

Every time Matt spent the weekend or any amount of time with my family, he'd jokingly ask my parents, "When are you guys going to adopt me? You better hurry before I get too big to cuddle." The sad thing is, I could see behind Matt's eyes that he meant it.

Family is pretty much everything to me, even more to me than my friends, now that we've moved. I suppose I don't understand how Matt's dad could have left him because my own parents ever doing anything remotely similar is as alien to me as flying a spaceship. I wish a part of me could have stayed in California to look after Matt, make sure he will be all right without us.

After I knock and go into our home office, my dad takes one sidelong glance at me and asks, "What's on your mind?"

I sit down in the chair across from his desk, pick up a commemorative baseball from its stand on a shelf, and toss it from hand to hand. He spins around to face me, lacing his fingers behind his head and crossing his right leg slightly over his left. It's his usual listening stance, letting me know he's all ears.

"So," I begin, realizing I'm a little nervous to talk about it, "I met this girl today in the cafeteria at school—Cara." I wait for his response.

He smiles, raising both eyebrows. "Aaand?" he draws out.

"Well, she's gorgeous," one side of my mouth involuntarily quirks upward, and without a beat, I add, "but it's not only that; there was, uh, something that happened when we looked at each other, something huge." I'm not doing my emotions justice with my inadequate words and finish trying. "Anyway, I sat beside her at lunch and hope to again tomorrow."

"Do you know anything about her? Did you get to talk with her?"

"That's what's so weird. We didn't get much time to talk at all; it was just these looks that passed between us and these feelings that were stirred. It's like we couldn't take our eyes off each other."

Shaking my head, I continue, "I've never experienced anything like it. I'm almost positive she felt it, too. At least, I hope so." I waggle my eyebrows. "Have I gone off the rails here, Dad? Should I be this crazy about a girl I've only just met and know almost nothing about?"

My dad chuckles, and I inwardly cringe, waiting for him to make light of what I'm saying, but he doesn't. "It sounds very much like what happened the first time I laid eyes on your mom,

Jamie. It took her a little longer to come around, but it's what some people might call 'love at first sight.' Of course, it's way too early to tell anything like that, but you never know, it could turn out to be."

Dad's expression changes to thoughtful. "This is where I should probably begin a lecture on how you're still too young to get overly serious with a girl, but," there's a long pause as he looks closely at me, "you're smart. I suggest you get to know her and see where it goes. Only time will tell."

I'm more than a little relieved he doesn't invalidate my feelings for Cara, yet I still have a niggle of uncertainty. "You think she felt it too, though, right? Would I have been so attracted to her if she wasn't feeling it as well?"

"You said you both couldn't take your eyes off of each other." He sort of grins knowingly. "If you ask me, that's confirmation she's at least interested in you." He stops and looks more solemn. "But I don't want you to be too disappointed if you find out she isn't."

"Honestly, Dad, I know I sound crazy again, but I would be *really* disappointed."

I thank him for talking to me about Cara and move to leave. He gives my thigh a quick, firm clap and says, "Good luck, Son. Maybe we'll get to meet Cara soon," and offers me a reassuring smile.

Cara

The next morning, Tuesday, I awaken easily, no need to snooze or use a second alarm like I usually do. Not today, because it takes only an instant after I wake for Jamie's face to flash behind my eyelids. My heart rate quickens with the anticipation of seeing him again. I spring from my bed and rush to the kitchen for coffee, knowing a fresh pot will be waiting like it is every morning.

My father, a habitual early riser, will have finished his two cups of coffee, read his newspaper, and be ready to leave for work when I roll out of bed. If I sleep later, he knows not to bother me, but I enjoy the mornings when we're able to say goodbye to one another.

Like clockwork, I'm pouring a cup of hot coffee when he appears in the kitchen to rinse out his mug. He kisses me on the forehead. "Make it a great day, sweetheart," his usual mantra.

It's only my dad and me now that my mom has been gone for over four years. She was a mother any kid would want to have, and she married a great man who has turned out to be the best single father to me, like the wonderful father described in a classic book we're reading in AP English. I find myself testing the similitude of boys I meet against Dad's example. Not that guys around my age should be what my father is at his age with all his years of experience and wisdom, but I try to make the comparison based on a guy's future potential.

Very few come even close.

If given the chance to know Jamie better, I can't help but wonder how he will stack up against the expectations such a good father has taught me to have of boys. I wonder if my dad would approve of him? This triggers more questions about Jamie: What is *his* family like? Does he have both his parents? Does he have brothers or sisters? Pets? Has he suffered loss like I have? How can it be that after only an initial encounter with Jamie, I am dying to know more about him?

I retreat to my bathroom to get ready for school and feel the caffeine from the rich morning coffee do its magic. I start the shower, and while the water warms, I examine my face in the mirror. There is some sort of new gleam in my eye, a new excitement born yesterday, the very moment I met Jamie and felt that intense current flow between us.

It's as if my shower rinses away the doubts I've had about Jamie's interest in me. I keep picturing the way he looked at me, the way he chose *me* to sit beside; and, of course, I can't forget the stomach flutters when he pinned me with his penetrating gaze. The attraction was seemingly reciprocated from what I could discern behind Jamie's gorgeous ocean blues. My heart beats quicker in anticipation to find out.

Invigorated after the coffee and shower, I wrap my hair in a towel and begin to get ready for the day. I work to apply a subtle amount of makeup so it won't appear I'm trying too hard to impress. Yet I do want to look good today, which happens to be more than I've cared about my appearance in a long time.

I'm reminded of my short stint in the goth-girl phase after my mom died. I was pissed that God took her, and with my dad, the pastor of our church, being kind of equivalent to God in my finite fourteen-year-old mind, I took it out on him—not speaking to him for the most part and only snapping at him when I did. I drew dark liner all around my eyes and painted my nails black, but all in all, it was a pretty pathetic attempt at being dark, lasting little more than a few weeks. The eyeliner seemed to gradually fade right alongside my inner anger until they were both just... gone.

I take that memory, fold it neatly, and return it to the emotional box delicately embossed with the label *A Daughter's Sadness*. No dark eyeliner this morning, but a little more mascara than usual emphasizes my large eyes. I apply some light, shimmery gloss to lips I have always considered too large for my face and am satisfied.

After drying my hair and leaving it long and loose, I choose my favorite jeans and pair them with a periwinkle top and brown boots. I move to the full-length mirror hanging outside of my closet door. Turning, I try to see myself with fresh eyes, the way Jamie will see me today. The semi-tight shirt accentuates my full breasts. I look lower over the length of my long legs—a curvy, yet well-proportioned body.

When I complained recently about my "big booty" to Jessica, she simply shrugged and said, "So, you've got some junk in your trunk, but it's some pretty good junk if you ask me."

I guess I could be considered beautiful by someone who likes my bolder features; my dad tells me I am anyway. I usually chide myself when I compare myself to petite Jessica or any other girl. Beauty is in the eye of the beholder, or whatever. Yet today, I just might rival the beauty of Jessica, even though I'm the antithesis of her darker, Hollywood-type facial features. Maybe Jamie likes me the way I am. Maybe I'm exactly his type.

Ready before the usual time to leave for school, I step outside, lock the front door, and head to my car. It's nearing the end of October and still pretty warm, even in the mornings, but it won't be long before cooler weather makes its appearance, usually around Halloween here in Fort Worth.

I live less than a mile from the school, and the drive takes the same amount of time to listen to a song on the radio. I park my used car I received for my eighteenth birthday last month into my reserved parking spot.

Seniors are given the opportunity to pay for the space and paint it to make it their own during their last year of high school, which is what I did. My dad even helped me with it over the summer. It's an enormous sunflower painted in bright yellows and greens, two of my favorite colors, with the words *Carpe Diem* written in large letters underneath—a nice welcome every weekday morning when I pull into the school parking lot.

I rush into the building for no other reason than the hope of seeing Jamie somewhere in the halls before school begins. No such luck, though, and my morning classes crawl by, especially second-period AP English. It's my favorite class, but it takes me about half the time to do my work than most of the students in the class. This gives me time to think about Jamie and anticipate seeing him at lunch.

I sneak out my phone and search his name on social media, but I don't find him. I wish we had at least one class together, but it's a big school, and I guess I'll have to wait patiently every day for our lunch period to see him.

When lunchtime finally arrives, I waste no time walking to the cafeteria, and there he is. The remarkable thing is that I *sense* Jamie first rather than actually see him. I look toward the table where I sit every day but am suddenly drawn to turn and look to my left. He's walking into the cafeteria opposite the side I enter, watching me.

He smiles and simultaneously hitches his chin in a quick nod of acknowledgment when our eyes meet. *Oh. My. Gosh!* I return his smile with one I'm sure will remain permanently plastered to my face when I'm in Jamie's presence, and I meet him at the table.

I set down my backpack in my usual spot and feel bold enough to address him first. "Hey there! You liked school so much yesterday, you decided to come back today?"

"Yup," arms crossed, kind of rocking back and forth on his heels, he leans in closer to my ear and flirts, "but there are some things about this school I like more than others." He raises one eyebrow and grins.

My stomach does a perfect backflip.

His tall presence and confidence make me feel something I can't quite pinpoint. Jamie seems so settled into himself. It's like he is sure and confident enough for the both of us, and I don't feel as shy or anxious in his presence today as I thought I might. He feels as comfortable as sinking into a hot bath when I'm shivering with cold—warm, calm, safe.

Jamie looks toward the food lines forming. "Unfortunately, I'm going to have to try the school food today and see if it's as bad as they say it is. I'm starving."

"You need to hurry and get in line then if you want to beat the crowd," I urge.

"Let's go!" He motions for me to follow him. I do, not caring which food line he chooses as long as I get to be with him.

He makes his way to the pizza line, but in my excitement of seeing him again, I absentmindedly forgot to grab money from my backpack.

"Crap," I say, "save my place in line; I'll be right back."

Walking briskly to the table to retrieve my lunch money, I sense Jamie's eyes following me like a missile homing in on its target. He's still watching me as I grab my money and return to his side.

"Wow," he voices, looking into me the way he did yesterday, kind of shaking his head.

"What?" I ask, smiling, thinking he's impressed with how I snatched my lunch money and returned to the line in record time.

"Nothing." He blinks hard, shakes his head again, and averts his gaze from mine.

I get it then and feel my cheeks flush. His "wow" is in appreciation for what he sees.

There shouldn't be any more doubt in my mind that Jamie totally digs me. There's just no mistaking it. I can see it again today in the way he looks at me with enough heat in his eyes to start a bonfire. My insides are melting into some type of warm goo, because, of course, I'm totally into him as well.

Jamie shifts gears and asks, "Do you want to take our pizza out to the courtyard where it's quieter so we can talk? It's way too loud in here."

"Yeah, sounds great." I try not to sound too eager, but the prospect of talking alone with Jamie excites me more than anything has in a long time. It's as though I've just been chosen first by the team captain to play ball on his side.

We move farther up the line together. Jamie takes a paper plate and places two slices of pepperoni pizza on it, while I choose a large slice of cheese for myself. We each pay for our own pizza and a bottle of water. I grab napkins, go pluck my backpack from the table, and head outside into the courtyard while Jessica, Eric, and the others at the table watch us quizzically as we exit the cafeteria doors together.

Once in the courtyard, we are met with quiet. Warm sunshine filters through the oak trees where picnic-style tables sit beneath. There are only a few students scattered throughout the large courtyard: a group of boys in a circle attempting to bring back the now-defunct game of hacky sack and a few students sitting around tables. I follow Jamie to an empty table in the shade and sit beside him. He straddles the bench with his long legs so he's facing me.

Jamie looks around, back at me, and then through the wall of glass into the cafeteria. "There's not a guy who'll be upset I brought you out here alone with me, is there?" he asks, eyes narrowed with wariness.

I think I know what he's asking and assure him, "No, I don't have a boyfriend if that's what you're asking."

His expression relaxes, and he smiles again. "Good! But if I'm not mistaken, Eric was giving us both the stink eye as we walked past their table." Jamie glances back into the cafeteria.

"Oh, he's probably just watching out for me. We've practically been best friends since kindergarten." I wave a dismissive hand in the direction of the cafeteria.

"If you say so." Jamie doesn't look overly convinced and maybe even a little worried?

He starts in on his pizza right away, and I ask, "What do you think? It's definitely not the great pizza-kitchen places they have back in California."

"No, but it's actually not too bad. Either that or I'm literally starving." He laughs. "I didn't eat any breakfast this morning, did you?"

"I did, yes. I eat the same thing every morning—a banana and a health bar, sometimes cereal if I want to mix it up." I lift a shoulder, wincing inside at what a boring creature of habit I am with my entire morning routine.

"What's your favorite kind of cereal?" Jamie asks. "No, wait, let me guess. "Wheat O's?"

"No," I giggle, "although I do like them."

"The crunchy, fruity kind? The one that has little marshmallows in it?"

"Ha, no," I say, smiling. "I think you're totally listing off your own faves."

"And you would be right. Okay, tell me what brand of healthy cereal you eat."

"How do you know I eat *healthy* cereal?" I tilt my head to the side and pretend smugness.

"Well," he begins, "you eat a banana and a health bar most mornings, which are both healthy; you like Wheat O's which is a healthier breakfast cereal than most; and, well, look at you." His eyes skim over me like a feathered touch, making my face grow suddenly hot. "You're fit. It's obvious you're careful about what you eat."

I look down and then back up from my pizza, swallow hard, and nod. "It's the wheat biscuit kind." I pause and primly point out, "But it absolutely must be the cinnamon ones. Girls aren't quite as lucky as guys who can eat all the sugar and whatever else they want and burn it all off in like five minutes. It's so not fair." I feign a pout.

He grins and says in a softer voice, "And I thought you were beautiful when you're happy, but you're just as cute sad." He gives my bottom lip a playful poke with his index finger.

He's only half-serious, but the compliment spreads warmth through me—or was it the soft touch of his finger on my mouth? Geez.

Already, in the short time we've been talking, he has given me two compliments besides the unspoken ones behind his eyes. Did he just call me beautiful? I feel beautiful when Jamie looks at me. He makes me believe it.

He's still watching me, but I don't know how to respond, so I take my napkin and wipe imaginary crumbs from my lips. His eyes follow the motion and stay fixed on my mouth even after I crumple the napkin and set it back down. His watchful gaze on my lips causes a heated flush inside me again and makes me want to use my paper plate as a fan to cool myself. I opt for a drink of my water instead.

I took one small bite to his every three, yet I still have some of my pizza left. Jamie's appetite must match his large frame, but I would think he's still hungry by the look in his eyes. I can see he has traded one type of hunger for another. Does he want to kiss me as much as I want him to? Would he? Here, right now, so soon after we just met?

Jamie and I do a lot of communicating with our eyes. He isn't the least bit shy expressing himself, which makes me feel pretty comfortable with him as well. He's a true miracle worker, but I'm still the first to break our gaze.

After a beat or two of silence, Jamie clears his throat, and we talk awhile about our favorite music, books (Jamie actually reads for pleasure!), and TV series, until it dawns on me that he is keeping our conversation light, allowing me to set its pace.

"Tell me about your family," I say. "Do you have any brothers or sisters?"

I take the last bite of my pizza and chew slowly while he answers. "Two sisters—one two years older than I am and one less than two years younger. Megan's in college back in Cali, and Amber is a sophomore here. She isn't in this lunch period, but I'll introduce you to her when it works out." He continues, "My parents have been married... well, for forever. They met and married in their first year of college."

"Did they both graduate?" I'm curious because of how important obtaining a college degree is to me, and that seems super young to get married, only a little older than Jamie and I are now.

"Yes," he replies, "although my mom never pursued a career in her degree field—criminal justice—which doesn't even match her personality. She stayed home with us while my dad worked the business. She began editing books from home when we all started school and still does. My mom's really a lot smarter than my dad, but don't tell him I said that." He laughs. "My dad has an MBA, which is what I eventually want to get."

Jamie pauses in thought, running a hand through the top of his thick hair. It makes it look messier yet somehow better. "I guess you could say we're a pretty normal family, whatever that means. There's not a lot of dysfunction or anything in my family as far as I know. Maybe some good cop, bad cop between my parents. What about you? What's your family like?"

"It's just my dad and me, no siblings," I begin. "My mom died when I was fourteen." I take a deep breath and exhale slowly. "She was only forty-four, and they had been married twenty-two years when she passed away. They tried for three years to get pregnant until I was finally conceived, and it just never happened again after they had me."

Jamie's face softens. "That's so young to lose your mom, Cara. I'm sorry it happened to you and to your poor dad. What happened? Was she sick?" His compassion is too sweet, and he jumps up several notches all at once on my swoon-meter scale.

I haven't told anyone about my fear that I will also die young like my mom did. If I die at the same age she did, I'll have already lived half my life after I graduate from college and settle into my teaching career. I quickly stuff that thought down and move on.

My bottom lip quivers ever so slightly before I answer. *Don't get teary-eyed, Cara. Don't you DARE cry in front of Jamie.* I attempt a steady voice. "Yes, for two years—breast cancer—and it had already spread when they found it. She had a lot of chemo treatments, which seemed to make her sicker and hardly touched the cancer. It's only been recently that I can talk about it without crying.

"Because I'm an only child and lost my mom young, I've learned to be pretty comfortable and content being alone. After she died, I felt different from all my friends, you know? Her illness and death forced me to grow up almost overnight. A lot changed inside me, too, but everything and everyone else around me seemed the same." I shrug and toy with my napkin.

Jamie nods, his brows drawn in a sincere show of empathy. He's an expert listener, I can tell, so I take in a shaky breath and go on.

"I felt like I was suddenly far removed from all the other girls my age; all the petty drama and worries most kids my age indulged in seemed trivial to me. My dad is great, but domesticity isn't his strong suit." I let out a rueful chuckle. "While I was worrying about what I'd make for dinner, what things I needed to add to the grocery list, or getting the laundry and dishes done, my friends were all worried about their bad hair day or making the cheerleading squad. I've kind of stuck to myself since then."

Jamie doesn't say anything, but I sense he wants me to continue. His sweet, sympathetic look compels me to. "It's all been really hard on me. People describe me as quiet if they know me and stuck-up if they don't, but the truth is, my mom's death caused me to be more selective with who I allow in my life and become friends with." I try to read what he's thinking and finish. "I keep a small circle."

Oh no, I'm being too personal, telling him too much too soon about myself. To lighten the morose mood I fear I've created, I tease, "So you should realize how lucky you are that I'm sitting here telling you all of this." I nudge him with my shoulder and half-heartedly laugh.

But Jamie's expression remains serious. He studies my face, and I wonder what he sees? I begin to feel self-conscious and fidget on the bench under his direct gaze.

Still unsmiling, he says, "I do feel lucky, very lucky, Cara, and I can see I was right about you."

"What do you mean?" I ask, taken off guard.

"I knew there was something different about you—good different," he quickly amends. He's squinting now, as though he really sees me and gets me. "I could tell there was much more to you than just a beautiful face. You're strong, and there's a quiet wisdom in your eyes. I saw it right away yesterday when we met. It makes more sense now, knowing what you've been through."

Jamie's perception lifts my spirits like breathing helium, and I don't want our time together to end, don't want this great feeling I have with him to end. His understanding enfolds me like a warm embrace.

The lunch period is almost over and there's so much more I want to know about him. "Man, how is it that the morning went by like a sloth on sedatives," I laugh, "and then as soon as I finally get to see you and spend time with you, it goes by in a flash?" I lean in a little closer to him, facing him on the bench, and add, "way too fast."

Smiling, but without breaking our gaze this time, I surprise myself with my boldness. I've suddenly been reincarnated into someone who can actually flirt. Jamie makes it easy.

He looks a little surprised himself, but pleasantly so, and exhales heavily as though he's been patiently waiting for me to reveal how I feel about him. I guess I've thrown him a bone. "Damn, you have no idea how happy it makes me to know you're feeling what I am."

"I felt it as soon as I saw you," I say honestly and shrug, looking straight into the sun-filled sky of Jamie's eyes.

His face goes completely slack. "Same here," he whispers. "*Shit...*"

The bell rings, but we both continue to stare at each other to soak up the moment.

Jamie blinks hard several times, and asks, "Before we go, can I get your number and text you?"

He rushes to dig his phone from his front pocket, and I give him my cell number. He punches it in quickly. "So, if you get a creepy text from an unknown number tonight asking what you're wearing, you'll know who it's from."

There's his deep, rumbling laugh again. Jamie possesses a great sense of humor and comes across as genuinely happy. So far, it's what I like most about him.

As we stand to head back in for class, he reenacts a gesture from your typical chivalric knight-in-shining-armor scene. He takes my right hand in both of his and places my palm over his heart. I can feel the warmth and definition of his pecs beneath his shirt, and it does crazy things to my insides.

He then keeps my hand in his as he bows low, looks up into my eyes under his dark lashes, and kisses my knuckles, lingering there a few long seconds. "Milady," he says in a British accent. He smiles up at me before letting go of my hand.

I laugh hard and tell him I will see him later as I hurry to make my way back into the building. But my hand tingles—marked, branded—where his lips have been, and I briefly touch the spot to my own lips to preserve the feel of his mouth on my skin.

It's as though my chest wall has suddenly morphed into a trapdoor, and the wings of my heart are frantically beating against it, begging for an urgent escape. Within an instant of leaving him, I realize my heart is indeed taking flight—it is swiftly becoming the sole property of the one, the beautiful, Jamie Gallagher.

Jamie

After seeing Cara again today at lunch and realizing the connection between us is very real and *very* mutual, I don't remember ever feeling this on top of the world, not even after winning an important basketball game. If no one else was home right now, I might steal a line from a movie, pretend I'm on the bow of a ship, and shout it at the top of my lungs.

Who would've thought just a week ago that I would soon be meeting a girl who would have such an earth-shattering effect on me? When she glided through the lunchroom entrance earlier today, my heart stopped. She looked even more beautiful today than yesterday, if that's possible. There was one solitary word that randomly snapped into my mind when I kissed her hand today and watched her walk away—

Mine.

Who is this girl who can bring out such a primal feeling of possessiveness? I don't want to move too fast for her and scare her away, but already, in the short time I've known her, I want her to be my girlfriend. I want to be the only one for her.

Even though I can tell when it comes right down to it, Cara can hold her own, her sweetness and vulnerability make me want to take care of her, to protect her. The feeling was overwhelming today when, with unshed tears in her eyes, she told me about losing her mother. I had the urge to lean into her and take her in my arms to absorb some of her sadness; but of course, I resisted.

I continuously think about Cara and the time, albeit brief, we've spent together. Her sweetness, her moves, her scent— reminding me of clean laundry and sunshine—and the way she looks at me with such admiration and respect. Now that about kills me.

And her mouth... Damn, her full, beautiful lips. I wanted to kiss her so badly today when she looked into me with those inviting eyes of hers. It took every ounce of restraint I had not to. Does she know even half of what she does to me?

I'm terrified that I'm light years ahead of her in relation to how much I already care about her. If that's the case, my hope is she will catch up sooner than later. If this isn't love at first sight, then it doesn't exist.

Nothing exists.

Today, Cara and I were tethered by the invisible thread of chemistry we share, but it was abruptly snipped in two by the shriek of the damn tardy bell. I would've preferred being gutted to leaving her and returning to class, and that's about how it felt. We might have had only one-and-a-half lunch dates—if you want to call them that—only a matter of minutes together, but I've fallen for her... hard.

The measly amount of time spent together at school isn't going to cut it for me, so I plan to ask her if she wants to hang out Friday night. I have no clue where to take her yet. She can ask me to go anywhere, do anything, and I'll make it happen so we can spend more time together.

After dinner, as I file paperwork Dad needs done before tomorrow, I overhear my mom and dad talking in the dining room. Mom asks him what he thinks about me being so quiet at dinner.

"He met a girl yesterday he really likes, and he's probably got his head in the clouds over her."

My mother seems surprised. "Jamie's never acted like that over a girl before, Brent."

"Yeah, I know, but he told me he's never instantly fallen for a girl like he did when he met her at school yesterday. Her name is Cara."

Mom raises her voice and asks, "How do *you* know all this?" as though my dad being the only one privy to this privileged information kind of hurts her feelings.

"He came in and talked to me about it last night. He hoped that after they saw each other today and were able to talk further he would find that she's interested in him, too. I'm sort of afraid to ask him how it went today, but I did tell him not to get his hopes up, just in case."

"Go ask him." Mom coaxes. "Maybe he needs to talk about it."

It's a little uncomfortable hearing my parents discuss my love life like they are, but I can't complain and say they're being meddlesome when I'm the one who told my dad about Cara and how I feel about her. I guess it's the price to pay for having a close-knit family. Most of the time, it's worth them knowing my business. They've never tried to control me, only steer me in the right direction when needed, and their involvement has never seemed suffocating.

I'm fortunate that my dad and I share a lot of the same interests and have the type of relationship we do. I've had some ass whoopings in my younger days and have had to be set straight a few times, but I've never questioned who's boss, and we seem more on an equal footing in the family hierarchy now that I'm older.

With their patience and guidance, I consider myself to be pretty well-grounded and well adjusted. Which is great, sure, but it can also make one feel like a bit of an outcast. There are things others put energy into that I simply don't give a shit about, like working too hard to be popular, attempting to prove their worth from how well they play sports, or trying to please people whose opinions don't mean jack in the long run.

Probably a reason the few girls I've been interested in ended it so quickly when they realized I don't like drama and won't play mind games. My parents were good at helping me learn priorities early on.

Mom taught me to ask this question when determining the importance of something: "Will it truly matter in a year? Even in six months?" We call it the "year test." When I worry about things or consider whether something is worth spending a lot of time on, I simply ask myself: *Does it pass the year test?*

My answer is "no" to the things I need to let go of and, of course, "yes" to the truly important things—goals worth pursuing. Playing on the basketball team failed the year test.

Cara definitely passes the year test.

My dad walks into the office doorway and comments on my progress after noting the dwindling stacks of folders I've been filing. He wants to ask me about Cara, and I wait.

"I've got to run to the store to get coffee for the morning. Need anything?"

"Nope, I'm good," I say.

He tries to read my mood. "How was your day? Did you see Cara again?"

I can't contain my smile. "Oh, yeah," I gush. "We're on the same page, Dad."

"You were so quiet at dinner. I thought maybe things hadn't gone the way you'd hoped."

"It actually went even better than I imagined," I tell him truthfully.

I'm sure I was more reticent than usual all day long because I've been imagining kissing Cara so often it's ridiculous. "Sorry I've been so quiet; just have a lot on my mind. As Mom would say, I'm processing." I laugh.

"I'm glad to hear it," Dad says before walking away.

After I finish all the filing, I tell everyone goodnight, get ready for bed, and text Cara for the first time.

J: *Hey, Cara. It's Jamie. You have my number now.*

I wait a few seconds and see the pulsing conversation bubble appear. My heart rate picks up speed.

Cara: *Hi, Jamie. What's up?*

J: *Not much. Just finished some work for my dad. Thinking about what a good time I had with you today.*

Cara: *Same here! My dad and I just finished a late dinner. I told him about you.*

J: *Well?*

It takes a few beats for her to begin writing again.

Cara: *I told him you're new to the school and told him everything I know about you so far.*

I finish reading the text when the bubble quickly appears again.

Cara: *And that I really like you.* She adds a smiley-face emoji, and my heart squeezes tightly at that.

J: *The feeling is mutual! Do I need to ask his permission to take you out Friday night?*

Cara: *No, but you should probably ask me first lol! My answer is yes, and yes, my dad will want to meet you if we go out.*

J: *I wouldn't expect less. What do you want to do? Where should we go?*

Cara: *Doesn't matter to me. Maybe a movie?*

J: *Sounds good. You choose. We can talk about it when I see you tomorrow. Same place, same time tomorrow in the awesome café?* I end with a laughing emoji.

Cara: *Yup, see you tomorrow.*

J: *Night, Cara.*

Cara: *Night. Sweet dreams.* She leaves a sleeping emoji with Z's billowing from its head.

Sweet dreams, huh? Only if they're about you, Cara. I lie awake for a long time thinking about her and how glad I am we moved to Texas.

***

The next couple of days pass in a blur, a sequence of smudges, really, except for the short time I get to see Cara at school. When I'm with her, life mutates into hyperfocus. I try to savor every minute of our time together and commit them to memory, which is not too difficult because everything about Cara is memorable. Friday couldn't get here soon enough, and I'm both anxious and excited about taking her out tonight... and about meeting her dad.

I've learned a few more things about Cara this week during our lunch "dates." Her favorite color is forest green. She is feminine and sensitive, yet she and her dad do a lot of camping, hiking, and fishing together (a girl after my own heart), and she's a huge fan of the local Texas football team, actually loves to watch football! I suppose I'll have to switch my loyalty from my favorite California team to hers, equivalent to a religious conversion around here.

I also learned Cara's favorite food is Mexican, which she and others in Texas call Tex-Mex. She explained, "It's not quite as spicy as authentic Mexican since it's a mixture of Mexican and American Southern cooking. I think you will like it."

"Cara, I'm from Southern California, a state also bordering Mexico, and we have Cal-Mex. I've come from another state, not another planet," I teased, and we both laughed about it.

Things are effortless between us. She's not like most of the girls I've dated who talked about themselves ad nauseam. Then again, if Cara did the talking, it wouldn't bother me at all. I could be with her and listen to her 24/7 and never get enough, but I love the way she asks questions about me, too. She's sincerely curious and absorbs every word I say, even later making connections by repeating things I've told her.

I can't say exactly how this works, how in this vast universe two people can meet and immediately click, can know one another for only a few days and be this into each other. It just happens, I guess, and it has undoubtedly happened to me.

At lunch today, Cara asked me to choose the restaurant and surprise her. We also decided we would look up movies and showtimes while we're at dinner tonight and choose one then. I know I want to take Cara out for Tex-Mex at her favorite restaurant because, well, favorite.

I've thought a lot about taking her to meet my parents tonight, but I don't think so just yet. One reason is that we will already be pressed for time if I meet her dad and we go out to eat *and* see a movie. The main reason, though—full transparency here—is I'm not ready for her to see my house and where we live. It shouldn't be embarrassing, but to put it bluntly, my family is wealthy, and our wealth is even more apparent since moving to Texas.

The money spent on houses in California buys twice the house and amenities in Texas. Our large home sits on almost ten acres—hard to come by on the outskirts of a suburb of Fort Worth. My dad has even talked about buying a horse or two in the future. Maybe he thinks owning horses will make us more "Texan." I don't know.

Anyway, from what Cara has told me, her father is a pastor, and they live on modest means. I'm afraid she will react the way some do to our lavish lifestyle and automatically think we're stingy, selfish, or snobby. If I know Cara the way I think I do, she wouldn't, but I still think it will shock her to see our house. So

I'll wait a while longer to bring her here to meet my parents and sister until after she gets to know me better.

As I get ready for Cara's and my date, I start to get pretty nervous, which is not my usual. Because she means so much to me, it's important that her dad likes me. My frame of reference is my own dad practically making Megan's dates turn in their resume before he allowed her to go out with them. He never let her go because he truly trusted the dudes, but because she was old enough to date and he felt obligated to.

Megan didn't date outright losers or anything, although there were a couple who were questionable. Yet my dad sat on the couch with a grim look on his face during the first several times she went out, and he was basically in the same spot when she returned.

Makes me realize I haven't asked Cara what her curfew is tonight. It might be better if I ask her dad the question instead. I'll do whatever I can to gain his trust.

I text Cara as I prepare to head out:

J: *Leaving my house now. Will be there in a few.*

Cara: *Thumbs-up emoji.*

The outside temperature is not nearly cool enough to wear a jacket, but I might need one later when the sun sets, so I bring one along. Cara and I live probably the farthest apart possible to both be assigned to the Oak Creek High School zone—about a ten-minute drive. I punch her address into the maps app on my phone and take off.

Lowering the window slightly to enjoy the outside air, I crank up the radio to a country-western station, not because I live in Texas now and country music is big here, but because I've always liked it. My nerves build to a crescendo right before I pull into the front of Cara's house, but I don't hesitate to get out and ring the doorbell.

Cara's house is nice, with a meticulously manicured lawn and assorted-colored flowers planted in the front and around two trees in the yard. Picturing Cara as the one who planted them fits their color and beauty. She opens her front door with a warm smile and motions for me to come in. I step into a bright, welcoming foyer and follow her into the family room.

Her father looks up from a book he's reading, something by C.S. Lewis, and removes his eyeglasses when he stands to greet me. There's an immediate surge of relief when I see his smile is very much like Cara's. In addition, his eyes are clear and kind. She indeed favors him.

"Chris Dawson." He reaches to shake my hand. It's a firm grip.

"Jamie Gallagher," I say. "It's very nice to meet you, sir."

"I've been hearing a lot about you this week, so it's great to finally put a face with the name," he says sincerely.

I glance at Cara and notice she has blushed bright pink at his comment. It's so cute, I can't help but smile. She looks incredible tonight, and although I want to take her all in, I stay focused on her dad.

"Let's sit down for a bit before you kids head out," he says.

I look behind me and see Cara sit down on the loveseat—how fitting—so I sit beside her.

"Cara tells me your family recently moved here from Southern California."

"Yes, sir," I answer. "My father expanded his industrial coatings business to Texas and a couple of other states."

I tell him a little about our family, our move, how much I like it here, and how we've taken on some big-name business chains in Texas as clients. He kind of whistles when I tell him the university Megan attends back in California, and I get his gist. It's a prestigious school. He then asks where I plan to take Cara tonight.

"If it's okay with her," I look at Cara for affirmation, "I'd like to take her for Mexican food, uh, Tex-Mex," I correct myself and chuckle.

"Sounds good to me." Cara smiles sweetly, tucking a strand of hair behind her right ear.

"And then to a movie, but it depends on what time you would like me to have her home."

He looks at me thoughtfully. "Just have her home by midnight, and that will give you plenty of time to see a movie, too. Call if plans change. I'd like you to put my contact information in your phone so you can reach me tonight or any time for that matter, Jamie."

"I appreciate it. I'll take good care of Cara and have her back home before midnight."

Her dad stands, which prompts Cara and me to stand, and I reach out to shake his hand again.

His grip is even firmer this time, and he looks me in the eye with the unspoken acknowledgment between us that Cara is his baby, his whole world, and he expects me to keep my word.

Cara

Jessica must have acknowledged early this week that Jamie and I were going to be a couple after she saw us eat lunch alone together in the courtyard every day. She seems to have resigned herself to the fact that, for whatever reason, the cosmos has obviously dubbed me better suited for Jamie.

She and I have talked briefly in the halls and in class this week. Of course, the first thing she wanted to know today is how it's going with Jamie and if I'd kissed him yet.

As we both rushed to our next class, I explained, "Jess, we are just getting to know one another and haven't even seen each other outside of school, so no, we haven't kissed yet. We plan to go out tonight."

She clapped her hands like a child. "You have to text me as soon you get home from your date, or I'll never speak to you again."

I can tell she's truly happy for me, and it's quite a relief to know there's not a competition between us.

As I get ready for Jamie to arrive for our date, Jessica texts me.

Jessica: *Where are you and Jamie going tonight?*

C: *Going to eat and see a movie. What are you doing tonight?*

Jessica: *Hanging out with Eric at his house.*

C: *Oh, just the two of you?*

Jessica: *Yeah, you don't mind, do you?*

C: *Of course not. Why would I?*

Jessica: *Cara, I didn't get to talk to you today about something I wanted to say. Please don't be offended, but since Jamie got here and y'all hit it off, it's like you have pretty much forgotten about me and the gang.* There's a frowny-face emoji.

My first instinct is to raise my hackles and defend myself because I would like to remind her how last year she totally ghosted me for three months while she and Bryan went out. But then I concede she's right. I've not sat at our lunch table since Monday when I first met Jamie after having eaten lunch with "the gang" every day since our freshman year. "Gang" is probably just a euphemism for "clique," but it is what it is, and high school is filled with them. At least Jessica invited Bryan to sit with us while they were dating.

It's true that I haven't reached out to Eric, Mark, or Jessica outside of school lately, yet they haven't contacted me, either. We usually chat on a group app, text questions about homework, or group-text memes and funny videos at least a couple of times a week. We regularly go to one of our houses to watch something one weekend night, sometimes on Sunday afternoons. Have they planned a movie party at one of their houses without inviting me? Are the others also annoyed with me?

C: *You're right, and I'm sorry. We're working on getting to know each other, and he's been my entire focus. I'm crazy about him, more than I've ever been about anyone. But I do see that's not fair to y'all.*

I send the text, then write another:

C: *Thanks for missing me.* I add a kiss emoji.

Jessica: *I only want you to be careful. Y'all BOTH seem to be focused only on each other, and I would hate to see you get hurt if it doesn't work out. Please don't neglect me just because you have a boyfriend now.* (smiley-face emoji)

C: *I'll do better, I promise. I'll make sure we eat inside at the lunch table Monday. Going to finish getting ready now.*

Jessica: *Have fun! Don't forget to text me when you get home!!*

C: *I won't.*

I don't have a lot of time to contemplate our discourse, but two questions come to mind: Are Jessica and Eric dating? Is it why she asked me if I minded that she was going to hang out with him alone? And two, do I care? I'll think about it later, but right now I concentrate on getting ready for my first official date with Jamie.

***

After we visit with my dad for a while and say bye to him, Jamie moves ahead of me to the truck's passenger door to open it for me.

"Well, aren't you the gentleman?" I say with a big smile.

"I aim to please, ma'am," Jamie drawls in an exaggerated Texas accent, making me giggle.

"This is a *really* nice truck," I say, as Jamie takes out his phone and asks me to text him my dad's contact info before we leave, which I do.

"Thanks, I'm proud of him," he says after he adds the contact. "My dad has made me work hard for every cent he gives me, but he compensates me well."

"Him? Your truck is a he?"

"Do you think a beast like this could be a girl?" he teases.

"No, I suppose not," I laugh, "but you're a little bit of a man's man, aren't you?"

He throws me a suspicious side-eye, but I'm momentarily distracted by his tanned bicep flexing as he steers the truck away from my house with his right hand.

"It's okay, I like it," I say, thinking how safe he makes me feel... and how giddy.

"His name is Shadow." Jamie glances over to see if I approve.

"Why Shadow? Because it's black or because he goes wherever you go?"

"I named him Shadow because he's gloriously all black inside and out, but I guess the reason could be both. Never thought of the reason you did. I might regret the color this summer. I bought him in California before I knew we were moving to Texas. It'll radiate a lot of heat when it's over a hundred degrees, and there'll be a lot more of those days here than I'm used to."

"I could sure get used to riding in Shadow," I tell him, trying to bite back my smirk.

"I hope you do." He looks over at me and smiles, causing the butterflies in my stomach to migrate south in one fell swoop.

When I opened my door to invite Jamie in earlier, cupid's arrow hurled itself straight into my heart. It was difficult to wrap my head around the fact that this guy who looked like he just stepped out of the pages of a fitness magazine was actually at my front door to meet my dad and to take me out with him.

His tight-fitting t-shirt totally shows off his grapefruit-sized biceps and defined pecs like nothing I've seen him wear to school. His jeans hug his muscular thighs and his narrow hips and waist. He has to work out on a regular basis. Surely no one can look that good without trying.

He's wearing boots, which make him look even taller than he is. My dad is six feet tall, and Jamie is at least three or four inches taller than he is. I can see why Jamie said his coaches were so disappointed that he wouldn't play on the basketball team this year. I bet he was like a machine on the court, and I would have loved to be the leader of his cheer section.

Watching Jamie drive gives me time to study his profile with unrestricted freedom. I skim my eyes over his strong jaw that always retains a tinge of darkness even after a shave—a match to his dark, slightly curly hair. A deep cleft in his chin under a perfectly shaped mouth contributes to giving his face the chiseled look of a Greek god. And here he is taking this mere mortal out on a date.

He's a masterpiece, and I want more than anything for him to be *my* masterpiece.

I think about the easy way Jamie spoke with my dad, a reflection of the good relationship he describes having with his own father. Early on, it was obvious Dad liked Jamie when at one point he looked over at me and gave me a knowing smile and a nearly imperceptible nod. While I never expected him not to, it's still a relief.

As if reading my mind, Jamie says, "Your dad is great. You two are a lot alike, huh?"

"Yeah, he's pretty great. We're alike in a lot of ways." I catch how that sounds and backtrack. "I don't mean that I'm great." I snicker, which comes out as more of a snort.

"But, you are," Jamie flirts, "no doubt about *that*."

His words spread liquid warmth through me, making me want to reach over and touch him in some way—in any way. I resist, twisting my hands in my lap instead.

"When do I get to meet *your* parents?" I ask.

"I thought about taking you to meet them tonight, but we wouldn't have time to go to my house and still do the restaurant and a movie. They'll want to visit with you for a while when you meet them. I know they'll like you."

"I hope so. I can read my dad well enough by now to know he was impressed with you."

"I'll just have to trust you on that one. I'm glad you think so, though. I was a little nervous about meeting him," Jamie admits.

"I could tell. But see, you didn't have to be." I assure him.

"No, I didn't. He's warm and friendly," he adds appreciatively, "like you."

We drive in silence for a while, listening to a slow country ballad on the radio. Riding beside Jamie in his truck, away from the restrictive climate of the school, is liberating. I'm the happiest I have been in a long time, and I'm looking intently at Jamie as I acknowledge this.

He catches me staring.

"What?" he asks, smiling.

I grin like a girl caught looking through a boy's bedroom window. "Nothing, I'm just happy to be with you is all."

His eyes brighten at that. "It will be nice to eat and talk somewhere besides the school cafeteria or courtyard, right?" He laughs, and I wonder what he would think if he knew just how much I've been looking forward to this date.

"It will, but it's more about just being with you than anything else," I say, boldness with speaking my mind to Jamie coming easier and easier for me.

His eyes are practically gleaming now, and I love seeing the different emotions dance across his face. He's expressive, and though some emotions are nearly indiscernible, they're there. I'm learning how to read them.

He loves it when I flirt with him, and I amaze myself that I can flirt so easily now. Jamie's presence paradoxically serves as an antidote to my shyness, the opposite of what I would have thought when I first saw him walk into the cafeteria that day.

We arrive at the restaurant, and Jamie continues to be a perfect gentleman, opening doors for me and guiding me along with his palm at the small of my back. His hand is warm, igniting the skin under my thin shirt with his touch and sending tingles up my spine.

The restaurant is dimly lit with little lanterns burning at each table. The hostess leads us to a booth well away from the entrance. My skin mourns the absence of Jamie's warm touch when he removes his hand.

We sit down across from one another, and our waitress is immediately there to take our drink order. I order water with lemon, and Jamie asks for one with lime. A young boy who doesn't look old enough to have a job brings us chips and salsa, and we dig in.

"If you ever want to know my weakness," I say, "it's tortilla chips and salsa."

"Good to know." He chews for only a few seconds and stops. His eyes widen as he looks quickly around the restaurant. "I need water," he says in a gasp. "I thought you said Tex-Mex is less spicy than authentic Mexican."

I can't help but laugh at his discomfort. "It's not spicy," I say, then reluctantly amend, "Okay, maybe a little this time. Sometimes when I eat here it's not spicy at all, but it depends on the day and who prepares it, I suppose."

I'm still laughing when our water arrives. Jamie thanks the waitress and gulps almost half of it down in one swallow.

He looks at me under his dark lashes wet with moisture. "How dare you laugh at my pain!"

"Sorry, I just didn't know, ahem," I falsely clear my throat, "you would be that sensitive."

"Sensitive? Ah, now you've gone and insulted me." He chuckles, but I start to worry that I might have truly hurt his feelings. His relaxed expression tells me I haven't. He's a good sport. "Really, it's good, and I'm fine as long as I have something to drink with it."

Still smiling, we look through our menus, and I confess, "I hate to say you're right. The salsa is too spicy. I can only eat a little or it will mess with my stomach; I guess it's a love/hate relationship tonight."

After a minute, when Jamie doesn't say anything, I raise my head to catch him studying me. I try to read his face, wondering what he's thinking, but he tells me. "You're so beautiful, Cara. I can't get over just how much. Here in the candlelight, you're killing me, girl."

I sense myself beginning to color, when he adds, "The way you seem unaware of it only adds to your beauty. You didn't even notice every guy at the bar checking you out as we walked through."

I turn and look at the bar area behind me. "I guess I didn't notice," I say honestly.

"Trust me, whether they were with someone or not, it was hard for them not to stare, but I can't blame them."

A muscle in his jaw tics and his eyes narrow as he looks toward the bar. Is that a little jealousy that crossed his features? If it is, it's gone as quickly as it appears when he refocuses on me.

It's hard for me to decide what to order because it all sounds wonderful, so we decide to order a combination of enchiladas and tacos to share with one another, Jamie's idea. As we wait for our food, we talk about our families and our plans for the future.

Sense of humor—check; honesty—check; ambition—check; beautiful—double check. I keep waiting for Jamie to reveal some sort of weird craziness that will keep me from swooning every time I look at him, but not a chance so far.

Our conversation continues as we eat and is as organic and effortless as always. When we're almost finished with our meals, Jamie takes out his phone and searches for movie showings at the closest theater. We agree on a whodunnit murder mystery.

"Let me pay for my meal," I say as Jamie snatches our bill and moves to take out his wallet.

"Nope, I've got it." He looks almost offended. He did say his dad paid him well, so I let it go.

When we slide from the booth, he waits for me to move beside him. I anticipate the feel of his touch at my lower back again; but instead, he takes my hand and laces his fingers with mine.

It's our first solid physical connection other than quick, light touches here and there. The gesture sends tingles up my arm and satisfies the ache I've had to touch him. My smaller hand fits perfectly inside his warm, much larger hand, and being Jamie's girl feels like the last piece of my life's jigsaw being snapped into place. It's the warm bath feeling, and I soak in its depth and solace as we walk to his truck.

"You're spoiling me, Jamie," I say when he opens the truck door for me.

"Only treating you the way I want to, the way you deserve to be treated." He looks back into my eyes and winks.

Every time he looks at me that way, my stomach drops as though I've just fallen over the highest peak of a roller coaster. It's like a drug I could easily get addicted to, and I want more of that feeling, more of Jamie.

It's a short drive to the theater from the restaurant, but we aren't in a hurry and arrive in plenty of time.

"Want popcorn or something to drink?" Jamie offers after we purchase tickets.

"No, thanks, I'm way too full." I lay my hand across my stomach and puff out my cheeks in an exaggerated gesture, and Jamie chuckles.

If I wanted anything, he would insist on paying for it. I already feel a little guilty that he's spent so much money on me tonight. He paid for our dinner and our movie tickets, another glimpse into what a gentleman he is.

My old-school dad would say Jamie's father sure raised him right.

Jamie

There are only a handful of people in the theater and no one around us. I don't know much about the movie we're seeing, and I probably won't be able to concentrate on it at all with Cara sitting right beside me.

The way her face brightens when she sees me after I return with a soda for us to share tugs at my heart. We both take a drink and recline our seats as far back as they will go. Instead of placing the cup in the holder between us, I place it in the one to my right as the movie previews begin.

I lift the moveable drink holder separating us into the raised position and take her hand in mine, moving closer until our shoulders touch. Cara turns her head to look at me in the dimming light, smiles, and kisses me softly on the cheek.

Her lips are soft and warm, and I feel my eyes widen at the unexpected, sweet gesture. Tightening my grasp of her hand, I whisper in her ear, "How am I supposed to watch the movie instead of you after that? Being this close to you..." I let my voice trail off and stare at her perfect lips before looking into her eyes already fixed on mine.

She holds my gaze with that familiar sultry look of hers that drives me half-crazy and whispers back mischievously, "I'm sorry, I couldn't resist."

"Don't be," I say with a forced smile that doesn't quite develop. It takes everything I have not to move even closer and take her mouth right here, right now. The thought of it slams my heart into overdrive, but I decide I don't want our first real lip-to-lip kiss to be in the middle of a movie theater. Maybe she'll allow me to give her a real kiss when I walk her to her door tonight.

I reluctantly break our gaze and pull our clasped hands to my mouth, kissing her knuckles before settling them back between us. A satisfied smile crosses her features, and we both focus on the screen. Or at least I try to. She smells like birthday cake and feels so warm and soft against my side, it's hard to think of anything else.

And I don't.

I think of how earlier at dinner, I was hypnotized in the most carnal way watching her speak and laugh—the creative ideas she shared with me, the way her lips moved as she spoke, and the way her hands gestured gracefully with animation when she talked about going to college to become a teacher. And, man, the way she held me with her soulful gaze was almost too much, like she was giving me an eye hug every time she looked at me.

It's a love punch to the gut when I imagine dipping my head to hers and touching her lips to mine, of holding her so close, her heartbeat indistinguishable from my own. *Jamie, you've got it bad, dude.* Yeah, I've turned into a sap in just under a week's time.

Cara doesn't have a clue how captivating she is. A far cry from someone like Jessica who knows she's attractive and uses it to her advantage, Cara seems oblivious. This fact alone makes her all the more beautiful from the inside out.

When we walked through the restaurant to our booth for dinner, a surge of possessiveness and sting of jealousy climbed up my spine when almost every dude sitting at the bar couldn't take their eyes off her. It quickly turned to seething anger when a sleazebag looked at his buddy and grabbed his crotch with a perverted half-smile as Cara walked by, something I'm glad she didn't see.

It's no secret my tragic flaw is a quick and hard-to-tame temper. I was so pissed, I pictured myself decking the guy and causing blood to spurt from his nose, washing the smug grin off his ugly face. But I let it go for Cara's sake. It took a lot of self-control to give him only a go-to-hell look and keep walking.

Where I'm salty, Cara is just so damn sweet. Other than being a little protective of my younger sister at times, I never imagined I could feel such intense protectiveness over the slightest threat toward someone I love.

Love?

Hell, yeah, I confirm the revelation. I would fight to the death to keep Cara safe if it came to it. If she knew how strong my feelings are for her, she might run the other way, but I can't just put the brakes on how I feel. I know how unsettled I am about all these new emotions, mostly about what to do with them. I don't see how they could get any stronger because she's already like looking directly into the sun.

I ask Cara a couple of questions about the plot during the movie, and we periodically whisper predictions of who we think the killer is. In the end, we're both wrong. It's a good thing the movie was fast-paced and entertaining because otherwise, it would've been torture to sit so close to Cara without constantly thinking about how her lips would feel and taste, not that I didn't think about it more than a few times anyway.

As the movie credits scroll up the screen and we reposition our chairs, I ask Cara how she liked it.

"It was great. The twist of the medicine labels having been switched after the nurse thought she was the one who poisoned her patient was clever."

"It was, wasn't it? I totally didn't expect that. I guess that's why it's called a twist, duh." I laugh at myself.

We stroll hand in hand to the back parking lot, which was full when we arrived, presumably with people seeing the earlier showings of movies. The lot is now deserted around our parking space.

"Our first movie together," I say, raising her hand to my mouth in a quick kiss. "I'll always remember it."

Cara smiles broadly up at me. "Me, too, thank you. I had a lot of fun on our first date. Well, excluding the salsa debacle." She snorts, and I just smile because even that part was fun for me.

When we return to my truck and I open the door for her, I'm pleasantly surprised when she scoots across the bench seat closer toward the driver's side. She wants to sit close to me, which plants a smile on my already love-sick face.

It's nice to be alone again with Cara in the dark seclusion of the truck. Before I start the engine to leave, I turn to her. "Cara, listen, I'm crazy about you, and I know we are just getting to know each other, but I've been thinking... You'll be going off to college next fall..." I'm a little nervous about what I want to say and my voice catches.

Cara takes my hand and looks at me intently, searching my face. "But you're not really looking for a serious relationship right now?" she blurts with a panicked expression.

"What? What the—? No... Hell no. Is that what you thought I was going to say?"

"I don't know, I just..." she looks as though she's been slapped, "I thought you were about to—"

"God, Cara, no." I take her into my arms to reassure her, and she feels as good there as I imagined she would—soft and inviting. She rests her cheek on my chest as I smooth her hair from the side of her face. I speak softly into her ear, "Just the opposite. I was going to ask you to be my girlfriend, ask if you'd be willing to see only me and no one else even though you'll be going off to college in a few months and things will change."

I confess to her, "I don't want to even think about anyone but you, or especially think about you with anyone but me. I was hoping you feel the same?" I pause and decide to tell her exactly how I feel. "Hell, I've been thinking about you every waking minute. I wish I could be with you every waking minute. That's the blunt truth here."

Cara keeps her cheek against me for a beat longer and murmurs, "I love hearing the deep rumble of your voice against my ear when you talk."

She moves her head from my chest and looks up at me. The interior lights in the cab of the pickup have gone off, but I can see her eyes shining in the moonlight streaming in from the window. There's relief in them.

She says softly, "It's exactly what I want. You had me terrified. It seemed like we had a great time tonight, but when you started talking about me leaving for college, I assumed you might be wanting to slow things down with me."

Her voice quivers, and it feels like a tourniquet cinched tightly around my heart to see the genuine distress on Cara's face at the thought of me backing off from her.

Her words and expression reveal she wants to be with me as much as I want to be with her. I can't resist her any longer. I need to *show* Cara how much she means to me.

Taking her face in my hands, I ask her point-blank, "Is it too soon to kiss you?"

She doesn't answer. Her permission is granted silently when she moves her lips closer to mine. I fall into the depths of her gaze, which hasn't faltered from mine, and leisurely skim the pad of my thumb across her full bottom lip. I've wanted to touch her lip like that since day one, and it causes my stomach to take a free fall. There's also a sharp intake of breath, and I can't tell if it's mine, Cara's, or both.

Her eyes trail to my mouth before returning to my eyes.

When I have no doubt she wants this as much as I do, I brush my lips lightly across hers, once... twice, testing their softness, relishing in the feel of them. She tastes amazing, and her mouth feels so good against mine that a sigh escapes me.

I pull back a fraction and search Cara's eyes to gauge how comfortable she is with going further when all she says is "Jamie" on a ragged breath like a frustrated plea.

It's then that I'm lost. I let go of my former restraint and move back over her mouth, gently nudging her lips apart with my own. Cara opens to me without a beat, and when the kiss deepens, her tongue boldly moves across the inside of my upper lip as though she's tentatively tasting a new flavor of ice cream.

"*Damn.*" I hear myself groan aloud. Her kiss is like my oxygen, and I want more, need more.

Her hand moves around to the base of my neck, and her fingers curl into my hair, holding me to her. She moans a type of "Mmm" sound, and it makes me kiss her harder, deeper.

We both get fully lost in this first kiss of ours, occasionally breaking for air and then promptly re-angling ourselves and returning to one another's mouths, frantic and hungry for each other. I've never in my life felt so connected to another human being. At this moment, Cara has become an extension of me, the better part of me. The kisses become deeper and stronger, but the need for more only intensifies.

I move my hands from the sides of her face to rub her back. Her shirt has ridden up, and her skin is warm and velvety smooth above the waistband of her jeans. *So smooth.* I feel her shudder beneath my hands, and it makes me want to touch her everywhere.

Who knows how much time passes, how long we are like this? I let my hands move up and down her warmth, and she moans openly into my mouth. It turns me on more than I care to admit, and my hands send any previous caution to a quiet corner, as they move lower to cup her perfect round bottom in my palms and press her against me.

God, the feel of her!

She moans again, but stronger this time, and pulls me down with her as she moves to lie back across the seat. I'm above her now, and I can feel her warmth (or is it mine?) radiating through our clothes. I try not to crush her in the confined space of my truck, but her body fits perfectly beneath mine, like two pieces of a puzzle.

I stop only long enough to tell her, "You're driving me crazy here, Cara."

She lets up to breathlessly say, "Same, Jamie. God, I haven't been able to think about anything else lately but kissing you," and then our mouths are back together. We kiss and kiss and kiss. Cara moves her right leg up and around me. I feel the heat and pressure of her inner thigh against my hip, holding us tightly together.

I'm a goner.

Being with her like this feels natural, like breathing, and *way* too good. For a split second, I picture us removing the barriers that are keeping us from skin-to-skin contact. My heart is pounding in my ears, and I think how I can just reach between us and...

I scare myself with where my thoughts are going, and some sense abruptly returns to me like a splash of cold water. I force myself to pull away.

"What's wrong?" Cara pants.

I can barely get the words out through my own labored breathing, "We should stop, Cara, before it gets too hard for us to."

"I'm already there, Jamie; please, don't stop. I don't want you to. You're incredible."

She begins to arch herself back up toward me and pull me back down with her. I mindlessly start to follow until I think again.

"Shit!" I groan. "You think I want to stop? Come on, sit up; we can't do this, especially not here."

Cara sits up, breathing as heavily as I am. She adjusts her shirt and brushes her hair back from her face. Releasing a long, ragged breath, she agrees, "You're right, I... I'm so sorry, you must think I'm..." She doesn't finish, but I know what she's implying.

"No, no," I say, with a vigorous shake of my head, "I don't, and I definitely don't want you to think all I want from you is to get inside your pants."

"I know you're not like that," Cara says, not meeting my eyes.

We sit in silence for a few seconds, catching our breath before she looks back at me. "You're being the stronger one here."

Still a little disoriented and more than a little ashamed, I'm the one to blink away now. "Yeah, you don't know the direction my thoughts were just headed."

I take both of her hands in mine, transfixed on our laced fingers.

I must be deep in thought because I barely hear Cara ask, "Jamie, what are you thinking? Talk to me here."

I glance up at her, and then back down at our clasped hands, rubbing my thumbs against the inside of her smooth wrists. I feel her shiver.

"It's just... this... us ..." I return my gaze to her face. "There's something crazy special between us, Cara." I search her face for confirmation.

"Yes, there absolutely is. I don't believe it's the norm. It's beautiful and—"

I don't let her finish; I take her in my arms and embrace her again, holding her close. Her arms come around my waist, squeezing me tightly in return.

I stroke her soft hair and whisper, "There's never been anything like this for me, not even close."

She draws back a little and looks into my eyes again. "For me, either, Jamie. You need to know, I've never kissed a guy like that... I mean, I've kissed boys, but definitely not anything comparable to *that*."

The thought of her kissing another guy intrudes on my imagination and doesn't sit well with me. But what does is knowing that what is happening between us is both unique and special to us both.

"I didn't mean for it to go down like that on our first real date. I only wanted to kiss you; hell, I've wanted to kiss you since I first met you. I was only going to give you a brief kiss, and then..."

I don't say it aloud, but that so-called brief first kiss, in actuality, was like a spark that quickly ignited a fire burning hot inside me, the heat between us begging to be quenched.

"My face is still burning," is all I say.

"Mine too." Cara smiles, touching her cheek, and we both release the tension between us by laughing together.

I raise my hand to stroke her cheek with my fingers, then cup it in my hand—so soft and small under my palm, and also very warm. "Yeah, it is." I grin mischievously as I take in all of her beauty. "Your just-been-kissed expression is about the cutest thing I've ever seen, especially knowing I'm the one who put it there."

"And you're the most handsome man I've ever laid eyes on. I could look at you all day long and never get tired of it... just sayin'." She runs her index finger lightly down my cheek, then looks away as though embarrassing herself.

I love her touch and the fact that she thinks I'm handsome, but what I love most is how she refers to me as a man. I tilt her chin up to see her eyes. "I'm *your* man," I say, "all of me, okay?"

She nods. "I'm all in, one hundred percent. I've never been happier in my life than when I'm with you." Her eyes glisten with moisture as soon as she says it, and she briefly closes them, blowing out toward her forehead. "Okay, wow. I think I might need a second here."

God, the sweetness of Cara, this moment, will remain indelibly seared into my memory as one of the best. "Ah, Cara, as far as I'm concerned, there will never be anyone else for me... ever," and I mean it, giving her a soft kiss to seal our agreement.

I suddenly realize I've lost track of time and look at my phone in a panic.

"What time is it?" Cara asks, eyes wide.

"It's late. I need to get you home. I would hate to lose your father's trust on our first date."

I start the truck, and after we're both buckled, put it in gear and take off toward Cara's house.

I drive with my left hand while holding Cara's in my right. All I can think about is how crazy I am about her. Our kisses bonded us tonight like nothing I've ever felt with another human. She rests her head on my shoulder and clasps my forearm with her right hand, staying close to me as we drive in silence—no radio, no talking, only the road noise and our thoughts.

Is she reliving our time together like I am? What began initially as an intense connection between the two of us that first day in the cafeteria has only grown deeper tonight, and I wish we could stay like this forever, wish I could feel this good forever.

There is no question that I'm totally crushing on Cara, and yes, I'm in "lust" with her, too, or whatever anyone would want to label what Cara and I have together in order to minimize it. Yet it's so much more than that. It might be a new love, a young love, but without a doubt, what I feel for Cara is unmistakably rock-solid L-O-V-E.

I freaking love her!

Cara

After we return to my house from our date, Jamie, the proverbial gentleman, takes my hand and walks me to my door. His hand is large and warm, and mine feels oddly small in his, but I reciprocate his need to remain connected. I don't want to say goodbye.

The porch light is on, and as soon as Jamie can see me better, he lets go of my hand and tilts my chin up toward him to look into my eyes. When we're standing, he's so much taller than my 5'6", I have to look up to see his face.

"Cara, you've been quiet; is everything cool with you?" His eyes are studying mine, concerned.

"Everything is amazing." I smile, but I can tell it's wobbly, conflicted. "I had a wonderful time tonight. Thank you for the best date I've ever had."

How can my voice sound so casual and steady when inside, one part of me wants to scream to unleash the overwhelming joy I feel, and one part wants to weep with the beauty of what Jamie means to me? I've been trying to reconcile the two the entire drive home.

Don't get too attached, Cara. He's a guy. This is probably just a fling. He will eventually get bored. I kept trying to tell myself that all evening and then we kissed and Jamie said things to me like, *"As far as I'm concerned there will never be anyone else for me."* Are we too young to make the kind of commitment we just did? Gah, I'm so torn between self-preservation and going all-in with Jamie.

He says, "I should be thanking you. Tonight was special. *You're* special." He looks at his phone and furrows his brows. "But the clock is about to strike midnight, and instead of the prince running after Cinderella, your dad's going to come running after me." He laughs.

He takes me in his arms to hug me, bending his knees so he's closer to my level, and I put my arms around his waist. I snuggle into his warm neck and grumble, "I wish we had more time. It's never enough." I breathe in his clean, masculine scent and decide he could bottle the formula, call it *Jamie,* and make millions of dollars.

"I agree with you on that!" He releases me, places his hands on my shoulders, and says, "Goodnight, Cara; I'll text you as soon as I get home." He gives me a quick, chaste kiss leaving me craving more.

It's two minutes until midnight when I walk through the door and lock it behind me. Of course, my dad is waiting for me in his recliner. He's either asleep or pretending to be. I tiptoe over and gently touch his arm.

"Hey, Daddy." I hardly ever call him that anymore, but it spontaneously flows from me for some reason. Being with Jamie tonight has fully opened a vulnerable and tender part of me. For an instant, a memory flashes of my father and mother expressing their love to one another as they once did, and my heart aches. "I'm home."

"Hi, Honey." He quickly sits upright. "Did you have a good time?"

"We had a great time. The food was good, the movie was good," I giggle to keep it light, "and the company was *very* good. I guess you could say we are officially a couple after tonight. Jamie is such a gentleman, Dad. He opened doors for me and wouldn't allow me to pay for anything."

I'm also thinking, but of course, don't add, *and when we got hot and heavy, he stopped me from seducing him to the point of no return.*

"Glad it went well. I like that young man. Never doubted I would because he would have to be something special for you to bring him here to meet me. And now to be going steady with him?"

"Oh my gosh, Dad, going steady?" I laugh loudly and roll my eyes. "It's called going out or dating."

"Giving you a hard time, but it's what my parents called it back in the day." He chuckles, the best sound next to Jamie's laugh. "It's obvious how much you like him and how well-suited you two are." He stands and kisses me on the forehead. "Your old man is off to bed now." He emphasizes the word *old*.

"I'm going to grab a snack and go to bed. See you in the morning," I say.

"Goodnight, sweetie."

As he turns out the light and walks slowly down the hall to his bedroom, my tears blur his silhouette. I sit down on the couch, feeling selfish that the thought only now occurs to me how very lonely my dad must be, as I guess I've been... until now. Sure, he goes to work most days at the church office and stays busy on Sundays with his sermon and all, but his evenings are, for the most part, spent alone after we have our usual dinner and evening visit.

I watched my compassionate, gentle father take care of my mother during the worst days of cancer's havoc on her body and observed the way he handled her subsequent death. How, after she died, he was the life raft that kept me afloat, kept me from suffocating in my personal sea of grief, all while drowning in his own.

I sometimes catch him with a forlorn look in his eyes when he doesn't know I'm watching. After my mom died, the thought of him dating or having affection for another woman bothered me, but now I only want whatever will make him happy. He is still young and very good-looking, which is not solely my opinion. I've been told so by both younger and older women. Does he ever think about dating? I make a mental note to discuss this with him at the right time.

I get up and go to the kitchen to grab a nut and date bar and a glass of almond milk to take to my room. When I check my phone, I've got three texts—two from Jessica and one from Eric. I read Jessica's first because I promised her I would text her when I got back from my date.

Jessica: *Hey, girlie, it's after midnight. Are you home yet?*

Then seven minutes later:

Jessica: *Cara, you home from your date yet?*

C: *Sorry, I didn't get home until midnight. Was talking to my dad and getting ready for bed. The date went great, better than I could've hoped.*

Jessica: *Details, please!!!*

C: *Jamie took me to my favorite restaurant and to a movie. We talked for a while, and then he brought me home.*

I make her suffer a minute before sending another text.

C: *Yes, we kissed, yes it was incredible, and yes, I'm even more head over heels for him!*

Jessica: *So he's a good kisser?*

Leave it to Jessica for this to be her main concern. She also thinks I'm an anomaly because I haven't had sex yet.

C: *Better than good. The best.*

As I type, I remember the feel of Jamie's lips on mine and the dark look of desire in his eyes mixed with something resembling pain. It revealed the inner battle going on between self-control and his strong passion for me.

It was more than difficult to keep from going all in. If Jamie moved us in that direction, I'm ashamed to admit I would have given my entire self to him—body and soul. I *wanted* to right there in his pickup truck. *Geez!*

Logically, I know it's too soon, of course, but the minute Jamie touched me, every bit of logic and clarity of thought fled like the good kid at a party when the beer's brought out.

I stare down at my "purity ring" on the ring finger of my right hand and gingerly twist it around and around with my thumb. Last year, I went through a ceremony at church where those in the youth group who wanted to make the commitment to keep their virginity until marriage received a ring symbolizing the commitment.

The idea is to give the ring to our future spouse on our wedding night as a gift of having "saved yourself" for them until after marriage. It seemed so straightforward and even easy to do at the time, but it was a year ago when I wasn't dating anyone and definitely never close to being in a position like I was with Jamie tonight. I feel conflicted and confused about the commitment now, even to the point of taking off the ring and leaving it off. But what would my dad say?

Thank goodness Jamie had the wherewithal and restraint to stop things before they went too far. My cheeks burn with heat from the memory, but also with a little embarrassment at my own forwardness.

When I apologized for that, Jamie didn't seem fazed by it, didn't think of me as easy or anything, *thank goodness*. I think we both understand the explosive chemistry between us; it's difficult to rein in. Obviously, what we share is new for him, too.

Jessica: *I'm happy for you! And a little jelly. Still hopeful my prince will appear soon to sweep me off my feet the way Jamie has you! Night, Cara Bear.*

Only my dad, Eric, and Jessica know my old nickname and still call me by it.

C: *Night, Jess. Sleep well.*

I leave her with a sleeping emoji and a red heart and then switch to Eric's text. While I'm reading it, I receive a text from Jamie.

Eric: *Hey, Cara. Just want to check on you. I hardly saw you at all this week, and I miss you.* A frowny-face emoji ends the text.

This makes me wonder if he and Jessica talked together tonight about me ghosting them. I go to Jamie's text:

Jamie: *Hi, Love, I'm home and in bed now. Whatcha doing?*

Wow, his endearment warms me to my toes and makes my heart skip a beat... or five. I'll text Eric quickly so I can get right back to Jamie.

C: *Hey, Eric, I've been busy, but I miss you, too. Will join you for lunch Monday.*

Jamie: *Eric?????*

Oh crap! I intended to send that text to Eric.

C: *Sorry, I accidentally sent that to you instead of Eric.*

There are a long few seconds before Jamie responds.

Jamie: *So you're texting Eric Baines?*

C: *He texted me earlier to ask how I was doing because he hadn't seen me much, and I was answering.*

Jamie: *Okay? And you miss him???? And you'll have lunch with him Monday??*

What's with all the question marks? I find myself getting a little perturbed. Jamie knows Eric and I have practically been best friends since we were in kindergarten, and I do miss seeing him, miss our conversations; but it doesn't negate anything I feel for Jamie in the least.

C: *He's a good friend, nothing more. Jessica texted me before we went out tonight saying much the same—she misses me and feels deserted by me. So I told her we would eat lunch back at the table Monday. I was telling Eric the same. Hope it's okay.*

A couple of minutes pass before Jamie texts back. I begin to think he's not going to.

Jamie: *Sure, of course, it is. I know you and Eric go way back. You had your friends for years before I arrived on the scene. Who am I to monopolize all your time? (male shrug emoji)*

After I received this text, I quickly received another from him:

Jamie: *Have I told you that I've discovered I have a bit of a jealous streak since I met you?* He ends with a laughing emoji this time.

The text stirs something deep within me because Jamie wouldn't be jealous if he didn't truly care for me, right? Should his jealousy make me feel good, though? Because it definitely does.

C: *If I'm honest, and the tables were turned, I would probably be a little jealous if you and another girl were expressing that you miss one another. But, if I knew it was strictly a benign friendship, what Eric and I have, I wouldn't be.*

Jamie: *Touché. I do trust that's all it is on your part. I really do. But are you sure you and Eric are on the same page with your interpretations of your relationship?*

C: *I've never given him a reason to think we're not.*

Jamie: *Okay, enough about Eric. I want you to know what a good time I had with you tonight. It will be forever etched in my memory. Every single minute of it.*

A sweet ache surges through the pit of my stomach at the image of us lying together on the seat of his truck, kissing deeply and desperately, feeling like we couldn't get enough of each other. I place the memory carefully into a new mental box labeled *The Best*.

C: *Same here! Again, thank you. I already miss you and can't wait to see you.*

Jamie: *Yeah, and I have to work with my dad tomorrow, so I can't come to see you. Can I come over tomorrow night, or is that too much?*

C: *It's not too much for me, but my dad might think so.* I pause and think. *I have to wake up early Sunday and go to church with him, so maybe we'll just see each other at school Monday?* It pains me to say it.

Jamie: *I understand. It'll be hard for me to wait, though. Get some good rest, and I'll call you tomorrow when I get a chance.*

C: *Goodnight. Talk to you tomorrow.*

Jamie: *I'll fall asleep thinking about you.*

C: *I'll definitely be thinking about you, too... and hopefully dream about you.*

Jamie: *heart emoji*

I text Eric what I meant to text him earlier and lie awake for a long time thinking about Jamie and our time together. I remove the memory again, unfold it, and attempt to relive how his touch felt—so tender at first and then fierce as we both teetered on the edge of taking things too far. I close my eyes only to remember the longing in Jamie's. They contained raw passion mingled with surprise. He was as shocked as I was by the unexpected intensity of our chemistry and desire.

Insatiable desire.

Ah, Jamie. How will we ever be alone together and keep from falling over the ledge of restraint? It will be as difficult as corralling wild horses off a Texas prairie, but it can be done. If I plan to keep this ring on my finger, we will have to work hard at it.

Cara

Monday couldn't come soon enough, only because it meant seeing Jamie at school. I have quickly gone from a girl who dreads the end of a weekend to one highly anticipating Monday to arrive. The morning classes each feel hours-long, as usual, which makes me all the more elated when the lunch bell rings. Of course, my elation has nothing to do with actually eating lunch.

As I place my things in my locker, I'm startled to feel a whisper through lips as soft as feathers on the back of my neck.

"Hello, beautiful."

I quickly turn around and there's Jamie with a devilish grin. He looks as hunky as ever and smells just as good. He brushes his fingers through the top part of his unruly hair, and I appreciatively watch his ample bicep strain against the sleeve of the gray Henley he's wearing today.

I laugh and say, "Right back at you," absently closing my locker behind me.

"I asked to leave class early so I could properly escort you to lunch. I hate that all our classes are so far apart from each other."

Jamie grabs my hand possessively and smiles at me with such radiance, my stomach takes a nosedive. A few students look at us and glance down at our clasped hands. I'm proud to walk with Jamie hand in hand for the first time at school down the hallway into the cafeteria.

Jamie bends down as we're walking and whispers in my ear, "God, I missed you," and all I can do in return is giddily smile up at him like I've just been told I'm going to Hawaii.

We enter the cafeteria and walk to the table to set down our backpacks. The only one of the gang already there is Mark Shelton, and he's his goofy, outgoing self. Sporting his signature brilliant smile and positivity, he greets us with a hearty, "Hi, guys, glad you're joining us today!"

I just smile, while Jamie gives him a nod and says, "Hey, Mark, how's it going, dude?"

We reach the food line to get our lunch, walk back to the table, and sit down together. Eric has taken the place beside me with Jessica sitting on the other side of him.

They have both brought their lunch from home and have already begun eating when Jessica asks, "How was your first date and the movie Friday night? We've wanted to see that one."

She's asking Jamie in order to get his reaction, I surmise, because I've already told her about it (*mental eye-roll*).

"The movie was pretty good and keeps you guessing all the way through. I would highly recommend it. We had a lot of fun." Jamie smiles at me and winks.

"I bet you did," Eric says under his breath but loud enough for me to hear. I look at him, willing him to turn his head to see my quizzical expression regarding his acerbic tone, but he won't look at me.

Mark speaks up, "Don't plan anything for Halloween night. I'm having a party, and I want y'all to come. More details later." He takes a healthy bite of a sandwich.

Again, Eric derisively mutters a comment under his breath, "I'm sure they'll be too busy counting the stars in each other's eyes to make it." And again, he won't look at me.

I've had enough of his bitter sarcasm. "Eric, can I talk to you a sec... out in the hall?"

Jamie watches me with narrowed eyes. He didn't hear Eric's rude comments and has no idea how badly I'm fuming inside at the way Eric is acting toward me.

"Sure, Cara." Eric gives Jamie a smug smirk as he stands to follow me.

I walk out into the hall and stop when we round the corner where we are out of sight and earshot from anyone.

"What's with the snide comments? What's going on to make you say those things?" The frustration in my voice is clear.

"Are you kidding?" he asks, words dripping with sarcasm again. "You even have to ask? Why haven't you texted me or called me? It's like you've fallen off the face of the earth in a week's time. Is that how important I am to you? And how can you spend all your time with someone you barely know and, poof, after one week, think you know him well enough to go out with him? Jessica told me you two are exclusive now." Eric looks down at the floor, sullen and sad.

"I did return your text Friday night. You never texted me back after that. No matter what you think, I do know Jamie well enough to be his girlfriend; he's a great guy. I think it's normal for a couple to spend most of their spare time together when a relationship is new, don't you? Please don't take it personally."

Eric softens a little and takes both of my hands in his, which feels awkward and somehow ominous. "Cara, you have to know how much I care about you. I've been waiting for you for what seems like years, waiting for you to come around and realize what we have together. This all just really hurts."

I'm taken aback and can't help but hear Jamie's prophetic words ring in my ears: *Are you sure you and Eric are on the same page with your interpretations of your relationship?*

"I do care about you, you know that. We've practically been best friends since I can remember, but I don't like you in the way you're talking about, Eric. I'm sorry," I say, shaking my head.

"I don't get why the hell not!" His voice is louder and has risen an octave. "Like you said, we've been inseparable nearly all of our lives. I've been here when you've needed me and have done everything I can to show you how much you mean to me. I've waited years for you," then speaking softer, he sighs, "hoping you'll love me the way I love you."

He forces a crooked smile and tucks a stray strand of hair behind my ear while gazing into my eyes. I start to panic because he looks as though he's about to try to kiss me.

Instead, he grabs me and pulls me close into a tight hug, speaking more frantically, "Don't do this; don't do this to us, what we have together!"

I immediately stiffen. The hug is too tight. I shake my head repeatedly and try to pull away, but Eric is unrelenting, squeezing me so hard I lose my breath, my arms pinned to my sides by his strong biceps.

My voice leaves my throat in a gasp, but it's louder than I expect when I cry, "Eric, you're hurting me!" and then "NO!" again and again, hoping he'll let me go.

Jamie appears from around the corner and stops dead in his tracks when he sees Eric squeezing me like a giant tube of toothpaste while I shout at him with what must be a very wide-eyed and panicked expression. My eyes lock with Jamie's and scream, *"Help me!"*

A hard look overtakes Jamie's face, one I've never seen before—pure, raw fury. He moves closer to us, but Eric's back is to Jamie, and Eric doesn't even notice him.

The blue in Jamie's eyes is no longer the usual cool Pacific blue, but the blue of the hottest part of a flame. His fists and jaws clench tightly, yet his voice remains steady.

Barely above a whisper, Jamie hisses, "Take your *fucking* hands off her."

When his command doesn't immediately seem to register with Eric, he shouts, "Now, dammit!" and Eric lets me go, a look of bewilderment etched on his face.

Jamie takes hold of my arm and pulls me close to him, away from Eric. He cups my face in both his hands and tilts my head upward to get a better look into my eyes. "Are you okay, babe?" His face is a grimace of concern.

In the shock of what just happened, all I can manage is a quick but weak nod.

Jamie drops his hands from my face and turns toward Eric. His fists are balled again. "What the hell were you doing, Baines?" he asks with such ferocity I'm afraid he is about to hit Eric.

Jamie outsizes Eric by quite a bit and could do some real damage. There are a few kids standing around watching now, probably hoping for some action.

Eric must realize he's about to get punched and tries to quell the situation. "It's cool, man, forget it. It just sucks how you've moved right in and poached my girl."

"She's not your girl, *Eric*." Jamie's teeth are still clenched, and he pulls me to him with one arm before moving me protectively behind him. He starts to raise his fist.

I find my voice, but it quivers and breaks apart like a fragile egg hatching. "Stop, both of you, please! This is ridiculous, and it's not the time or place for this. Eric, we'll talk later. Jamie, let's go."

"Sorry, not yet, Cara." Jamie doesn't take his eyes from Eric's and steps closer to him with flared nostrils and narrowed eyes, quite an intimidating look.

He puts his mouth about two inches from Eric's left ear and whispers, "If you ever, ever touch *my* girlfriend like that again, I will break your fucking face. Do you hear me?"

Eric looks at Jamie totally bereft, as though Jamie is an evil villain who has broken into his home and stolen his most prized possession. I can't help but feel a little sorry for Eric. It's only now I realize the depth of the feelings he must have been carrying for me for quite some time. I didn't have a clue he truly believed there was a romantic future for us. The thought leaves me feeling queasy and a bit sad for him at the same time.

Eric claimed he loved me. I'm slightly traumatized at that particular revelation, along with his desperate and pathetic attempt to show it. But the instant Jamie stood up for me and I saw the anger mingled with fear on his face when Eric was hurting me, I had another sudden revelation—It's hardly Eric I love at all.

I love Jamie. With every bit of my heart, I *love* him. *Oh, my God, this is what being in love feels like.*

Eric and the others disperse, and I try to keep up with Jamie's long strides as he rushes down the hallway toward the exit to the south parking lot. I want to hug him, to thank him, and tell him how I feel.

"Jamie, wait." He stops and looks at me, his expression remote and hard, eyes boring into mine. "You're upset with me. Why are you mad at *me*?"

"Texting Baines that you miss him the other night? Secret conversations with him? Hugging in the hallway? Why didn't you tell me there's been more between you and Eric than friendship?" he accuses.

Is it anger or jealousy? Whichever it is, he's not seeing the situation for what it is.

"There's not, Jamie, I promise," I say as more of a plea.

He looks me in the eye with a dejected expression. "I need some time alone to cool off and think."

With that, he walks off, leaving me staring at his back. I'm tempted to run after him again, but I respect his request and stay put.

I move to the window and watch him walk to his truck. He places both hands on the roof above the driver-side window and rests his forehead against the glass for a few seconds before rearing back and driving his fist into the side of his truck.

My throat tightens, and tears sting my eyes before I quickly turn away. I sure as heck don't want to go to class, but feeling alone and disoriented, I return to the cafeteria, snatch my backpack, and go to class anyway.

As soon as I enter the classroom, I walk straight to the teacher and say, "I'm not feeling well. May I have a pass to go to the nurse, please?"

She fills out a nurse's office pass for me; but instead, I walk to the girls' restroom, go into the farthest stall from the door, and sit down on the toilet. I'm trembling and let myself quietly cry. I'm shocked Jamie just left me standing there in the hall, but at the same time, it's obvious how angry he is and needs time to simmer down.

News to me—Jamie Gallagher has a temper!

I didn't actually mind it when his anger was directed toward Eric. If I'm honest, I thought it kind of heroic. But it's hurtful to know that at least some of Jamie's anger was directed toward me, thinking that there's more going on between Eric and me. I'm struck that the reason I'm crying is that for the first time, Jamie has questioned my honesty. It hurts like hell, feels a bit like a betrayal.

I wipe my eyes with some toilet tissue and take out my phone. My fingers itch to text Jamie, but I find myself growing angry with him when I start to. Doesn't he trust me by now and know how much I care about him? Eric and I have only ever been friends, that's it. Even if Eric has wanted more than friendship, I haven't.

There's not a snowball's chance in hell I would choose Eric over Jamie. That Jamie would even remotely think there's something between Eric and me twists my insides, especially after all that has passed between Jamie and me. So why should I text him like a groveling sycophant?

No, the ball's in his court. When we talk next, it will be Jamie who makes first contact. I didn't do anything wrong. I put my phone back in my pocket and decide to go back to class. It's better than sitting in a smelly restroom stall pining for Jamie. I can pine for him in a more comfortable setting than on a toilet.

When I return to class, I let my teacher know I went to the restroom on my way to the nurse, which made me feel better— not really a lie, although I still feel crappy. She smiles and takes back my pass as I head to my seat.

The rest of the school day drags, and I don't know if Jamie left or stayed at school, don't know if he's left *me*.

The thought of that only tightens the knot in my twisted gut.

Jamie

I skipped my last two classes and stayed pissed off the rest of the day, but I had to set aside any ruminating about what happened until I finished working on invoices for my dad. I had a lot to catch up on, but it was a nice distraction. I've been working since returning home from school, breaking only for a few minutes earlier to eat dinner.

When I finish in the office, it's late. I walk to my room, close the door, and sit at my computer desk tapping a pencil against it as I let myself go freely back over the day's events.

After a few minutes, I've come to the following conclusions: I was mad as hell when Cara asked Eric to follow her out of the cafeteria to talk privately, and raving mad at the shit-eating grin

Eric gave me when she did. When I saw them hugging in the hallway, a knife poisoned with jealousy stabbed straight into my heart.

Jealousy quickly became rage when I saw Cara's face and realized Eric was hurting her. Adrenaline flowing, I couldn't think straight—obviously. It took all I had not to beat Eric to a pulp right then and there, but I was afraid Cara might never forgive me if I did.

After having gradually calmed down throughout the evening, I admit I jumped to a lot of conclusions and, in essence, accused Cara of not being completely truthful about her relationship with Eric. Didn't she promise me there was nothing more between them than a deep friendship? I've definitely not given Cara the benefit of the doubt and know I overreacted.

I didn't stick around to let her explain and acted exclusively from my jealousy. I allowed my anger to consume me when I saw Cara being held, literally, against her will by Eric's suffocating hug—if that's what you'd call that damn stranglehold—the son of a bitch.

Now, I'm even angrier with myself for my lack of self-control. My adrenaline was pumping full force, and it was either Eric's face or the hard metal of Shadow. Still, no excuse.

Looking down at my bruised knuckles, I realize my worst fear is losing Cara, so I must've inadvertently tried to put distance between her and my feelings for her by leaving—maybe a subconscious effort to soften the blow of learning she has competing feelings for Eric?

Yet she promised she didn't, I continually tell myself.

Smothered by fear of losing her to Eric, I allowed anger to take precedence over my love for her. Clearer-headed now, I still can't seem to get past two questions: Why did she want to speak to Eric privately, as if there's something secret going on between the two of them; and why were they hugging in the hallway to begin with? I need to talk to Cara, *now,* and not a conversation through texting or over the phone.

Impulsively, I take my phone and text her:

J: *We need to talk. Can I come by?*

Cara: *It's too late, my dad's already in bed.* A curt reply that hits its mark and stings.

J: *Can I come talk to you through your window, just for a few minutes? Please? It's important!*

Cara: *I guess, but if you get caught at my window, my dad will not be happy. Park a good way down from my house and be quiet. Text me when you're getting out of your truck, and I'll raise the window.*

J: *I'll be there in ten. One more question.*

Cara: *Yeah?*

J: *Which window is yours?*

Cara: *Lol The first one on the right side of the house. See you in a few.*

Her virtual laugh gives me hope she's not irreparably upset with me. I plan to apologize and beg if need be.

My dad is still up watching one of his cable documentaries, so I decide to play it straight with him. "Dad, I know it's late, but I need to go see Cara and clear something up with her—a misunderstanding that happened today. It's something I really need to take care of that I should have earlier today."

He looks at me for a long while and nods. "Been there, I get it. Okay, but don't take too long, and text me when you get back in the house in case I've gone to bed. Don't forget to reset the alarm."

"Thanks, Dad. I'll explain later."

"You don't have to," he shakes his head.

I'm already practically running to the kitchen counter to grab my keys when he calls after me, "Good luck."

On the drive to Cara's, I think about how I surprised her at her locker today before lunch, how amazing she smelled when I nuzzled her neck—like her usual clean sunshine—and the big, surprised smile on her face when she turned around and saw me. I reflected on the feel of her soft hand in mine as we walked together to the cafeteria. Everything was going so well; it was a great day... until it wasn't.

I can't get the image out of my mind of Cara struggling to get away from Eric, or the crazed look on Eric's face when he finally let her go. The thought of Eric hurting her in any way was more than I could stand; I just snapped. I've at least now gotten past the point of repeatedly picturing myself rearranging Eric's face with my fists. I still don't trust that dude as far as I could throw him.

I turn onto Cara's street and pull up to a curb on a corner lot where there are no houses. I cut the engine and text Cara to let her know I'm walking toward her window. She is there waiting for me with her window raised, only the screen separating us.

I look around to make sure there are no neighbors outside of their houses watching us, but all is dark and quiet. I have to squat down to rest my elbows on the outside brick sill.

"Hey, Cara," I say, trying to discern her features in the darkness of her room. Her bed is under her window and she's sitting on it cross-legged. "How are you doing?" It takes a second for my eyes to adjust, but it looks as though she's been crying. "Cara?"

"I'm okay... well, I guess I've been better."

"If it's any consolation, I feel like crap knowing I'm partly to blame for that. I came to apologize. I'm sorry I left today without talking to you, without listening to you. I was angry, but it should've been about you, not me. I know Eric must have hurt you and scared you, and yet I just... left, wasn't there to walk you through that. I let my anger control me, and I—"

My words must bring everything back for her. Her shoulders slump forward, and she looks down at her hands twisting in her lap. "He did hurt me, and scare me, but... but what hurts most is that you didn't trust me, that you didn't believe me when I told you there was nothing going on between Eric and me." A sob breaks free, and she covers her face with both hands, crying into them. "Sorry, I'm being way too emotional here."

I can't bear seeing her cry like this. She had enough to deal with regarding Eric's craziness. Losing my temper and questioning her honesty only added to her pain.

"Cara," I say, but she doesn't remove her hands to look at me. "Shit..." I carefully remove the clasps on the window screen and set it against the house. "I'm coming in there."

This gets her attention. She drops her hands from her face. "Jamie, no, you can't, I—"

"Watch me." I climb through the window in one fluid motion and then lower it to half-mast.

I sit facing Cara on her bed and take her into my arms. She cries harder now onto my shoulder, and I give her a long minute before cupping her face in my hands. "It kills me to see you cry. Please don't." I use the pad of my thumbs to wipe at the tears, but more appear just as quickly.

When she looks up at me with pain in her eyes, it's like a sucker punch, and I begin kissing her cheeks in an effort to erase her tears, to erase her pain.

I rest my forehead against hers. "I'm so sorry I doubted you, doubted *us*. I allowed jealousy and anger to tackle my common sense."

Cara hiccups between sobs. "Have you forgotten all our conversations, all the time we've spent together? Haven't I made it clear how I feel about you?"

"Yes, yes, you have, and I'm an idiot. I fouled you... bad, and you deserve a dozen free throws right at my damn head. Please forgive me? Will you? I'm truly, truly sorry, babe."

The tentative twitch of one corner of her mouth as she swipes at her cheeks makes me feel a hundred pounds lighter.

"I do forgive you, Jamie. How could I not? From now on, though, I hope you know I won't ever lie to you or keep anything from you. I don't work like that. What I say is what I mean." Her look is strong and intimidating, and the censure is fully deserved.

I nod. "I know that, I do. Like I said, I'm an idiot to even think that you have feelings for Eric like you do for me. I was a very crappy boyfriend today."

"You're harder on yourself than I am, don't you think? I mean, if you didn't care about me, all of this wouldn't have bothered you like it did, right? A part of me wants to thank you, not throw a ball at your head." She smiles just a fraction more.

I study her, confused, and she says, "Thank you for coming to check on me in the hallway and for standing up for me, for making Eric come to his senses and let go of me. You *were* there for me when I needed it most today."

The mention of Eric's name causes my blood to boil again. "You're strangely welcome, but what the hell was up with him hugging you like that? Why'd you want to talk to him privately in the first place; what did you two discuss?"

She looks upset again, so I quickly reassure her. "Sorry, those are the lingering questions I've had all day. I promise I believe there's nothing going on between you two. But can you see, at least a little," I give her my best puppy-dog face, "why I questioned there possibly being some type of past or something between you and Eric you weren't telling me?"

She chuckles at my expression. "All right, I understand how it must have looked to you outwardly, but you didn't hear what was going on beside me—what Eric whispered for my ears only when Jessica asked about our date, and then again when Mark invited us to his Halloween party. Eric has never been so rude and condescending toward me—ever."

Cara describes Eric's sarcastic comments and how he tried to convince her they had a future together that she was allowing *me* to ruin—how angry he was at feeling ignored by her. She explains that what started as a hug, initiated solely by Eric, quickly became a desperate attempt to hold on to her, both figuratively and literally.

"It was like he thought he could will me to love him, to make me suddenly realize there is more between us than friendship. It all seemed so unbelievable and shocking to me. And then I remembered you suggesting more than once that you thought Eric had his sights set on me as more than just a friend.

"Now that I look back, there were some signs. If I had listened to my intuition, I would have known that his feelings toward me were different than mine for him. I see that now." She pauses, waves a hand, and finally initiates a real smile. "You know, hindsight and all."

"Yeah, but how will you and Eric move on from this? It's pretty clear from my end that he better not ever touch you again, and surely he knows now there will never be a romantic future for the two of you. Do you think you guys can remain friends?"

"Eric actually called me earlier apologizing profusely, and I have to give him some grace here and put myself in his shoes. If he likes me even half as much as I like you and then suddenly has to face the reality that those feelings will never be reciprocated..." she shrugs, palms turned up, "it must have crushed him."

"Cara, you'd give grace to Jack the Ripper." I chuckle. "You're such a good person; better than I am. I don't have to like him, right? I'll tolerate him for your sake. It would be a lot harder to ignore him because he'll pretty much be wherever we go together, namely school."

I sigh heavily, resigned. "You all have the same friends, so I'll learn to make the best of it. He'll be at Mark's party Saturday night and any other get-togethers the gang has. Also, we'll have to sit together at lunch every day after it gets too cold to eat outside. Will that be awkward for you?"

"A little, but I think he's truly remorseful about what happened. If I practice what I preach, forgiveness is important here. Eric wanted me to give him your number so he could call you to apologize, but I told him I didn't know if you were ready to hear from him just yet. I also didn't think it was my place to give him your phone number, so I said he could talk to you at school."

Cara's words and soft tone are soothing, making most of the anger I'm still holding on to dissipate. She has helped me see things from Eric's perspective, something I hadn't attempted to do until now.

She makes me a better person.

Jamie

S till sitting on Cara's bed, we both fall silent. All is quiet save for the sound of our rhythmic breathing and the night sounds floating in from outside the open window. Deep in thought, I concede that Eric will remain a part of her life and therefore a part of mine. The main thing that keeps me from hating Eric too badly is that he's the one who introduced me to Cara, which is the best thing that's ever happened to me.

I break the silence, my voice like a quiet rumble of thunder inside her dark bedroom. "I probably need to lighten up a little and apologize to Eric as well for losing my cool. I mean, I did threaten to break his face." I laugh faintly, but Cara is looking at me soberly, unmoving.

She's obviously been thinking about something else. Pinning me with an uncertain gaze, fresh tears shimmer in her eyes.

"Ah, man, have I upset you again? What is it?" I start to apologize for having threatened to bust Eric's face when she stops me.

"It's not that," she says. "He deserved it. There *is* something else I need to tell you, though. I told you earlier I'll always be totally honest with you, but there's one thing I'm holding back."

She looks down and my heart begins to thunder in my chest. "What's wrong, Cara? You're scaring me!"

A tear leaks from the corner of her eye, and when she looks back up at me, the stupid part of my brain fears she's about to reject me in some way.

"Nothing bad," she shakes her head, "I just," she hesitates before saying, "I need to tell you I love you. The realization hit me so hard today when all this was happening, but then you were angry and left, and I didn't get to tell you, and... I've been afraid I'd never get the chance to. I love you, Jamie, I do."

It's not what I expect—such boldness coming from Cara—so I'm surprised into silence, trying to absorb the fact that Cara could possibly feel as strongly about me as I do her.

Panic enters her eyes when I don't immediately say anything, and she adds, "I know it's too soon." Her speech picks up speed. "You probably think I'm confused for thinking I'm already in love with you, but I am; I know I am. That's why I was so hurt today when I thought we might be over." She's nervously rubbing the cuticle of her left thumbnail with her right when her bottom lip begins to tremble. She unexpectedly bursts into full-blown tears.

I take her in my arms and bury my face in her soft hair that smells like fresh flowers tonight. "Don't cry, babe, please don't cry again. I'm serious, it breaks my heart in two." I speak softly into her ear in an attempt to comfort her. "Why *are* you crying? This is a good thing, right?"

"Because I'm afraid you don't... or won't ever feel the same way. This has never happened to me before, and you already know how sensitive I am; I can't help it." She swipes at her eyes with the back of her hand.

"Look here, Cara." I gently tilt her chin so she can see I mean what I'm about to say. "I should have already told you how much I love you. I swear it's more than I can express to you in words, but, ironically, I thought the same thing—that you would think I'm moving too fast. You're right, it's early in our relationship to declare our love, but it's true that when you know, you just know." I shrug faintly and am surprised to feel my own throat tighten with emotion. It's the first time I've ever told anyone outside of my immediate family that I love them. I swallow hard and say, "I think I've loved you since the first day I saw you, honestly."

More tears surface, and she wipes at her eyes again before she rises to her knees to initiate a kiss. It's soft and brief, and oh-so-good. She puts her arms around my neck and brings my chest to hers in a tight embrace. "You have no idea; that makes me the happiest girl on the face of this planet."

Which makes me feel like I just won the friggin' lottery. We stay this way for a while, basking in the closeness and in each other's warmth. I stroke her hair, thinking how much I truly do love Cara and never want to hurt her again the way I did. It was wrong on so many levels.

The scent and feel of her are intoxicating. An overwhelming sense of desire grows between us through simply holding one another. In spite of the cool night air coming in through the window, warmth becomes a blazing heat with the feel of her body pressed against mine.

My brain tells me this is the time to say goodnight and leave.

I pull back enough to look into her eyes, but I go blank. Was I about to say something, tell her something? All thought is lost when her heavy-lidded eyes share a longing that must be a perfect reflection of my own.

I don't even attempt gentleness. My mouth crashes down hard onto hers, and she meets my kiss with equal passion—two people in love, kissing as though their very existence depends on it. Her mouth tastes something like sweet vanilla and is soft and hot. It's more than I can handle and remain a sane human being. Her kisses do this to me. *Every. Damn. Time.*

We become a tangle of lips and tongues, gliding, sliding, stroking. Mouth still on hers, I move my hands up and down her back like I did in my truck after our date. She feels as warm and smooth as I remember. I want to hang onto her and consume her—to press my love into her and never let her go.

I tell myself to end this kiss and get the hell out of Cara's bedroom before more can happen between us than a "make-up kiss." But the realization there's nothing under the wisp of a long T-shirt she's wearing makes me want to touch her more intimately, and I lose all reason.

Instinctively, my hands begin a journey from the middle of her back around to the sides of her body as we continue to kiss deeply. Any alarm bells signaling my entrance into the danger zone are drowned out by desire and the pounding of my heart in my ears.

I can feel the sweet curves, just under her arms, and I press my chest closer into hers, flattening her softness against my hardness. Her body is a perfect contrast and complement to mine. Cara's excited heartbeat thrums against my own thudding chest, yet somehow, I'm still not close enough.

She begins kissing my neck—soft, open-mouthed kisses that drive me closer to insanity. "You smell and taste so good," she whispers breathlessly onto my neck, and my own breath catches.

The break from her mouth on mine is too long, and I take back the kiss, hungrily—our tongues an unchoreographed dance of desire. Before my palms can mindlessly move farther around between us to travel where they're itching to go, Cara pulls back and takes both of my wrists in her fists. I feel scolded. My hands have roamed too far, have trespassed into forbidden territory.

I open my mouth to apologize when her eyes capture mine and paralyze me. Cara remains sitting on her knees, leaning back on her heels. With eyes drenched in desire, still looking into mine, it's as if she has telepathically read my thoughts. She guides my hands around in front of her, slowly placing my palms on herself. Her own palms cover my hands, holding them there, showing me what she wants.

For only an instant, I'm stunned into stillness before I allow myself to touch her, to move over her beautiful body, relishing her feminine curves. It's my downfall; she feels like magic. Her head tilts back, and I feel her shudder. Or was that me? Her eyes close, and her lips part in a moan of pleasure. My heart might burst out of my chest at the sight and feel of her.

It's too much. I've always tried to be a "gentleman" and have never touched a girl like this before—never wanted to like this— and my hands start to shake. My heart is pounding with all the newness and my need for her. I take her plump, swollen lips back to mine. "Cara," I whisper between kisses, "damn, I need you. I want to love you. I want to show you how much I love you."

"I think I'll die if I don't have you, Jamie, all of you. Don't stop."

"I-I won't."

I lay her down on her bed and move on top of her, my firmness pressing into her softness. She feels like heaven on earth. I need to be closer, to feel more of her. Straddling her thighs, I raise up and lift my T-shirt over my head and toss it to the floor.

The heat in her eyes when she looks at me is exquisite pain. The way her hungry gaze roves over my bare chest turns me on more than a touch. "The way you're looking at me; I don't think I can take it."

I want to see her, too. To touch her with nothing separating us. The thought of seeing her body sends a fresh wave of burning heat through me and causes my heart to pound even harder.

"I can't help it. You're so beautiful. I've always thought so." She smiles, pulling me back down to her, holding herself close to me. Her smooth hands run up and down my bare back, and *damn*, it feels good, makes me want to feel her soft touch on me everywhere.

My hands have a mind of their own. I take both of hers and stretch them above her head, my palms clasping hers. Our kisses become deeper, more desperate. I move my palms slowly from her hands down the underside of her arms to trail down the sides of her body. Her fingers of her right hand move to the nape of my neck and tangle in my hair that is badly in need of a cut.

I've lost all reason. Coming up for air, I say as a question, "I want to see you, all of you?"

She nods while pulling my mouth back to hers.

I begin inching her long T-shirt up with one hand to follow the journey of my own shirt to the floor when a loud noise stops me.

She stills only for a beat but seems lost in oblivion. I take my hands from her body and grab both of hers, holding them still as she practically fights me to let them go, to return to what we were doing.

"Wait, listen, what was that? Did you hear it?" I whisper. "It sounds like someone is right outside the window."

She must detect the fear in my voice and see my right hand shaking when I run it through my hair to push it from my eyes. But, admittedly, my unsteadiness is more from the effect she has on me than from being frightened by the noise. She sits up quickly, looking startled yet heartbroken that we've been interrupted.

I pull her shirt down for her and grab mine from the floor, pulling it back on. I scoot over to the window, raise it a little more, and sneak a look in both directions. It's then I see the wind has blown over the window screen.

"It was the screen I propped up outside the window. It fell and made the sound we heard." I sit back down on the bed and let out an unsteady breath.

"Thank God," she whispers, clearly relieved. "I thought maybe my dad heard something and came out of the house to check on it."

The thought of that happening is shockingly sobering. My own relief is palpable.

"It would be so easy," I let my voice trail off as I scrub both hands down my face, trying to rub away the desire I'm still feeling, "to finish what we started."

"I wouldn't stop you," Cara whispers matter-of-factly, moving toward me again.

As much as it pains me, I hold her at a distance. "Being with you feels perfect." I'm still breathless, practically panting. "You feel so good, but I'm not prepared for this, are you?"

She hesitates before saying, "No, I guess not," dropping her gaze and toying with the hem of her T-shirt.

I think about the unopened box of condoms sitting in my nightstand drawer my dad discreetly left on it last year—with a note not to tell Mom—when I dated a cheerleader named Katie. But the relationship didn't last, and I never even remotely wanted to be with her the way I want to be with Cara.

"Just because we both want to, doesn't mean we should," I add. "Can you imagine your dad walking into your room to find us like this, or worse? I've already disrespected him by coming in through your window in the dead of night. I promise I came only to talk with you, but damn, when we start kissing—"

"No, no, you're right." She shakes her head and then nods, remaining silent for a few more seconds. "I even vowed to myself after our date to do better the next time we were alone. I'm not going to lie, when we're together, all my self-control flies out the window, no pun intended," she lets out a rueful laugh, looking out into the night from the partially-raised window. "Like last time, you seem to be stronger about this than I am."

"I love your honesty," I say softly. "I'll never doubt it again, but we both have a self-control problem here, Cara. It's not just you. I take full responsibility for how far we go. Any strength I have comes from my love for you and not wanting to hurt you in any way. I won't let that happen." I pause. "You *are* just too irresistible, though." I kiss her nose, wanting to see her happy again.

"So are you, Jamie; that's the problem. What are we going to do? If we vow that this can't happen... for now, at least, we're going to have to have a plan, some boundaries... and it will still be hard, because I *want* to be with you. I can't get to the point we were tonight and stop. It's torture." She looks down at the ring on her right hand, twisting it with her thumb. Letting out an exasperated breath, she says, "I'm the biggest hypocrite."

Cara tells me about the commitment she made at church not to have sex before she's married, how easy it was to make the commitment then, but how hard it is to keep it now.

"After my mom died, my dad told me he's prayed for my future husband since I was a little girl, prayed that both our hearts would be kept pure and safe for each other. Do you see what a hypocrite I am?"

The knowledge brings completely conflicting emotions. On the one hand, I'm selfishly relieved to know that no guy has ever gotten as close to Cara as I have, or touched her like I have. Yet it also brings a surge of guilt. This is a girl who's conflicted over what she wants and what her dad and the church want for her. Until she figures that out, we need to give this time.

My heart lurches at the thought of how I could have easily caused her to break her promise tonight, how we surely would have if the window screen hadn't fallen and scared us back to reality.

Was that God intervening to stop us from doing something we would regret? Did we have to be stopped because we are too weak to stop ourselves? I admit I don't exactly know how the spiritual realm works.

My family hasn't been to church since we moved to Texas, but Mom is notorious for reminding us that "God works in mysterious ways." Was this one of those ways? Am I the one

Cara's dad has prayed for all her life, and through no merit of my own, but because of his prayers, I've been kept a virgin, too? To be Cara's first and her mine? Does it mean we'll get married someday?

The thoughts are mind-blowing.

"You're not a hypocrite; it's a real struggle. I'm selfishly grateful to know you've kept yourself from other guys. Obviously, this is something important to you, and I respect the hell out of that, Cara. I want to be your forever. Knowing that someday I'll be your first, that you'll be mine... that prospect is amazing," I stop, actually imagining it, swallow, and can't help but add, "more than amazing."

I think about how compatible we'll be together when that time does come, how Cara has given me a glimpse into how passionate and giving she is. I look forward to giving her all of myself in return... at the right time.

"But until then, like you said, we need a plan, need to set some boundaries," I say, and she nods.

"First of all, I'm going to have to be more careful about getting you alone in intimate places, not allow myself to barge in on you when it's dark and you're half-dressed." My gaze wants to move lower. I try hard to keep my eyes only on her face, all the while remembering how she looked and felt under my hands.

"What's the second thing?" she asks expectantly.

"Is there a second thing?" My mind is clouded with sensual thoughts of her.

"You said first of all, so I was expecting something else," she teases. "Earth to Jamie." She playfully nudges me with her shoulder.

"Okay, then," I smile, "second of all, it would help if you weren't so beautiful and sweet. I can now add forgiving to that list of attributes."

"You can also add that I love you," she says softly, looking sweetly into my eyes and grinning.

"Yes, and that, especially that," I say and kiss her. "I swear I loved you the second I saw you, when I walked into the cafeteria and was blown away by you."

"Seriously?"

"Seriously. You can even ask my dad; he knows."

Her eyes widen. "You told your dad you love me?" she asks, incredulously.

"Sort of." I wince, knowing most guys don't tell their parents their intimate feelings, hoping she doesn't think it's too weird. "That night of the day I met you, I talked to my dad about you, told him how I was hooked after taking one look at you. I shared my fear that you might not feel as strongly about me, a fear I now know you and I separately shared since day one. When I explained how we seemed to completely connect the instant we saw one another, he's the one who told me it sounded like love at first sight."

"I wouldn't have believed it even existed until now." She stills, and her eyes take on a far-away look—wistful. "You and your dad have a unique relationship, huh? You sound more like brothers than father and son." She sighs reflectively. "It sounds like what my mom and I had. I can't wait to meet your parents."

"How about meeting them Saturday before we go to the Halloween party? For now, though, I promised my dad I wouldn't be long, yet here I still am. I'm going to put your screen back on when I leave. Close and lock your window quietly, and I'll text you as soon as I get home."

I kiss her quickly and make my way out the window.

"Wait, before you leave, I have an addendum to what I said earlier." She pauses in thought. "It had to have been love at first sight for me, too. I mean, it's grown every day since then, the more I get to know you, but the seed was planted that day, positively. And tonight... tonight it definitely grew." She blinks away, self-consciously crossing her arms over her stomach.

As I click the window screen back in place, I ask, "So what does that make us if we were a seedling after we met? Are we a sapling now, a shrub, or what?"

She returns a smile that pulls at my heartstrings. Here in the soft glow of moonlight through her window, with her hair tousled, no makeup on, and her mouth swollen from my kisses, Cara is the most beautiful I've ever seen her.

I become serious again. "I knew the instant I saw you, something happened between us that was the end of me... and the beginning of *us*." I turn and leave her to her thoughts.

Cara

I wake up bone-tired Tuesday morning. It had been a stressful Monday and a short night of sleep after Jamie left. However, since Tuesdays are busy with school all day and community service at the church in the evening, I don't have time to be tired. The adrenaline from remembering the time spent with Jamie last night should be enough to keep me energized, along with some much-needed caffeine.

As I sip my morning coffee and get ready for school, I can't get Jamie off my mind. I picture his passionate yellow-blue gaze, a reflection of his personality—cool and hot rolled into one. He's a dichotomy of gentle tenderness and possessive fierceness.

And I love it all.

I figure there are very few people in one's lifetime who will truly love you. I have felt that love, for the most part, solely from the family circle I was born into. I suppose if one is lucky, she will also find deep love outside of that circle. I've never felt so loved and cherished by anyone other than my parents and grandparents.

Until Jamie.

I relive our time together last night, his adept hands and lips on me, *I want to see all of you. I want to love you.* Remembering his words creates a tingling sensation throughout my body as if he were still touching me.

We had come too close to going all-in after I asked Jamie not to stop—*I won't,* Jamie had spoken urgently when we both lost all control. Rather than feeling relieved that we didn't succumb to our passion, I feel regret this morning. Isn't the typical morning-after cliché regretting what you did, not what you *didn't?* This unnerves me because it's a sharp detour from the path I chose for myself based on my upbringing and values, but it's the honest truth. It feels natural to want to be with Jamie unreservedly and wholly.

One day. I exhale a wistful sigh.

While sitting in my first period, I receive a couple of texts and wait until the teacher is busy so I can check my phone. There is a no-phone policy in most of my classes, but I don't want to wait until the passing period to check. It's Jamie.

Jamie: *Morning, babe. How's my girl?*

I suppose after I didn't respond right away, he knew I wasn't able to and texted me the news he wanted to share.

Jamie: *Baines found me outside of my first period and apologized for everything, so we're cool now, even shook on it.* (thumbs-up emoji)

I glance over at the teacher who is speaking with another student and type a clandestine text under the desk.

C: *Morning! Was it awkward? No hard feelings?*

Jamie: *Well, he's never going to be my best friend or anything lol but it's all good.*

C: *I'm glad. Sorry it ever even happened. So we still plan on eating lunch with him and the others today?*

I send this and send another right after.

C: *We don't have to!*

Jamie: *We will today. It'll break the ice. But tomorrow, I want you all to myself... compromise.* (winking-face emoji)

C: *Fair enough. See you at lunch.* (red heart emoji)

Jamie: *I love you, Cara. Forever.*

My heart melts into a puddle. Those incredible three words coming from the incredible Jamie.

My Jamie.

At lunch, Jamie and I talk more with one another than with the gang. Eric acts as if nothing happened, but from my end, I can sense the tension in him. Jamie is his usual cool, collected, and witty self.

After we finish our lunch, Jamie laces his fingers with mine under the table and absently rubs his thumb back and forth over mine as we talk, lighting every nerve ending in my hand on fire. I relish the intimacy, relish knowing I'm his girl.

I turn to him and ask, "What are you doing tonight?"

"The usual; doing whatever my dad has for me to do in the home office. But I'm flexible. Are you asking me out on a date?" He smiles teasingly and squeezes my hand.

"Yeah, kind of," I reply. "Do you want to go with me tonight to do community service at my church?"

"Sure! Wait, I don't have to cook or anything, do I?" The stricken look on his face is hilarious, making me laugh.

I try to reassure him. "Haha, no, the food will already be prepared; we just serve it to the families who come through. We usually play games with the older kids after dinner while the parents, mostly single moms, visit with one another. It's also their weekly grocery pick-up time, and we'll need to sort the grocery items into bags before they all arrive."

"I can do that. What time should I pick you up?"

"Around six? It doesn't give you a lot of time at home after school, but we can eat at the church after everyone is served. I usually do."

I look over to see that the others have gone quiet and are covertly listening to us. Mark seems to be waiting for a lull in conversations so he can say something.

When we stop talking, he announces, "Okay, gang, my house Saturday night at 8:00. Everyone needs to bring something to munch on. I have all the drinks covered—adult beverages." He waggles his dark eyebrows. "So if you want a kiddie beverage, bring your own. My parents and little brother will be out of town visiting my grandparents like they do every Halloween weekend, so no worries. It's gonna be epic."

"What superhero are you going to be for Halloween this year, Mark?" Eric asks, smiling.

"Ah, man, we have to dress up?" Jamie asks, looking in my direction.

"Hell, yes, Gallagher, it's a gang tradition," Mark pretends to be insulted.

Jamie searches my face and says, "Really?"

"Yes, really. It'll be fun." I then say to him more quietly, "We'll come up with something as a couple," and playfully nudge him in the ribs.

"Whatever you say, Cara." Jamie smirks obediently as Mark turns to him.

"Gallagher, you're one of the gang now, so if you don't dress up for Halloween, the council might have to oust you."

Jamie concedes, rolling his eyes, "All right, okay, I'm sure we can think of something."

Jessica encourages him, "The costumes allow us to see our classmates in a whole new light. It's always a good time. Mark's thrown a Halloween party every year since he moved here in fifth grade, and trust me, he goes all out."

I turn back to Jamie. "We can do something simple, not too outrageous since it will also be the first time I meet your parents, right? I want them to be able to recognize me the next time they see me." I laugh and make a goofy face at him.

The only one not looking at us is Eric. He remains quiet with a neutral expression on his face—his "resting dick face," as Jamie has called it before.

Jamie takes out his phone, brings up the camera, and holds it out in front of us. "Lean in and say 'cheese.'"

I do as I'm told, trying not to giggle.

"What is that for?" I ask.

"I realize I don't even have a picture of us. I can show my parents a photo of you beforehand in case you dress up like a witch or something. It will reassure them." A hint of a teasing smile plays on his lips.

"Trust me, I will *not* be dressing up as a witch or putting any kind of scary makeup on my face Saturday. I can send you some better pictures of myself." I wince as I stare at the photo.

"What, you don't like this one?" Jamie leans into me and says sweetly, "It's perfect, as I'm sure every picture of you is."

I feel his warm breath on my cheek and wish we were alone so I could turn my face to his and kiss him. "It's okay, I guess."

I notice Eric from the corner of my eye leering at us. As I start to look over at him, his eyes dart away. It causes me to wonder if he will ever truly be okay with Jamie's and my relationship. I somehow doubt it.

***

Jamie picks me up promptly at six o'clock. When we arrive at the church, the volunteers, some of whom have known me since I was a baby, are excited to meet him. I introduce Jamie first to two of our most faithful volunteers, Sally and Norma, and then the others who have gathered around us. Curious eyes look from me to Jamie as he shakes hands with them. They're all still watching us as we move to the grocery assembling area.

"Put me to work, Cara," Jamie says, rubbing his hands together.

I show him the routine of sorting groceries into bags. The food is in bulk, and a list dictates how much of each item goes into a bag. There will be up to twenty families coming through to eat dinner and pick up the groceries.

Some food is taken out of the bags and left on the tables by the families who have allergies or a dislike for particular foods. These become the "extras" that are quickly taken by the families who have more mouths to feed, so nothing is ever left over. Helping the struggling families who come through each week is a reminder of the plenty I have in my own life. I always leave feeling grateful.

Jamie works by my side efficiently. With others helping, we are finished in less than thirty minutes and move to the dining area, or "fellowship hall" as we call it. Jamie raises an eyebrow at the plastic gloves I tell him he must wear, which makes me laugh. I don't dare attempt to ask him to wear the plastic shower-cap-looking hat some of the older women wear.

Jamie's aversion to wearing anything other than his normal attire is quite funny to me. He also balked at the thought of dressing up for Halloween.

He whispers for my ears only, "Who would've ever thought my aspirations of becoming a coveted lunch lady would finally come to fruition."

I nudge my shoulder into his as we both laugh to ourselves and get to work.

After we finish serving the families and sit down with the volunteers to eat our own dinner, Jamie comments, "I would like to meet the chef who cooked this wonderful food. It's delicious."

Norma, a petite woman in her seventies, beams at Jamie. "You're looking at her, young man."

"Now, Norma, you're not the only one who cooked tonight, are you?" Alice glares at her. "I made the rolls, and Sally made the pecan pies."

This flusters Norma, and she clarifies, "I made the chicken tetrazzini and salad," she shoots daggers at Alice, "and as you can *see*," she emphasizes, "that is exactly what this young man is eating."

All eyes trail to Jamie, so he intuitively retrieves his roll and takes a bite. He has Alice's rapt attention as he chews. "Wow, these have got to be the best rolls this side of the Pecos." Jamie feigns a bit of a Texas accent the ladies don't pick up on.

When he steals a mischievous look at me, I have to look down to keep from busting out laughing. I turn my head toward him and mouth, "Pecos?"

He smiles and shrugs.

My shoulders bounce with barely contained laughter as he speaks in the same southern drawl. "If the pecan pie is half as good as dinner, ladies, you might have won yourselves a permanent volunteer."

They all sit up straighter and beam under Jamie's flattery as though his pronouncement is better than receiving a blue ribbon at the county fair. He gives the ladies his best smile, and it's clear they adore him. Who wouldn't?

When Jamie walks over to get a piece of pecan pie from the dessert table, Norma, who is sitting beside me, says, "My, my, little Cara, wherever did you find such a fine young man?"

Alice chimes in, "Handsome as all get-out, too. Reminds me of my Harold when we were young." She watches Jamie as he retrieves two pieces of pie from the table, walks back to us, and sets one of them down in front of me. "And polite," she adds.

I thank Jamie, look at the ladies, and then back up at him as he sits down. "I got very lucky," I say, as Jamie's and my gazes meet.

Even within the walls of a church, the carnal butterflies don't cease flitting their wings against my stomach when Jamie looks into my eyes the way he does.

The ladies all give one another a knowing look and smile back at both of us.

Jamie's charisma is equally apparent when after dinner during game time, the kids all flock to him. Earlier, when I asked him if he would lead the activity, he had no qualms about saying yes even before I explained the game and what would be required of him. There are nine children aged six through ten, and after we all walk outside, he motions for them to gather around for instructions.

He introduces himself, "Hi, everyone. My name is Jamie. I'm Cara's friend," he looks over at me and winks, "and I'm ten years old."

Some of the younger children take that at face value while the older kids smile and say in unison, "Noooooo."

"I'm not?" He laughs. "Okay then, how old am I?"

The kids begin blurting out numbers from twenty to sixty-five, and now we are all laughing.

Jamie gives them a riddle: "I'm a third of the way to fifty-four and halfway to thirty-six."

This leaves most of the kids briefly baffled, and Jamie is about to move on when one of the girls standing behind the other children speaks up, "You're eighteen!"

Jamie steps over to her, and says, "You're right!" and high-fives her. "Also, smart."

She brightens at his compliment, and I can't help but think how Jamie has that effect on people of all ages.

He has taken less than a minute to win the children's trust. They are all paying better attention to him than they ever do to me, and I'm the one who wants to be a teacher someday—*not fair!* But I smile to myself.

He announces the game and gives instructions on how to play it while tossing a ball into the air and catching it. He's a natural with kids and watching him makes me sillily think of sunshine and rainbows, invoking the same happy, nostalgic feelings I still get when I listen to the theme songs to my favorite childhood television shows. Jamie has gotten under my skin in the best way possible, his joy and zest for life burrowing everywhere inside of me.

His big, strong hand palms the ball before he throws it to each child. They have to catch it, say something good that happened to them today, and then throw it back to him. This is a warm-up to the actual game, I guess, because it was not part of the activity I gave him. It's a good idea, though, and his way with children causes me to fall in love with him yet a little more.

After the game is over, the boys don't leave his side and all charge him. He just laughs and creates rules for them to take turns wrestling with him on the grass. He's still accommodating them all when my dad appears in the doorway to announce it's time to go back in.

"But it's my turn, my turn," a small boy around six-or seven-years-old cries. "I didn't get to go again like the others."

Jamie ruffles the boy's hair and kneels to his level. "How about when we wrestle again next week, you can be first?" He moves closer to the boy and whispers, "And I'll let you wrestle me an extra-long time, all right?"

This seems to satisfy the boy, a tentative smile unfurling on his sweet little lips.

As we walk back inside the church, I say to Jamie, "You do realize you just committed yourself to come back next Tuesday, right?" I arch a brow, waiting skeptically for his response.

"Of course, I wouldn't miss it," he replies eagerly. "That is, if it's okay with you?"

"Are you kidding? You're incredible with the kids. They will love to have you lead the game again, and the ladies will love your help in the kitchen... and your company." I laugh. "I'll love you being here, too," I say, flirting with him and taking his hand in mine.

"I used to help with Vacation Bible School every year after I got too old to attend myself. I enjoy working with kids. Maybe I'll have a dozen or more with you one day." He says more quietly into my ear, "We would make beautiful babies, you and I," and looks at me half-serious.

I feel my eyes round to small planets. "I do want kids someday, definitely, but a dozen? Uh, no way." I laugh, shaking my head.

After the families all leave, Jamie, Dad, and I visit in the foyer of the church. I tell my dad how much the kids enjoyed Jamie playing with them and that he plans to volunteer next week, too.

He thanks Jamie for helping out and says, "Let me show you around the rest of the church and my office real quick before we go."

He leads Jamie through the halls where the classrooms are and then to the sanctuary where the services are held.

"This is nice, Mr. Dawson."

"Please, call me Chris from now on, Jamie." Dad smiles at him. "We remodeled recently—all new carpet and paint. You and your family are welcome to visit us any time."

"I'll let them know that. We'll probably take you up on the offer. We've discussed finding a church here."

My dad must be glad to hear that because he whistles as we make our way to his office.

"This," he says, sweeping his hand through the air of his office, "is my home away from home. A lot of people walk through these doors for help or just to talk. Ironically, it's really where most of the magic happens, more than in the church services."

Jamie looks around, taking it all in. "Do you prepare your sermons here as well?"

"Some," my father says, "but if I want true peace and quiet with no interruptions, I study in the evenings at home. That is, if this little brat doesn't pester me."

He looks over at me and smiles as Jamie picks up a framed photo from the desk and studies it.

"Cara, you look so much like your mom." Jamie then says unabashedly, "She was beautiful, like you." He looks from the photo to me.

It feels as though Jamie is meeting my mom for the first time, and my chest tightens.

"That she was," my dad says, staring at the photo alongside Jamie.

"I never asked her name." Jamie turns to look at my dad.

"Charlotte," he answers. "Her name was Charlotte." He speaks her name with such reverence, the backs of my eyes sting.

My dad smiles pensively when Jamie softly says, "Well, I look forward to meeting her one day."

Jamie's belief in heaven, my mom's place there, and his intentions of also being there someday cause my eyes to completely cloud over. *Ah, Jamie, such a sweet remark.*

Jamie returns the photo to its place on the desk, and I can tell my dad sees the unshed tears in my eyes. He quickly switches off the light.

"Okay, kids, let's call it a night. Jamie, do you want to drive home from here, and I'll take Cara home with me?"

Jamie must sense this is what my dad wants and acquiesces. "Sure, that sounds good."

However, Jamie's expression reveals his disappointment at not being able to see me home. I'm disappointed, too... disappointed I can't thoroughly kiss him the way I want to.

"I'll walk Jamie to his truck while you finish locking up, Dad."

Jamie takes my hand as we leave the church and enter the parking lot.

"Thank you again for volunteering tonight," I say sincerely. "You made it even more enjoyable than usual."

"It was fun. Thanks for asking me, and I look forward to next Tuesday." He looks over at the door as my father is turning to lock it. "I guess I'll say goodnight now."

He frames my face in his hands and kisses me. The kiss is quick, but not brief enough to stop the tingling sensation it causes.

"Text me," I say as I turn to walk the short distance to my dad's car.

"I will as soon as I get home." Jamie calls out, "Goodnight, Mr.—" he stops and corrects himself, "Uh, Chris."

"Goodnight, Jamie. Be careful."

Jamie

When I ask Cara again on Friday what she thinks we should wear to the Halloween party, she says, "I've got us covered, but it's a surprise. Wear straight-legged jeans with your boots over them. Wear riding boots if you have some—that will look best—and wear any shirt you want. I'm using my mom's old sewing machine to make a couple of things to complete your costume."

"Sounds easy enough," I say. I'm a little worried about it being a surprise, but it doesn't seem like much of a costume. "Why can't you just tell me what it is?"

"So you can tell me no and take me back to square one? I don't think so. Trust me, I'm making it easy for you. I thought of a way to add a couple of things to make your regular clothes a costume. That way, you can simply take off the costume pieces after we make our appearance and take pictures in the photo booth Mark will have set up. I'm doing the same with my outfit. Halloween costumes aren't really my thing, either."

"How cringe-worthy can it be, then?" I shrug. "As long as it's not a tiara and a pink tutu you have for me to wear."

Cara's expression flattens, and she deadpans, "How did you know?"

For a millisecond I almost believe her until she laughs and reassures me, "I promise it's nothing like that."

Saturday is unseasonably warm for October thirty-first from what Cara has told me. She thought it might be chilly on Halloween, but no true cold front has made its way into the DFW area yet this fall. I pick Cara up at 7:00 p.m. so we have time to go by my house to meet my parents and sister before the party.

She is as pretty as a picture when she opens her door to me, wearing a hot-pink dress with gold sandals. Her hair looks different; it's in curls falling softly over her shoulders and back. I stand dumbfounded a minute before I can say anything.

"You never cease to amaze me. You look gorgeous." Chris isn't anywhere around, so I grasp her shoulders to kiss her pretty pink lips before stepping inside.

"Thanks, but this isn't the complete outfit," she says, reaching into a bag she's holding.

She removes a plastic jeweled princess crown that matches a pink-jeweled costume necklace she's already wearing. She places the crown on her head and slips on elbow-length gloves almost the same color as her dress.

"Voila! I don't think you'll be able to guess who I am until you see your costume."

"All I know is you are some type of beautiful princess, but I could have told you that before you put on any type of costume." I give her my best wink and nuzzle her neck, breathing in her scent that has the power to set my blood on fire.

Cara sighs and says, "Jamie, you're too sweet to me," while removing a red bundle of material from her bag and unfolding it. "This is your cape," she says, "and this is your hat." She hands me a triangular hat made of soft felt with a long point in the back. It looks like a Robin Hood hat.

"Okay?" I say as a question and wait.

"You still don't know who we are?"

"Sorry, no, Cara, I don't."

"I'm Princess Aurora, and you're my Prince Jamie!" she announces as if that should be enough explanation for me.

When I stare at her blankly, she feigns annoyance. "You know, from *Sleeping Beauty*."

"Oh, yeah, it seems vaguely familiar," I fib. I'm obviously fairy-tale impaired; not my type of books or movies.

I would have never known who these characters were, but when she searches the pair on her phone and shows me, I can see her choice holds more merit than I initially gave her credit for. I think I remember my sisters watching the movie. We both actually resemble the animated characters quite a bit, especially Cara with her long, blonde hair and dark eyes and lashes... and her kissable pink mouth.

"Wow, you do look a lot like Sleeping Beauty, or she looks like you, especially dressed up like her."

"And you will look like a prince with your hat and cape on— enough anyway. Go on, put them on."

I begrudgingly put on the hat and cape and let Cara adjust them as I give her the stink eye. She just laughs at me as she raises her phone to snap a photo of us.

Chris walks into the entryway where we're standing. "Here, let me," he insists and takes Cara's phone. "How are you doing, Jamie?"

"Doing well, thanks. Actually, I was better before Cara started playing dress-up with me."

He chuckles and takes a couple of photos of us. "She has an uncanny ability to coax people to do what she wants them to, that's for certain. She's hard to say no to."

"I completely agree. Can I take this off now?" I ask Cara.

"Yes," she laughs, "but, I must say, you look very dashing. I'll carry this bag with our costumes and snacks in it. We can put them back on before we go into the party."

We say goodbye to Chris and make our way to my house. On the drive, Cara tells me the story of Sleeping Beauty, aka Princess Aurora. It seems Uglyane, an evil fairy, is jealous of Aurora and places an evil curse on her. The curse is intended to kill Aurora when she pricks her finger on a spindle. But, with the announcement of death, her guardian fairies turn the curse of death into a sleeping curse only to be broken with true love's kiss. At age 15, Aurora pricks her finger on a spinning wheel and falls into a deep, deep slumber. Her guardian fairies, at the request of her father, force the kingdom into a deep sleep, only to awaken when she does. Many years pass and Aurora's prince finally arrives to kiss her. She awakens from the curse, and they live happily ever after.

"What's with kissing a sleeping princess? That just seems wrong. I hope she kissed him back when she woke up... after she brushed her teeth, of course," I tease.

"You just took all the romance out of one of my favorite fairy tales," she says with an exaggerated eye-roll before turning her head to stare out the window.

I think about it for a beat and glance over at Cara, all kidding aside. "I happen to like the fairy tale we're actually living best of all, don't you?"

Cara turns back toward me, looks into my eyes, and says, "You're right, yes. And it's not make-believe, is it?"

"Nope," I say without any doubt, "it isn't."

•••

Cara was astonished when I pulled up to our front gate and punch in the security code.

"This is where you live, Jamie?"

As the gate slowly opens, I try to downplay it. "Not what you expected?"

"Uh, honestly, no. It's breathtaking, though." She looks straight ahead in awe as we wind our way down the long drive to the front of the house. "Now, I really do feel like I'm in a fairy tale traveling to the prince's castle. I love all the acreage, too. It's so green, and all the trees—like you're in the middle of the country. Really lovely," she says with wonderment.

It's a beautiful look on her.

I drive under the porte-cochere and come around to open her door. My parents and sister are already at the front door waiting for us, most likely having seen us drive up on the cameras at the gate.

Cara stops looking up at the expanse of the house from the truck window and is now focused solely on my family waiting excitedly to meet her. I've talked incessantly to them about her but never ended up showing them a picture, so this is their first look at her.

My mom steps forward, takes Cara's right hand in both of hers, and says with the friendliest of welcomes, "Hi, Cara, it's so nice to finally meet you. I'm Susan, this is Brent, and our youngest daughter Amber."

"It's very nice to meet you all," Cara says. "Your home is absolutely beautiful."

My dad and Amber shake Cara's hand, and Mom says, "Come on in, and I'll show you around."

I follow behind and watch Cara as Mom gives her a tour and as she interacts with my family. I should have never worried about her reaction to our lifestyle and to them. After her initial amazement, she seems perfectly relaxed. She fits right in, and for the first time, I give free rein to a recessive thought—this is who I would really like to spend the rest of my life with. Can I truly already know this? It sure seems so.

We visit with my parents in the great room after finishing the tour of the house and grounds. Cara seems comfortable disclosing details about her life. She talks about her dad, his profession, and about her mom. I've already told my family that Cara's mom passed away, but they listen with sincere sympathy as if hearing it for the first time.

It's obvious this information so freely entrusted to them endears Cara to my parents all the more. Her strength and intelligence are revealed through her words and demeanor. They are as taken with her as anyone would be upon meeting Cara. She's a wonderful person.

Cara seems equally enthralled with them, especially my mom, and I can't help but think that there's a sunny future for their relationship to bloom. If I lived a million lifetimes, I couldn't find anyone as perfect for me as Cara.

When it's time to go, Amber and Mom walk through the door toward the truck with Cara, while my dad and I hang back a little and follow.

"Wow!" Dad mouths to me with raised brows and whispers quickly, "You did not exaggerate. She's stunning, Jamie."

"Yeah," I say. "Now you know why I'm in love."

●●●

Cara and I don the prince and princess costumes when we arrive at Mark's house before getting out of the truck. Cara grabs the chips and dip, a package of cookies, and her purse to take in.

"Here, let me carry the snacks. You look beautiful, and I look ridiculous," I feel it necessary to tell her, "but let's go."

Even before we leave the truck, we can hear the pounding bass of the music. Although Mark's and the other houses nearby are separated by a couple of acres, I'm sure it's got to be annoying to the neighbors.

There are a lot of people already at the party when we enter the house. Mark is in a full-fledged all-black superhero costume that looks pretty authentic.

"You look badass, Mark," I tell him, hoping he hears me over the music.

"Yeah, who says superheroes can't be black, right? Get with the times, Hollywood!" he shouts, flashing his brilliant smile beneath the mask.

"Hell, yeah," I say, returning the smile.

Others are dressed as everything from a bottle of ketchup to Hawaiian-themed costumes to no costume at all.

We spot Eric and Jessica right away standing in the large living room snapping a selfie in front of the photo booth screen. Eric is a caveman, holding a plastic club, and Jessica is a cavewoman with a bone in her hair. They're both dressed in animal print furs and look pretty good.

"I guess they're together now?" I ask loudly over the music into Cara's ear. She shrugs as if whether they are or not isn't of any consequence to her.

"Hey, Cara, Jamie, glad you made it," Jessica has to practically yell. "I like the Sleeping Beauty costumes. Y'all look the part."

Cara looks at me smugly and says, "See, Jessica knows exactly who we are supposed to be and I never told her." She calls over to Eric, "How about you, Eric? Do you know who Jamie and I are dressed up as?"

"Sure," he says, "you're a prince and princess."

"Good answer," I say, nodding.

Cara rolls her eyes, not even attempting to clarify for Eric.

Mark comes over with two beers. "Hey, guys! Wanna beer?" He holds them between the fingers of one hand.

"Thanks," I say, taking them from Mark and handing one to Cara before I notice the wary look on her face. "Here, I'll set yours on the counter for someone else if you don't want it."

"I normally don't drink, really," her expression is conflicted, "but, hey, I'm at a party, and I'm an adult now, right?"

"Yeah, but don't do anything you're not comfortable with just because I am."

"No, I wouldn't. Will you open it for me?"

I set the snacks Cara brought on the table with the rest and open our beers.

Nestled beside all the food is a large punch bowl resembling a witch's cauldron containing red punch and dry ice to create the effect of spooky fog rising from it. Jessica was right when she said Mark went all out every year.

Cara and I finish our beer quickly while we nibble food from the table. She talks with a few people from school I've never met. It's hard to hear much over the loud music, but it's fine with me. I'm content watching everyone else, especially Cara. I enjoy seeing her in this festive atmosphere talking animatedly with others. I'm having a good time watching her have a good time.

After we take our own selfies and have someone snap our full-length pic in the photo booth, Cara introduces me to a lot of people whose names I'll never remember. After listening to yet another lengthy conversation, I get bored and take a cup from the table to sample the punch.

"This is good," I tell Cara and pour us both some. She smiles at me as a thank you and continues talking to a girl with braces dressed as Medusa.

I start to feel pretty good and relaxed after the beer and downing half my punch, which is flavorful and sweet enough not to notice the alcohol too much. I can tell Cara feels the effects, too, as she laughs more than usual while watching others dance to the music in the middle of the living room. All the furniture has been pushed aside to create a makeshift dance floor, and a table-top disco light beams swirls of color across the dancers' faces and clothes.

I pour us another drink, and we watch the dance floor for a few more minutes until liquid courage takes over Cara.

She grabs my hand and says, "Come on, let's dance."

"I need more of this before I get out there," I say, and down the rest of the cup of punch while laying my costume cape and hat on the counter.

We stand by the punchbowl awhile longer, filling our cups and sipping them by the dipperfuls. I've lost count of how many. Cara drinks the rest of hers while I pour more punch into my cup and chug almost the whole thing. She takes the cup from my hand, drinks the rest, and says, "Ready now?"

Still holding my hand, she drags me toward the others dancing. We both immediately begin spinning and laughing too hard to dance with any real finesse. I lift her in the air and twirl her around a few times before returning her to the floor. We laugh excessively at the effects of the alcohol and our dizziness.

When Cara's equilibrium returns, she impresses me by showing off her dance moves. She raises her arms above her head, her hips swaying in perfect rhythm to the music. She throws her head back in abandon and moves it from side to side, causing her hair to follow—a trail of spun gold moving back and forth to the fast beat of the song. Although her intention is to be a bit silly, the effect she has on me is definitely not one of laughter.

We dance this way for a while until she turns away from me and moves her backside against me, hips swaying a little slower now, more provocatively. She flips her hair back and looks over her shoulder deeply into my eyes, as our bodies intermittently brush against one another causing friction where it probably shouldn't be on a dancefloor. She looks sexy as hell and must not have a clue what she's doing to me, or she would stop.

"If you're trying to drive me crazy, you're succeeding," I say into her ear over the music.

Her only response is a mischievous grin, eyes smoldering.

To hell with it, I place my hands on her hips, pull her closer into me, and sway with her, feeling her rhythm, her heat, her sensuality. I bend my knees and brush her neck lightly with my lips under her ear, enjoying the clean, floral scent of her shampoo, and she tilts her head to the side to give me better access.

Man, it feels too good to be moving to the tempo with her so uninhibited. It causes me to think of other, more intimate things I would like to be doing with her that mimic the same type of cadence.

Thank goodness a slower country song plays next because I don't know how much longer I could handle that type of dancing and keep my hands off her. I turn her to face me, take her hand in mine, and pull her close. Her warm body fits snugly to mine. Heat floods through me when Cara sweetly rests her head against my chest and looks up into my eyes with that blazing awareness.

Damn, I love her.

We dance like this for a brief eternity, gazes deeply fixed on each other, speaking only with our eyes and speaking the same language through our booze-laden haze.

I want to get inside your soul, to know you and feel all of you, my eyes plead drunkenly.

I'm an open book to you, and only you. Come inside. Read me, know me, love me, her eyes reply.

Still swaying to the slow song that follows, I finally admonish her, "Don't look at me like that unless you want to get thoroughly kissed right here in front of everyone."

She has intoxicated me as much as the alcohol has.

She doesn't look away but instead says, "I can't think about anything else but you kissing me, Jamie." She looks at my lips—a blatant invitation.

In turn, my eyes indolently drift over her full, sensual mouth. She briefly licks her bottom lip, and it's too much. I go in for it, right there with everyone around us. When my lips reach hers, her mouth is already partially open and waiting. The kiss is hot, hot, hot and crazy good. As far as I'm concerned, we are the only two people who exist in the room.

The kiss would have gone on longer had the next song not been a fast one. The quick staccato breaks the spell, and we grudgingly move apart. I lead Cara back over toward the food and grab some cookies, trying to get my sluggish mind on anything that doesn't have to do with ravaging her.

Eric sees us from the other end of the table where we are standing. He comes closer to ask if I want to play pool and hands me a cup of punch. I can tell I've had more than enough but accept it as an olive branch and say, "Sure."

Jessica and Cara pour more punch for themselves and follow us.

Jessica exclaims, "This ought to be good," and we all follow Eric into a game room adjacent to the living room.

After the first couple of rounds, I discover Eric thoroughly sucks at playing pool. I can't decide if I should play the way I normally do on the pool table we have in the center of our pool house or let go of trying to win and allow the game to be more on par with Eric's skill level.

Yet, ironically, as the game progresses, each time I try to shoot, my arms feel like limp noodles, and I truly begin to suck at the game as much as Eric. It hits me that I am dead-on drunk.

I decide when I finish this drink, I'm done—should have already been done a few drinks ago. I straighten up after my next shot and shake my head like an animal shaking water from its fur, trying to rid my brain of the cobwebs that seem to have been spun there from all the alcohol.

Cara watches me and laughs as she takes my drink and slurs a bit, "Jamie, you've had enough of Mark's punch. I'll trade you for some water."

Cara hands me a bottle of water while she finishes off my punch. Since she doesn't usually drink alcohol, I want to tell her she shouldn't be drinking anymore, either, but my mouth doesn't seem to want to form the words.

"While you boys finish your game, Cara and I are going to go join the other girls in the backyard," Jessica says, sauntering off arm in arm with Cara.

I try to stay focused on the game that up to now I was winning. It's hard for me to believe Baines is getting the upper hand here. I sluggishly take the next shot and almost miss the ball entirely.

Eric eyes me curiously as he moves to take his next shot. He looks from the table to me and says, "You okay, Jamie?"

"I'm great, Baines, couldn't be better," I garble.

"So you and Cara are... enjoying each other... as a couple?"

I'm not sure what he's getting at, what he means by "enjoying," but it somehow registers as sinister. My brain is functioning in slow motion, so I decide to give him the benefit of the doubt.

"Hell, yeah. I love her more than anything. What's n-n-not to love about her, though?" I stammer.

"Hmph." Eric doesn't hide his disgust. "You know Jessica and I are going out now, right? I'm sure Cara has told you. Is she upset about it or anything?"

"Nope," I say a little too harshly, popping the *P* for emphasis, "she hasn't said anything about it, but I'm sure she's thrilled for you both."

This conversation is exhausting. It takes too much concentration to enunciate my words. I want to stop playing this stupid game of pool with Eric and go sit down.

The next thing I know, there is a commotion going on outside. A few people have gathered at the window that overlooks the backyard.

At about the same time, Mark opens the back door and yells, "Oops! Girl in the pool. Jamie, it's Cara!"

Jamie

I haphazardly throw my pool cue on the table. As quickly as I can, I trudge my way to the back door. It's as though I, too, have fallen into water and have to fight gravity to make my heavy legs follow my lethargic brain's commands.

When I reach the pool, Jessica looks at me, concerned. "Jamie, she's had too much to drink. We were just walking by the pool, and I noticed Cara staggering right before she fell in."

Cara is sitting next to the pool laughing hysterically, her crown tilted sideways on her head, her hair and dress clinging to her with rivulets of water cascading down her face.

I take hold of her to help her lean against me. I try to turn her toward me, away from two gawking guys I notice nudging one another, grinning, and staring at her chest where the material clings like a thin coat of paint to her cold, full breasts. She's not easy for me to maneuver, considering I've had too much to drink as well.

"Damn, Shelton, what the hell is in that punch, a hundred proof?" I slur.

Mark answers with only a lopsided grin while everyone around laughs and goes back to what they were doing.

Jessica takes control. "Here, I'll take Cara to get out of these wet clothes and put them in the dryer before she catches pneumonia. Mark," she calls out, "can you bring me a robe or something of your mom's for Cara to wear while her clothes dry?"

Cara and Jessica go into a hall bathroom, and I stand outside the door, waiting. I hear rustling, giggling, and banging.

"Jessica, is she okay in there?" I shout.

"Yeah, she will be. She's pretty wasted."

Mark comes around the corner holding a robe and knocks loudly on the door. "Here's a robe, Jess."

Jessica opens the door wide enough to grab it and quickly shuts it again. It takes a minute or more—who knows, though, time seems to be elusive and too abstract now—before the door opens again and Jessica helps Cara out.

Her hair has been towel-dried and brushed, and she looks a little better. I try to take hold of her and almost fall. Luckily, Mark is still standing near us and grabs hold of my arm.

"Whoa, buddy, how much did you two drink? You both need to take it easy for a while." Mark looks at Jessica. "Help me get them into my brother's room where they can lie down. We can put Cara's clothes in the dryer after we get them settled. They're both toast."

The floor and walls move like a carnival funhouse, and even with Mark's help, I struggle to walk. Through mangled words, I try to thank him for helping me down the hallway. Cara is even worse off, and Jessica is barely able to keep her upright. Mark opens the bedroom door and helps me to the bed.

"Okay, you guys, we'll check on you in a bit," says Mark, looking at Jessica with a concerned expression. "For now, you two need to sleep."

Jessica sits Cara down and takes off her wet sandals still on her feet. She lifts Cara's legs up onto the bed for her and covers her with the bedsheet.

Cara continues to giggle and insists, "I'm fine, I'm fine."

"No, you're not fine, Cara. Lie down and rest," Jessica commands, scowling.

She and Mark leave and close the door behind them. I sit on the edge of the bed and take off my boots. As I watch my arms move, they look like they belong to someone else and feel like melting gelatin.

There's a sliver of light coming from the restroom door, which reminds me that I need to use it. "I'm going to the bathroom."

"Don't leave me." Cara reaches clumsily for me and takes hold of my arm.

"I'll just be a few feet away." I attempt a laugh. "There's a bathroom in this bedroom."

I have to grab the bed and then the wall to keep my balance as I make my way into the restroom.

Cara is sitting up when I return to the bed. She reaches for me, puts her arms around my neck, and asks, "Why did you leave me, Jamie? Please don't leave me again." She looks panicked and is not making a lot of sense.

I try to reassure her that I didn't leave, will never leave her, but I don't know if I'm actually speaking aloud or only thinking the words.

Her face tilts up, and she lifts her lips to mine as she presses herself into me. She is so soft and pliable, she simply melts into me.

Consciousness is a strobe light coming to me only in millisecond increments. My head is fuzzy. Is this thing sitting on my shoulders even a head, or is it a pillow stuffed full of feathers or cotton? My thoughts have become incoherent.

Cara and I are lying side by side, legs intertwined, worshipping one another's mouths hungrily. As lethargic as I am, this aspect of my senses is actually heightened. Cara feels like electricity, charging my skin with every touch.

Her hands move up into the front of my shirt and over the bare skin of my chest—soft, generous hands. In the next flash of the strobe, her hands are running along the length of my back, moving sensuously up and down, lulling me into an inexplicable stupor.

Some part of my brain vaguely remembers that we have promised one another not to allow ourselves to be in this type of predicament again, so I try to remove Cara's arms from around me and whisper, "No, Cara, remember our pact? We've both had too much to drink."

My God, why am I so sleepy? Why am I slurring so badly? Memory becomes tiny bubbles blown through a wand, promptly popping and disappearing forever.

"Let's sleep this off for a while before I have to leave, and Jessica takes you to her house."

"Sure," Cara says groggily.

But she puts her arms back around my neck, kissing me again, although my eyes are now too heavy to stay open—

My last conscious memory.

I fall asleep experiencing a mishmash of dreams. First, I dream there's a pirate ship approaching a tiny lifeboat I've thrown myself into to escape the pirates' treachery. My arms are like two heavy iron rods trying to row the boat. It's like rowing through sludge, but I keep at it, pumping the oars in and out of the water in rhythmic succession in my effort to flee the wake of the ship. I turn to see the lights of the ship gaining on me with every stroke of my oars.

In the next sequence of dreams, Cara is lying in the bottom of the lifeboat with me, and I touch her as she moans into my ear. I enter softness and pleasure beyond belief, Cara's hands on my backside holding me there, keeping me safe inside the boat with her while waves of pleasure threaten to knock me over the side. There's an explosion of brilliant light. I try hard to decipher its origin but cannot.

It's the pirates! They have fired cannons at my little lifeboat and knocked me into the waves and into darkness. All feeling is gone, and I'm floating, floating... floating away from what's left of the burning orange glow that was once my boat. I'm then plunged into utter darkness, but all is calm—the bliss of nothingness.

When I wake up, I am downright disoriented. *Where am I?* There is total stillness, total silence. In the faint light burning through the crack of the bathroom door, I don't see Cara lying beside me and panic. I glance over the bed and see her lying on the carpeted floor beside the bed.

She must have fallen off in the night, but her chest rises and falls evenly in sleep. Her robe came undone when she fell, and

I quickly pull it together for her and tie it, lifting her back up onto the bed. She doesn't even stir.

What time is it? How long have we been asleep? I reach for my phone from my front pocket. 3:34 a.m.!

What the hell?

I hurriedly text my dad, explaining that I meant to text earlier to let him know I was staying the night at Mark's but fell asleep. He must have not been too worried and assumed that's what I had planned because there were no texts from him or my mom. Or maybe they fell asleep waiting to hear from me? Regardless, there will be questions.

I spot my boots on the floor and pull them on. I stand and button my jeans. How could I have been so wasted that I didn't even refasten them after using the bathroom? Damn.

"Cara, wake up." I kiss her forehead. "We fell asleep, and it's already 3:30 in the morning."

It dawns on me that it's November first, which is daylight saving time, so it would actually be 4:30 a.m. without the time change. That means we have been asleep for six hours.

"What?" She stirs but doesn't open her eyes. "No, let me sleep. I'm so tired." She grabs my arm and uses it to pull herself closer, attempting to snuggle against me.

"Cara," I say louder and more sternly, "wake the hell up!"

She opens her eyes, but they're not cooperating. I can barely see her eyeballs trying to make out their surroundings through small slits. Acknowledgment surfaces as she sits up too quickly, cradling her head in both hands.

"Whoa, easy, babe. You okay?"

"I'm dizzy. Give me a second. What time is it?"

"It's 3:30, and your dad's going to kill us both if he finds out about this. It looks bad, Cara."

Her eyes open wider, shocked. "No, don't worry. Remember, he thinks I'm at Jessica's. Where is Jessica?" she asks, looking around, obviously disoriented herself. "Ugh, remind me never to drink that kind of alcohol ever again. Or to never drink again, period."

"Yeah, must've been a hundred proof they spiked that punch with. I'm still pretty groggy, too, and it gave me weird dreams. I never drink hard liquor, only a beer with my dad occasionally... or another if I sneak it." I let out a derisive laugh. "From now on, I'm sticking to the weaker stuff."

"I need to pee." Cara giggles.

"While you use the restroom, I'll go see what everyone else is doing."

I open the door quietly and step out into the hallway. There is complete silence as I tiptoe to Mark's room. The door is slightly ajar, and I slowly push it farther open until I see the sleeping silhouette of Mark across his bed. I close it back and walk quietly to the main room.

It's a disaster. Cups are strewn all over the place, bottles and cans and half-eaten food are also everywhere. Someone—who is that, Eric?—is asleep on the couch. Jessica is asleep on the loveseat with a crocheted afghan atop her. I make my way back down the hallway and back into Mark's brother's room as Cara is buckling her sandals.

"I need to find my clothes and my purse," she whispers.

"Jessica put your clothes in the dryer last night," I say quietly. "Your purse should still be on the counter where you left it when we came in. The others are all asleep. Let's go get you dressed and get out of here."

"I can't go home now. My dad will know something's up. I don't want him to know I've been drinking and fell asleep like a drunkard." She giggles again, which lets me know the alcohol has not entirely left her system.

"We can go get coffee and breakfast, drive around, whatever, until I can take you home or to Jessica's later. She's asleep in the living room."

"She probably told her parents she was spending the night with me. What about you? Your parents don't know where you are."

"I texted them to let them know I stayed the night at Mark's but forgot to text them before accidentally falling asleep. It's the truth, but they'll be upset and ask some questions."

We make our way to the laundry room and find Cara's dress and underthings sitting in the dryer completely dry. I wait for her outside the hall bathroom while she changes and think about how out of hand all this feels. My jaws tighten as I grow angrier and angrier with myself.

Cara reappears, and I take her hand and whisper an apology, "I'm sorry, I didn't take very good care of you last night. I once again sucked as a boyfriend and should have never let this happen." Shaking my head, trying to shake off all the events of the last several hours, I lead Cara into the hallway and say, "Let's go."

"All's well that ends well," Cara quietly chimes a lot more cheerily than I feel.

We tiptoe past the sleeping Jessica and Eric and shut the door behind us. We are halfway to my truck when Cara stops abruptly. "Wait, where are our costumes? My crown? I've lost my crown."

Cara

Jamie and I drive around town and its outskirts for hours, filling the time with random conversation. We see which one of us can name every one of our elementary school teachers, and I win that one. He beats me by a long shot on naming all the national football teams and their respective cities. We then discuss the craziness of last night.

"My last clear memory was watching you and Eric play pool," I reflect. "I don't remember much after that. I very vaguely remember falling into the swimming pool and Jessica helping me change out of my wet clothes, then nothing." I shrug sheepishly.

"After Mark and Jessica helped us into the bedroom, I remember using the restroom and lying next to you, kissing you goodnight. Well, I suppose it was a much more intense kiss than a goodnight kiss," Jamie grins, "but I couldn't keep my eyes open and fell asleep—bizarre dreams. Seriously, I won't be drinking for a long time. Just the thought of it makes me wanna hurl."

"I hear ya," I laugh. "I don't remember even being in the bedroom, didn't know where I was when you woke me up."

We spend well over another hour eating breakfast at a restaurant several miles outside of the area so no one local will recognize us. Even hungover, we enjoy ourselves, and it feels natural being with Jamie like this—very everyday. It's like we seamlessly fit together no matter where we are.

"How are you feeling, Cara?" Jessica asks when Jamie and I return to Mark's house around mid-morning. "We all woke up and you two were gone. I tried to text you," she scoffs.

Jessica is the only one still at the house helping Mark clean up. It already looks almost a hundred percent better than it did when we left early this morning.

"Sorry, I didn't see your text. I'm fine now after some food and caffeine. We left super early and drove around, watched the sunrise. Then we had a nice, long breakfast," I say casually, hoping she won't make a big deal about last night. "I'll help y'all finish cleaning up here. Can you take me home later so Jamie can go ahead and head home now?"

"Sure, I'll take her home here in a few, Jamie."

"Thanks," he says, glancing from Jessica to Mark, who is wiping down the kitchen counters with a paper towel. "And thanks for letting us crash here last night. Sorry if we caused trouble for you guys. We obviously need to keep a better check on our alcohol consumption."

In typical Mark fashion, he shrugs it off entirely. "There wasn't really any trouble. There was no fight, no blood, and no broken glass or furniture." He chuckles. "All in all, a pretty tame night, I'd say. We've all been drunk before and needed help, right?"

Jamie and I look at each other and laugh. "First for me," I correct Mark.

"Me, too," Jamie says, lifting his shoulders in an exaggerated shrug. "First time for everything, I guess."

Mark nods and grins like a child caught in mischief. "You would think I would have learned my lesson by now, but it seems I never do. I passed out not too long after you two did, even before everyone left my own party. Who does that?" He laughs again. "I'll blame most of it on being exhausted from preparing for the party."

"Eric and I held down the fort just fine." Jessica smiles broadly at Mark before turning to me. "I gathered your costumes for you." She points to the bag sitting on the arm of a chair. "I couldn't find one of your gloves, Cara."

"Thanks, no problem. They're cheapies, and I won't be wearing them again anytime soon," I say.

Jamie yawns behind his hand. "I'm going to head out now. Thanks again for everything. Great party, Mark, what I remember of it anyway." He lets out a self-deprecating laugh, and I can hear the frustration in his tone.

"I'll walk you out," I tell Jamie. We reach for one another's hands at the same time and head to his truck. "Jessica will take me home after I know my dad's home from church. Call me or text me later?"

"Of course, but I plan to go home and sleep, so I don't know what time it will be."

"If I don't respond, you know that's what I'm doing, too. I could probably sleep all day." Saying the word *sleep* causes me to yawn.

Standing at the driver-side door, Jamie takes my other hand and pulls me closer to him. "Sorry again that the night turned out the way it did after only having a couple of hours or so to actually enjoy the party."

"Those hours were extremely fun, so I'm not complaining," I assure him.

I think about the way we danced for the first time together, up close and *very* personal, his hot gaze on me, the feel of his hard body swaying against mine, and his kisses—*Wow*, those kisses.

"I would give you a long goodbye kiss, but I need a toothbrush and a shower." Jamie kisses me briefly and pulls me in for a hug he doesn't immediately let go of. "I love you so damn much, Cara," he rumbles into my neck, causing me to shiver.

I hug him tightly in return and say with a resigned sigh, "Ah, Jamie, I love you, too. I wish I never had to say goodbye to you."

He steps back looking truly torn to leave me. "Yeah, it always sucks. I'll call you later."

"Talk to you then. Tell your family how much I enjoyed meeting them," I say as he opens the truck door and climbs in.

I wave as he starts the engine, and then turn around to walk back into Mark's house.

Jessica is in the kitchen when I return. I spot Mark through the window cleaning up the backyard and pool area.

"What can I do to help?" I ask.

"I'm almost finished with these dishes if you want to vacuum. Then the only thing left will be to mop the kitchen. Unless Mark's neighbors tattle, his parents won't ever know there was a big party at their house last night."

"And if no one who was here tattles at school, it won't get around that the preacher's daughter got drunk and fell into the pool."

I try to make light of it, but saying what happened aloud makes me cringe, acknowledging how awful it sounds, and that I'm worried about my reputation. I don't want to pretend to be a goody-two-shoes, but I also don't want to come across as a reckless partier because neither is an accurate picture of me.

"You don't need to worry about anyone who was here saying anything. They would just implicate themselves. Everyone knows you and knows last night wasn't typical of you. It's probably already forgotten."

"I hope you're right. As long as my dad doesn't find out about it, I'm good."

Jessica looks at me for a long few seconds and says, "You and Jamie have something really different, don't you? I was going to say he is crazy about you, but it's more than that. He loves you; I can see it. He's very protective of you. The way he looks at you... man! It makes me happy for you but sad for myself. I wonder if I'll ever have anyone look at me that way?" She sighs dreamily.

"I'm sure you will, Jess." I give her a quick hug. "But if we're being honest here, I don't foresee that look ever coming from Eric."

"Oh, hell no." She laughs. "I've gone along with him telling everyone we're dating because I know he's heartbroken over you right now and it helps his wounded pride. I'm not blind; he's only trying to make you jealous. We don't even kiss. Poor guy has been desperate to have you. Surely, he's got to see what is obvious between you and Jamie." She pauses briefly. "By the way, you two sure were hot on the dance floor. Maybe after seeing that last night, Eric's given up."

"I certainly hope so. There was still a lot of tension when he was around, though. I hope it gets better with time because he's been a good friend for as long as I can remember. I would hate to lose that."

"Can I tell you something else?" Jessica asks, her expression uncertain.

"Of course; what's wrong?"

"No, I think something is very right, but it's complicated." When I arch a brow, Jessica says, "Last night, after watching Mark in action when he took charge of you and Jamie and then spending time with him after we got y'all settled..." she inhales deeply for dramatic effect, "well, he was a real-life superhero, and it was so hot!"

"I can totally see it happening with you two," I say. "Go for it!"

"We kind of already did." She blinks away. "He kissed me last night before he went to his room. He must've sensed my interest in him and then snuck it in when Eric walked away. Totally gave me all the feels. He thinks I'm with Eric and still went for it... *very* hot."

"Tell Eric to get lost, Jess. Especially if he's only using you to make me jealous. He doesn't deserve you."

"Thanks, I don't know why I never noticed—"

"Here comes Mark," I blurt quickly as he opens the door to walk back into the house with a large bag of trash.

Jessica turns around, and Mark shoots her a mischievous smile as if they're both carrying the same secret. Jessica's cheeks color, and I think, *well, Jessica, your prince might just be closer than you think.*

We finish cleaning, gather our things, and say goodbye to Mark. Jessica is hungry so we pick up some lunch for her at a drive-through restaurant and drive to my house. My dad has not returned from church, and I figure he has been invited to someone's house for lunch, which happens often. I plan to shower and change while Jessica eats.

I notice a small spot of blood on my underwear before showering and wonder if it's already time for another period. It's as if I just had one a couple of weeks ago, but my periods are so irregular, it's hard to say. I go months without having one and then have a heavy one for days, like the last one I had.

I need to ask my dad about seeing a gynecologist. Many of the girls I know have already been to one for a checkup, even Jessica. Most of them go to get on the pill, which I'm not opposed to doing to straighten out my hormones and help regulate my periods. This is something I could have easily spoken to my mom about, but I feel a bit timid attempting to speak to my dad about female matters.

When I've finished showering and am fastening my robe, Jessica speaks loudly so I can hear through the bathroom door, "Cara, I'm going to go ahead and jet."

"Wait." I open the door and pad across the carpet to her. Hugging her, I say, "Thank you again for helping me last night and for bringing me home, Jess."

"What are best friends for?" She beams, and for the first time in a long time, I feel Jessica is a true best friend.

✦✦✦

December

"You got your wish, Jamie," I say as we enjoy the fire in the giant double-sided fireplace. Its hewn-stoned presence stands in the middle of the great room of Jamie's house like a bulwark, the other side opening to their large dining room.

"What wish is that?" He turns his head to look at me, picks up a long strand of my hair, and twists it between his fingers.

We're sitting together on the sofa watching my favorite classic Christmas movie while his mom types away on her little laptop in the nearby recliner. She's working on her latest editing commission.

"For your first Christmas break in Texas to feel like a true Christmas." I give him an incredulous look as if offended he doesn't remember.

He looks confused, so I remind him. "The first time we met in the cafeteria that day? You said you were looking forward to experiencing the different seasons in Texas and that you wanted to have a Christmas break that wasn't warm like it is in Southern California."

"You remember I said that?" Jamie is genuinely surprised that I do.

I teasingly flutter my eyelashes at him. "I remember everything you said that day. I was so smitten with you, I hung on every word."

My confession puts a smile on his face. "Yeah, I'm glad it's cold enough for a fire tonight. Even better that I get to snuggle with you in front of it. Which is only one of the things I love to do with you," he whispers in my ear and kisses my cheek.

Susan looks over at us and smiles before quickly returning to her work.

Over the last several weeks, many weekend evenings have been spent like this, either at my house or Jamie's. Now that we are out of school for winter break, it's been even more often. I have fallen in love with Jamie's family, and they treat me as a fixture, like I'm supposed to be here. I am no longer considered a guest.

It's the same with my dad and Jamie. They watch a lot of football games together, and my dad is thrilled to have a watching buddy with whom to do so, especially now that Jamie has declared himself a fan of our Texas team.

Christmas is only a few days away, and everyone in Jamie's household is eagerly anticipating the arrival of his older sister, Megan. She is due to fly in on the twenty-third from California. Apparently, according to Jamie, she's bringing her new boyfriend with her, and his parents are somewhat leery.

Susan sets aside her computer. She stands to stretch her arms above her head and inhales deeply with the grace of a yoga instructor. It's obvious Jamie's entire family makes good use of their home gym.

"Cara, do you mind helping me in the kitchen? I'm going to start dinner. You are staying, aren't you?" she asks, hopefully.

"Sure, I'd love to," I say, as I let go of Jamie's hand to follow her into the kitchen.

He smiles and quickly looks back to the television, changing the channel. I guess my favorite Christmas movie is not his jam, yet he didn't say anything or try to change the channel when I got excited about it coming on.

That's Jamie.

Susan begins setting things on the counter to prepare dinner. "Do you mind throwing a salad together while I get the pasta boiling?"

"Of course not," I say, happy she's asked me to help. "I've made a salad or two over the years."

"And a lot of full-course dinners over the years, too," she adds knowingly. "Jamie tells me you're a wonderful cook." She turns toward me.

"It's something my mom and I enjoyed doing together. She bought me my first cookbook when I was seven. Before that, I had lots of practice with my toy oven." I laugh, and she smiles, looking thoughtfully at me.

"While I have you in here, I would like to ask you if you'll be able to join us for Christmas Day dinner?" She looks excitedly into my eyes—expectant.

When I hesitate to accept because I think how I couldn't possibly leave my father alone on Christmas Day, not even for part of it, it's as though she reads my thoughts. She turns back to an open cabinet and rushes to add, "Of course we want your father to come, too. Do you think he would like to?"

She said, *"we,"* implying this has already been something discussed among the family, which touches a hollow place inside me, filling it.

"Yes, I believe he would like that," I answer, grateful for the invitation given as though we are all family. "We're going to my grandparents' house—my dad's parents—on the twenty-third and my mom's mother's apartment at her assisted care living facility on Christmas Eve, so that will work perfectly. I'll talk to Dad and let you know."

"We would love to have you. My motto is always, 'The more the merrier.'"

"Are you sure we won't be intruding on your family gathering?"

Susan stops what she's doing and closes the space between us. Peering into my eyes, she takes both of my hands in hers and says softly, "Can I tell you something that has been on my heart?" When I nod, she continues, "I know you and Jamie are still young, and I don't know what the future will hold for you both, but I can speak on behalf of Brent, myself, and even Amber. We consider you family. Even if you and Jamie at some point decide to part ways..."

I start to speak and she holds up her hand. "I would hate that, of course, but hypothetically, if you do, I will always want to be a part of your life. We've grown to truly love you." Tears brim in her caring blue eyes, and I feel my own forming, stinging. "You're very special to me, and I would be honored to serve as a sort of mother figure in your life if you will allow me to."

Her words reach in and soothe me to my core, miraculously closing a portion of the raw, open wound left by the loss of my mother. Tears threaten to spill over when I step forward to hug her. My intention is to hug her quickly so as to keep in check these raw emotions that have decided to surprise me.

But she keeps her arms around me, prolonging the embrace. The comfort and warmth of a mother's love is something I didn't know how much I missed—*longed* for. I might as well be five years old again, and she's kissing away my boo-boo while simultaneously ripping off a four-year-old band-aid from another. I relax, sinking into her embrace, cherishing it. Swiping at my face with one hand, I attempt to hide a tear that has tracked silently down my cheek.

Sensing the meaning of my gesture, she murmurs softly into my hair, "Oh, sweet Cara, I am so very sorry for all you've lost. I love you, sweetheart."

That's all it takes for the box I thought was tightly closed to spring open without my permission. There is no stopping a sob that leaps into my throat as Susan continues to hold me, whispering comforting words.

"I'm here for you, whatever you need, Cara. We will always be here for you. Your mother would be proud of who you are now, how much you have overcome. You've been so sweet and strong."

She holds me this way for some time, allowing me to let go of years of suppressed sorrow. It's like discovering I have an injury or bruise only after it's been prodded. My continuous attempts to appear strong over the last four years by not allowing my grief to fully surface have taken their toll—feeble attempts to carry on seemingly unscathed with a new life irrevocably broken by loss.

The stress of keeping my grief inside continues to pour out of me. It's a cleansing I didn't know I needed, but Susan must have. We stay like this until my sobs begin to dissipate and she's certain I have cried it all out.

She steps back and takes my hands in hers again, holding me at arm's length now. "We're all so grateful that you were brought to us, or that God brought us to you." She smiles. "It's okay to admit that it still hurts, that you have times of extreme sadness. I also lost my mother pretty young and can relate. You can call on me any time you're feeling this way or just need to talk."

I nod, thinking that the woman in front of me is one of the kindest people I have ever known, and she happens to be Jamie's mother.

"You have no idea what you all mean to me, what Jamie means to me," I confess through my sniffles.

"Oh, I think I do," she says, squeezing my hands and smiling the brightest smile she's ever given me, "I think I do."

Jamie

"**M**ay I help you, sir?"

"I'm just going to look around first, but thank you," I tell the older, well-dressed sales representative.

She allows me to walk freely around the cases for a few minutes before she asks, "Are you shopping for an engagement ring?" and adds sweetly, "Can I take one from the case to show you?"

"Not an engagement ring," I say, still looking inside the cases, my head spinning from all the choices, "more like a promise ring, a ring symbolizing our relationship as exclusive. It's a Christmas present for my girlfriend."

"How nice. I can help you find one if you want to follow me a little farther down here."

I'm relieved as soon as I see the selection of smaller, less extravagant rings. Cara wouldn't like anything too large or fancy.

"Are you looking for sterling silver, white gold, or..."

I don't hear what she asks me because the perfect ring catches my eye. "That one, there." I point. "I think it's exactly what I'm looking for." I had already looked online at a few, and this one checks all the boxes.

"Wonderful, let's take a look at it," she exclaims dramatically, unlocking the case to retrieve the ring.

It's a heart with a small diamond in the middle and smaller diamond accents on each side. I hold it between my thumb and forefinger, turning it back and forth, appreciating how it catches the light. I envision Cara seeing it for the first time.

"She will love it," I confirm.

"If you know her size, I can check to see if we have one in stock. If we don't have her size, I can place an order for a resizing."

"She wears a size six," I say confidently, recalling how I was able to extract this information from Cara after I decided what to give her for Christmas.

We were holding hands while sitting on my sofa watching TV one evening, and I feigned interest in Cara's purity ring, as she calls it. I removed it and commented on how small it looked compared to my larger fingers and placed it on my pinky finger as far as it would go—only to the first joint—which made her giggle.

It was the perfect opportunity to comment nonchalantly, "It's so small; what size ring is this?"

"It's a size six. Do I have bony fingers?" she asked while examining her hand.

"No, they're long and elegant," I said and returned it to her right ring finger, kissing her hand.

Easy shmeezy.

"A very common size," the saleswoman assures me.

She unlocks and opens a drawer under the case, locating the ring in Cara's size.

"I'd like to have the inside engraved. Would it be done by Christmas?" I ask.

"Yes," she replies, "we send all our engraving over to a company located inside the mall. They usually have a one-day turnaround, but I would give it two days. We'll call you when it's ready."

She hands me a form to fill out, and I write what I want to be engraved inside the ring. After paying with my credit card and leaving the jewelry store, I drop into the mall's card shop to buy Cara a card before heading home.

◆◆◆

The anticipation of Chris and Cara's arrival on Christmas Day about kills me. I'm excited to be with Cara on this special day, but truth be told, I'm dying to give her my gift. I'm sure she will like it, but will she think it's too much? I couldn't care less about the cost, and I hope she doesn't overthink it like I am.

After the events of last night, the house has returned to peace. Since Megan has come home with her boyfriend, Decker, whom she met at college, there have been two incidents of drama—one between Megan and Mom, and the second between my dad and me.

I couldn't help but overhear Mom and Megan arguing about sleeping arrangements the first night of the day she arrived. Dad had taken Decker to the store with him while the women and I stayed to get dinner ready and visit with Megan.

"Mom, we are adults here. Decker can sleep in the same room with me; there's no need to get two guest rooms ready," Megan protested when Mom was retrieving clean sheets for the beds.

Normally, our housekeeper, who comes twice a week, would be preparing the beds, but she's off for the holidays.

"No, I am not putting you both in the same room, Megan. You two are not married, and it would set a bad example. Stop being selfish and think of Jamie and Amber." Though Mom was trying to be quiet, I could hear their heated exchange from my bedroom while I lay on my bed playing a game on my phone.

"So you think Decker and I aren't having sex?" Megan asked defiantly. "This isn't the Dark Ages."

"Be that as it may, placing you both in the same bedroom is tantamount to giving you my approval. I won't do it."

"Fine! We'll end up in the same bed anyway; you just won't know about it!"

"Megan, you are infuriating," Mom said resignedly. "Are you two using protection? Are you on the pill? Because I'm not quite ready to be a grandmother yet."

Huh. What do you know? Mom could bite back with her own sarcasm.

"Mom, again, it's not the Dark Ages; of course, I'm on the pill. Trust me, as much as you're not ready to be a grandma, I'm not ready to be a mother." Megan spat back.

"This is how it's going to be: When Dad and Decker return, I will show Decker his room and have him bring his bag up. What you guys do after that, I don't want to know about, and I would appreciate it if Jamie and Amber don't, either!"

I heard Mom's angry retreating footsteps and a loud "Ugh!" from Megan as she practically slammed the door to the bedroom.

The second incident was the next evening, which was last night. Dad and I were sitting out back on the deck enjoying the warmth of the fire pit and talking football—voicing our predictions for the big game.

"I'm going to grab a beer; want one?" Dad asked. It was the first time he'd asked since my Halloween party experience with alcohol.

"Nah, thanks," I said, glancing away.

"What?" He looked at me strangely. "First time you've ever turned down having a beer with me."

He walked over to the outdoor kitchen fridge we keep stocked with drinks, took out a beer, and opened it. He sat down again, watching me.

Since I turned eighteen, he has asked me a few times to have a beer with him. "Only one beer, though," he had said, "until you turn twenty-one." Then, he'd told me, there would be nothing he could do about how much I choose to drink or whether I decide to drink at all.

I think Dad is attempting to demystify the drinking experience for me and trying to teach me moderation.

It's also been a bonding time for us, kind of a rite of passage that he chose for me instead of taking me out to shoot a deer or something. He has always told me, "You will never feel as good as a couple of beers will make you feel. Any more than that only takes away the good feeling and invites trouble."

I had always stuck to his rules and advice until Mark Shelton's party. I hadn't even thought about his advice during the party when Cara and I were feeling good and carefree, carelessly drinking more to get more of the good feeling. I should have heeded Dad's instruction that alcohol doesn't work that way; but instead, I learned his lesson the hard way and still feel guilty two months later.

"Something bothering you? You got quiet on me after I asked if you wanted a beer."

"Yeah, it just doesn't sound very appealing to me," I said. The glum in my voice was audible, and Dad noticed.

He didn't say anything, just looked into the fire and waited for me to speak.

After a minute or so, I decided to tell him. "I got drunk at Mark Shelton's Halloween party."

There. It was bluntly out in the open.

Again, Dad said nothing, so I hesitantly looked up from the fire and attempted to read his thoughts. He gave a couple of quick nods and said, "Hmm."

Since he didn't seem too shocked or about to tear into me, I continued, "It honestly didn't seem like a lot, but it was a spiked punch I couldn't gauge well and overdrank. I guess it had some pretty strong stuff in it. That's why I didn't text you until late. I literally passed out. And learned a huge lesson from it," I added apologetically.

"Did you throw up?" he asked me gruffly.

"No, but I had to be helped to walk." Dad's mouth formed a thin line at that admission. "And I feel really bad about it. But what I feel most guilty about is that Cara was with me, and she was a lot worse off than I was."

"Oh, Jamie, no." Dad shook his head and scowled at me, clearly upset. "Does her father know about this?"

"Hell, no," I said too quickly. "Sorry, no, Cara would die if he found out. She's terrified of disappointing him. She doesn't drink alcohol much, so this was also the first time she had ever been drunk. I feel horrible about not watching out for her better, but in all honesty, it didn't seem like we drank that much." I shrugged. "Live and learn," I added quietly, but without a bit of levity.

We sat in silence a few seconds more before I said, "I also hate disappointing you, which I know I have. Sorry I disregarded what you've tried to teach me about drinking responsibly. It won't happen again."

"I trust you learned a lesson from it like you said you did." He paused and said, "You did the right thing by staying put and not trying to drive home or anything stupid."

"Ha," I laughed derisively, "I couldn't have walked to my truck, much less gotten behind the wheel. I don't even remember anything past lying down in the bed I was led to, making sure Cara was okay, and kissing her goodnight."

My dad raised an eyebrow and opened his mouth to speak, but seemed to reconsider and shut it, saying nothing else.

The doorbell rings, startling me back to the present. This will be the first time both Cara's and my family will be together in one place, besides the times we've been to Cara's church. This more intimate setting makes me a little anxious because I want everyone to relax and enjoy themselves. Mom answers the door and shows Cara and her dad into the great room where most of us are hanging out.

I stand when Cara walks in, and we immediately lock eyes across the room. My heart rate accelerates at the sight of her—it's been a few days. I've *missed* her.

She looks beautiful in a red sweater-type dress and black boots. The red dress hugs her curves and is a beautiful contrast to her blonde hair flowing down over her shoulders. She has more color on her lips than I've seen, and all I can think about is getting her alone soon so I can kiss them.

After introductions to Megan and Decker, Dad takes Chris to show him around. Cara takes a couple of gifts she's carrying and places them under the tree. Amber and Mom make their way into the kitchen to finish preparing dinner, and Cara is quick to volunteer to help.

"No, Cara, you and Jamie relax and visit. We've got this. There's not much more to do." Mom smiles broadly, seemingly thrilled to have them over.

It's not quite cold enough for a fire in the fireplace tonight, but we have one anyway to contribute to the ambiance of Christmas cheer. The saying in Texas is if you don't like the weather, wait a minute. All four seasons can make an appearance within the same day here, so who knows what later will bring?

Cara and I sit on the loveseat and Megan and Decker on the couch. Megan's preference for boyfriends sheds a little more light on her carefree personality.

I whisper into Cara's ear, "They're so stoned."

Cara looks shocked and asks, "How do you know?"

"Just watch them."

Which is what we do, and Megan and Decker seem oblivious to us even being in the room. Both are glassy-eyed and laughing at nothing at all. When either of them opens their mouth to say something—anything—the other begins to laugh as though they've just received laughing gas at a dentist's office.

Cara giggles as a result, and I decide to try to engage them in conversation. "So, are you guys hungry? About ready to eat?" I then say quieter, under my breath, "Got the munchies?"

Cara gasps and nudges me in the ribs with her elbow.

"Yeah, brah, I know I am. How about you, Meg?" Decker asks.

"I'm so hungry, I could eat a horse, as they say in Texas. Or do they?" Megan laughs hard at her own statement, and Decker joins in again.

Cara and I look at each other, and I roll my eyes while mouthing the word, "See?"

She gives a faint nod and chuckles quietly.

Dad and Chris come back into the house after taking a tour around the property and sit in the two chairs next to the couch opposite the loveseat. Megan sits up straighter, and Decker loses his smile.

"So, how was school this semester?" I look at them both, but Megan answers.

"It was fine. I've almost got all my basics out of the way, so I'm sure it will get better once I'm able to dive into more of the film classes. Decker is also studying film; that's how we met," she says, taking his hand and smiling at him. He seems disinterested until she says, "He wants to create documentaries."

I say only loud enough for Cara to hear, "Yeah, and I bet they'll be about legalizing weed in every state."

She nudges me again, trying not to laugh.

Dad is an avid watcher of documentaries, and this has piqued his interest, so the two of them discuss the topic for a while. It seems to break the ice for us all to join in. I notice Decker staring at Cara more and more throughout the conversations when Megan's either talking or not paying attention—I never noticed how close to zero Megan's attention span is until now. I can't decipher if Decker is just intrigued by Cara's beauty and fully appreciates it, or if he's got a wandering eye. I'll keep my own eye on this dude.

Mom announces dinner is ready and we all stand to go into the dining room. For the first time in my life it's as though I've replaced Megan as the oldest sibling, and I wonder when, exactly, our roles got reversed.

Cara

The eight of us sit down to dinner at the large, beautifully set table, decorated in all reds and greens. Jamie's dad, Brent—although I still don't feel comfortable calling him by his first name—asks my dad to say the dinner prayer. It is brief but heartfelt, asking blessings for our families, the food, and the year ahead.

I watched my dad uncertainly for a few minutes after we arrived while he interacted with the others to make sure he was having a good time; but he's been smiling and enjoying the conversations. Dad is quiet yet naturally good with people and enjoys being around them, which is the main reason he is so good at his chosen profession. He's also not one to pass up good food or wine, and tonight, they're plentiful.

Walking into Jamie's house tonight flooded me with warmth and memories of the lively Christmases from years past when my mom was still alive. Mom loved Christmas as much as Susan and always made them special for us by going all out with decorating and cooking. Jamie's Christmas tree is larger and the decor more elaborate than we ever had, but the effect is the same—simply a peaceful, incredible feeling of home and family.

The food was delicious, and we all complimented Susan and thanked her for the work that went into its preparation; but lately, I haven't been able to eat much.

Jamie noticed, of course, and while we are cleaning the kitchen, he comments, "You didn't eat a lot. Are you still having trouble with your stomach?"

"Yes," I say, "but I think it's getting better."

I began having bouts of queasiness recently where food of any type just hasn't been appetizing, yet I always feel much better if I go ahead and eat a little. I researched my symptoms, and they all lead to one condition. It's the same thing I was diagnosed with after my mother passed away.

"I have IBS," I tell Jamie, "Irritable Bowel Syndrome. It causes a lot of digestion issues when it acts up. I won't go into it all, especially the 'B' part of it." I attempt a laugh but think about all the cramping and bathroom visits that are a part of my life, and cringe instead. "If you look it up, I have almost every symptom, especially food sensitivities and fatigue, sometimes nausea. It was pretty bad after my mom died, but I haven't had it flare up like this since then. I started taking a probiotic, and it's helping."

"I'm sorry, babe. I hope your appetite gets better. You need to stop losing weight or you'll only get more fatigued," Jamie lectures, brows drawn in concern. "Maybe Shadow and I need to take you out for more ice cream. That's what always makes me feel better." He grins, and I catch a glimpse of the cute little boy he used to be. It's adorable.

Susan listens to us as she loads the dishwasher. "Jamie, ice cream isn't the remedy for every ailment, especially not for IBS. Dairy can sometimes exacerbate it."

She looks at me and says, "I have a tendency to suffer from it occasionally, too. Along with the probiotic you started, try drinking a little kombucha daily. It might also help balance your stomach bacteria. I drink it when I have symptoms of imbalance."

"I do like kombucha," I say. "I'll put it on my next grocery list."

"That stuff is nasty," Jamie grimaces in disgust, "like drinking vinegar. You both can keep all your healthy foodstuff, and I'll stick to ice cream."

I just laugh, while Susan rolls her eyes.

"Before we open presents, let's make some hot chocolate with almond milk. I have a dark chocolate mix that would have very little dairy in it. Does that sound good to you?" Susan asks in her soothing voice.

She's perpetually ready to nurture and comfort me, and I am beginning to love her like a mom—a real mom.

"It really does," I reply. "I'll help you."

Jamie and Amber return to the great room while Susan starts the hot chocolate, and I take down a few mugs from the cabinet. I find the mini marshmallows in their giant pantry and put a few inside each mug to pour the hot chocolate over.

When it's time to exchange presents, I take my mug of hot chocolate and one for Jamie and sit beside him on the sofa.

Decker and Megan opt for the floor and sit cross-legged, furthering their bohemian look and vibe.

The gift exchange is mainly for the guests. My dad gave me some pro earbuds this morning I've wanted, and I got him the same thing I'm giving Jamie, with the ability to invite a plus-one.

Brent passes out three of the few gifts left under their tree. He gives one each to Decker, my dad, and me. They all have a label, *"From the Gallaghers,"* attached.

"Go ahead and open them," Brent says.

We open the gifts simultaneously, and my dad interjects, "The invitation here tonight and the wonderful meal were more than enough."

The gifts are all the same beautiful, expensive-looking frames but with a different photo in each. Decker's is a photo of him and Megan on a beach in California, both looking completely in their element. My dad's is one I had taken recently of him standing in front of a stained-glass window at the church dressed in his finest suit. It's my favorite photo of him looking quite handsome. When I look at Susan quizzically, she knows what I'm thinking.

"The beauty of social media," she says. "You had posted the picture, and Amber snatched it and saved it from your photos after you accepted her friend request."

Amber smiles proudly, and I let her know she chose the perfect picture.

Clearly moved by their kindness, my dad exclaims, "I love this photo, and the frame is beautiful. It will look great on my office desk... very thoughtful."

My photo is the selfie Jamie took of us in the cafeteria the day after the incident with Eric.

"It's the first picture we ever took together," Jamie explains. "I know you said at the time you have better pics of yourself, but I love this one; and it being our first photo together makes it special."

"I absolutely love it," I say and thank them all. I whisper to Jamie, "I'll put it on my nightstand so yours will be the last face I see when I turn out my light. It will help me dream about you."

He places his warm, heavy palm on my thigh and squeezes. My heart overflows with appreciation for their thoughtfulness and how it was a family effort to put my dad's and my gifts together.

I take Jamie's gift and the one we brought for Jamie's family from under the tree and hand that one to Susan. "This is just a little something from us to say how much we appreciate you all."

She opens it while Brent looks on. "A beautiful desk clock." She removes it from the box and holds it up for all to see. "Thank you both."

"I chose it to match the decor in your home office, but it's like a cuckoo clock if you turn on that feature. Instead of it making the cuckoo sound, though, turn it on with the switch in the back and see what it does," I say with excitement.

Brent snatches it from Susan playfully and says, "I want to do it."

He switches it on, and the opening line of the California state song plays, "I love you, California..."

"In case you ever get lonesome for California and want a taste of home," I say, now suddenly self-conscious.

"It's brilliant," Brent says and plays it again.

"Thank you both again so much," Susan says sincerely, her eyes a bit misty. I appreciate that she's sensitive like I am and makes no apologies for it.

My dad replies, "Thanks again for having us, and for all the love and hospitality you've shown my girl here." He looks over to me and winks.

Susan beams. She always wants everyone to be happy—just another sweet thing I love about her. "It's our pleasure. She's become a part of our family, and we love her very much," she assures my dad.

"Okay, before you all get too mushy here and make me cry..." I say, handing Jamie his gift from me.

He holds it next to his ear and shakes it teasingly. He takes his time opening it, looks inside the box, and pulls out an envelope.

It's a card I finally found after searching through a few shelves. On the front are two intertwined hearts, and inside, it states my feelings very simply yet perfectly.

Jamie opens it and reads it aloud: *"The moment I met you was like waking up from the longest dream. Love, Cara."*

"Aww," everyone chimes in collectively, and my cheeks grow hot.

Jamie looks at me. "You're blushing, Cara." He doesn't seem to care that anyone is watching and leans over to kiss me softly on the cheek.

He takes out another envelope that was tucked beneath the card and unseals it. "What?" His face lights up when he recognizes what's inside. "Heck, yeah!" he whoops loudly.

"What is it?" everyone asks at once.

"Two tickets to my first Texas football game, a home game. Thank you, Cara!"

"But look who they're playing that day," I prompt.

"Oh, oh, wow! Now you're killing me here." He laughs. "My California team!"

I shrug. "Look at it this way, whoever wins, you'll be happy."

"True, and now I just need to decide who I'm going to take with me," he says, biting his lower lip and rubbing his chin with his thumb and forefinger.

"Haha," I say, poking him in the ribs.

My dad speaks up, "I got the same gift from Cara—two tickets. I was wondering if you would like to be my partner in crime at the game and keep an eye on these two, Brent?"

"Are you kidding? I'd love to. Seems to me I'm the one who got a twofer deal here today with the Christmas gifts." Brent and Dad both laugh at that.

I didn't know my dad planned to ask Brent to take his extra ticket, but I can't help thinking how special it will be for two fathers to take their children to a game together—their children who happen to be in love.

"My turn." Jamie stands and walks over to the tree to retrieve a large, nicely wrapped box. He brings it back to the sofa and hands it to me as he sits down again. "Last, but certainly not least."

There is a hand-sized card attached to it. The first few words let me know it's a personal card, and my cheeks grow warm again because I can sense everyone watching me. I decide in half a beat not to read it aloud and continue reading silently, *You're the pep in my step / My comfort through pain / My joy through sadness / My sun after rain.* Below the poem, it is signed in Jamie's handwriting, *My heart beats only for you... Jamie.*

I look up at him, but before I can speak, he says, "Cheesy, I know, but very true."

"Thank you, Jamie. I love it; it's really sweet."

I untie the large ribbon on the box and lift the lid. The box is stuffed with a lot of tissue paper, which seems endless as I remove piece after piece. There, at the bottom of the box, is a small, velvet, pastel-pink box. I take it gingerly out of the larger one. My heart begins to pound in my ears. *A ring?* I can feel Jamie watching me closely.

I lift the hinged lid slowly and can't believe my eyes. I'm suddenly unaware of anyone else in the room. "Jamie! Oh my gosh, it's beautiful."

I remove the ring while Jamie says more to everyone else than to me, "Don't worry, it's only a promise ring. Look at the inscription, Cara."

I have to hold the ring close and move it around slowly as I read it aloud, *"My heart beats only for you."*

"Hence the heart with the diamond in the center. I'd like to think it's your heart, and the diamond represents me inside of it."

"Yes, it's perfect... too much," I exclaim, as I place it on my left ring finger, "but I love it. It fits perfectly, too." I look into his eyes and around at the smiling faces. "Thank you."

I will have to wait to get Jamie alone to fully express how I feel, to show him how much I love the gift, but especially the giver. For now, I give him a tight hug I'm reluctant to let go of.

My eyes fix on my dad's. The look on his face is a mixture of happiness and resignation. His expression turns slightly sorrowful when he catches my gaze, and I can read what it's saying: *I have lost my baby girl's heart to another man.*

✦✦✦

May

"Cara, stop!" Jamie holds my upper arms still. "You're stressing way too much about this."

Jamie and I sit at my dining room table with my laptop, textbooks, folders, and papers scattered about. Evenings like this have become the norm. Tonight, it feels too overwhelming to deal with, and I'm experiencing a bit of a meltdown.

"It's easy for you to say, Jamie, you aren't even taking any of the AP exams. You know doing well on them means not having to take the classes in college. Do you realize how much time and money that will save me if I do well on the tests? Studying is a priority right now."

"I understand. I'm just trying to talk you off the ledge here. You're going to crash and burn if you don't take a break and sleep. For weeks, you've studied and fretted, staying up half the night doing homework. I'm worried about you, babe."

It's true, I'm working hard to stay in the top ten percent of my class. The high ranking helped me get accepted into my first choice of Texas universities for the fall. With the scholarships I've been granted, I will already have a lot of my college paid for after weeks of filling out applications and obtaining letters of recommendation from teachers. The last couple of months have been a flurry of activity, each day like a pixelated photograph leading into the next.

"Please don't be. I just need to finish this one assignment and then I can get some sleep tonight. Overall, I'm doing better. Physically speaking, I feel better than I have in quite a while."

"Your tummy is better?" he asks.

"I still have the bloating and constant rumbling, but I don't really pay attention to them anymore. All our ice cream trips, well, frozen yogurt for me, and all the takeout have definitely contributed to gaining back all the weight I lost... and then some," I add, smiling.

"I tried to tell you and Mom ice cream is the answer to everything." He shrugs, holding a smug grin. "Seriously, though, I've been worried about you." His eyes rove over me. "But I like the way you look; you look healthy now."

"Healthy, huh? Is that a euphemism like *fluffy* is?" I jest. "I'll blame finally getting my appetite back after all the flare-ups for some of my clothes not fitting, along with stress eating. Thank goodness Boho fashion is still in vogue. After the exams, maybe I can schedule some workouts with you in your home gym?" I say, meaning it. I'm so ready to be done with high school.

"Only if I can be your personal trainer," he says, nuzzling my neck and laying a soft kiss under my ear, making me shiver. "I'll admit to being selfish here, too. I miss my time with you. It's been too scarce lately. Even when we're together, your mind is in another zip code."

My eyes catch his as I start typing again, "And I'm sorry, but the classes were already difficult this semester, even more so now that the tests are next week. I'm not as concerned about the AP English exam as I am the others."

"No one could ever accuse you of not being ambitious and hard-working. I wish I could say it will get better after the exams, but graduation is only a couple of weeks after the exams, so, unfortunately, there's no slowing down just yet, is there?"

Jamie—perpetually concerned with my welfare and faithfully looking out for me. He's been overly patient the last few weeks, even though I drive him crazy with my school obsession. He seems satisfied to just finish high school and take his basics at the community college when he's ready. Unlike me, his future career with his family business is set, and money is not a concern for him. He says he plans to eventually get an MBA, but he's in no hurry. He also seems to earn good grades with a lot less effort, which unnerves me.

I, on the other hand, want to get a college degree as quickly as possible to start my teaching career and earn a salary. Jamie jokes that he will take care of me, that I won't need to work if I don't want to "when we get married," but he knows how important starting a career is to me, thus the patience he's shown. I need to do this for myself and for no one else.

He has made many runs for takeout so I wouldn't have to cook on the evenings that I have a lot of homework. He even cooked breakfast food—basically, the only thing Jamie knows how to cook—for my dad and me one evening, and it was good.

"Are you sure there's not anything else wrong besides the stress of school?"

Jamie knows me too well. My mind immediately jumps to my dad. He and Rachel had their first date on Valentine's Day—about three months ago—and they have been nearly inseparable since. They met at church on a Tuesday evening when she and her two children came to eat and pick up groceries. She's been attending ever since, but it took months before Dad asked her to dinner.

Rachel and Dad are about the same age, but she has younger boys, one twelve and the other thirteen. According to Dad, her husband was in the military and was killed in Afghanistan almost six years ago. After dating a few weeks and realizing they clicked, he has spent a lot of time at her house—where he is tonight.

It's difficult to arrange spending much time at our place with her kids at home to take care of, so we haven't spent a whole lot of time together yet. Rachel is very pretty in an understated way. She's nice, incredibly quiet, and seems a little guarded around me. Maybe she is only reflecting my own uncertainty about her. We'll be able to spend more time together when school is out and I finally have the summer to chill and recuperate.

I'm genuinely happy for them, I am, but it's hard to accept that, in essence, my dad has an entirely new family. I have a feeling it won't be long before I have a stepmom and two stepbrothers. They seem great together, and it's what I wanted for him, sure. But the selfish side of me misses having my dad to myself whenever I needed him—something I took for granted before circumstances changed.

Too much change.

Cara

With the completion of my AP exams, the level of stress and anxiety has somewhat subsided. Now, it's the two-month waiting game for the scores to be posted—sometime in late July. The highlights of last week were sitting through graduation planning meetings, graduation practice, and picking up our regalia. Today, we receive our cords unique to our various designations and achievements to wear around our necks over our graduation robes.

When we were trying on our robes before taking them home with us last week, I jokingly commented to Jessica how I hoped mine would fit since gaining almost ten pounds over the last several weeks, even with my stomach acting up.

Jessica asked, "You're not pregnant, are you?" only half-joking.

"Well, Jess, don't you think someone would need to have had sex first before that could happen?" I laughed. "And don't you know I would have shared that with you if I had? You know Jamie and I are waiting."

"Yeah, of course, Cara. I was only kidding. In all honesty, I've gained at least five pounds this semester, too, and I'm short so it shows more. We are going to celebrate big and then get on a better schedule once our senior year is over."

"We probably shouldn't be so concerned about our weight, but haven't you heard of the 'freshman fifteen'?" I asked, quirking a brow as Jessica aligned the zipper of my robe for me.

"Omigosh, I can't afford to add that much weight my freshman year of college to what I've already gained from sitting on my ass doing homework this semester!" She looked horrified, and I'm sure she probably was at the prospect of putting even one more pound on her tiny frame.

"My sentiments exactly. But as stressful as our senior year has been, it's also been a blast. I met Jamie, and I wouldn't change a thing about it." I sighed.

"And I have Mark now. The end of the school year is bittersweet, though, isn't it?" Jessica turned to me, somber. "I'm gonna miss seeing you and the gang. We will all go our separate ways. So much will change..."

So much change.

***

It's Monday, the day before school is out, and three days before graduation. I wake up early, so sick my entire body is covered in a cold sweat. I lie in bed for a long time hoping it will pass, but the pain in my lower abdomen only grows worse. It comes in waves, and it feels as though I have the worst menstrual cramps ever, combined with a progressive need to use the restroom.

I try to think back on what I've eaten in an attempt to pinpoint the culprit of the worst flare-up of IBS I have ever experienced, but I can't think of anything unusual. I hear my dad leave for work, and when it's apparent my hope of feeling better so I can get ready for school is not going to materialize, I text Jamie. I let him know I'm sick and won't be at school. I tell him I'll go later if I feel better.

Jamie: *I'm sorry, babe, can I bring you anything?*

C: *No, thanks. I'm sure it's just a bad flare-up of my IBS, but it's the worst ever!*

Jamie: *Will you be sure to text me if you need me to come over? I'll skip school if you want me to. No big deal since we're pretty much done.*

C: *No, go on to school, I'll be fine.*

Jamie: *Okay, get some rest. I think part of your problem is your lack of sleep. You need more rest.*

Severe pain hits me when I receive his text. I have to wait a few seconds before I can reply.

C: *I will. I'll text you later. Love you.*

Jamie: *Love you too, babe.* (kissing emoji)

I take my phone and slide carefully off the bed. The pain is so intense, I can't stand up straight. All I can think about is getting to the toilet.

I slowly make my way there, each step amplifying the sharp pains coming more steadily now. Sitting down on the toilet yields some relief, but the pain comes in almost constant currents, and it hits me like a literal punch to the gut how utterly sick I am.

Something is very wrong.

After a few minutes of the pain and pressure intensifying, I place both hands on either side of the toilet and bear down with a cry. This happens several times in succession, and I've broken out in a drenching sweat. All I can compare the sensation to is having the worst constipation ever—which must be what's going on—and I am about to fill the toilet.

Which I do.

But it is not what I was braced for, not in a trillion years! I spread my legs to look down between them, and still attached to me by a cord-like tube is what looks like a tiny baby doll with flailing arms.

In my wildest dreams, I would not have imagined this. I cannot, *CANNOT* absorb what is happening.

In all of one second, my brain works to comprehend. I must have been pregnant—somehow; I've had a baby, and I need to do something quickly. In a far corner of my mind, questions only begin to take shape: *When did I get pregnant? HOW?*

I don't have time to fully process any of my thoughts before my hands, without hesitation, scoop up this tiny creature covered in blood, and cradle it in my arms.

I slide off the toilet and slither my bottom down to the bathroom floor. My phone, at some point, must have dropped to the tile. Picking it up with my shaking right hand, I think first of calling my dad or Jamie. But foggily comprehending the situation as dire, I dial 911 instead.

"911, what is your emergency?" a female dispatcher asks in a flat tone.

"Please, please help me, help me! I just had a baby, and, and, and, I don't know... Oh my God... I don't *UNDERSTAND!*" I yell into the phone. "Help me! Please help me!" I cry.

A sob leaps into my throat, choking me, and I force myself to hold it together. I try to switch the audio on the phone to the speaker with my bloody, trembling right hand and finally get it on the fourth attempt. I lay the phone on the floor beside me so I can comfort the whimpering infant.

I can't reconcile the warring emotions between denial and acceptance—*This can't possibly be happening,* one part of my brain is screaming, *SCREAMING!* While another part thunders, *This is happening; it* did *happen. I. Had. A. Baby!*

How? How?

HOW?

As the 911 dispatcher on the phone asks me questions, I look down at the baby in my arms and recognize it's a boy. He's little, but he's perfectly formed; a beautiful baby boy. Yet this can't be real. Am I still asleep and dreaming? Have I been dropped into an alternate universe? How in the *hell* did this happen?

I answer her questions as best I can, as errant ripples of thoughts emerge:

Jamie.

Does he know?

No, he doesn't.

How?

Mark's party. Mark's party. Mark's party.

But Jamie didn't remember, either?

No, he would have told you.

Or did he?

He would have told you...

The dispatcher tries to calm me. "I'm going to give you some instructions now. Listen, you need to wipe the baby's nose and mouth. Do that for me now."

Through the haze of uncooperative comprehension, I follow her instructions. It's as though I am a spectator, looking down, watching a person who is not me perform the tasks.

Upon command, I watch gentle hands wipe the baby's nose and mouth with a clean washcloth from the under-sink cabinet. The disembodied hands dry the baby with a towel and wrap him in it to keep him warm. The same gentle hands place a towel between my legs to soak the blood that is turning the bathroom tile beneath me crimson.

Within only minutes, the dispatcher lets me know the fire department is arriving. "You're going to be just fine, Cara. As soon as you see the firefighters and paramedics, you can end this call, okay?"

A few seconds later, I hear a deep voice boom, "Paramedics!"

"In here!" I yell.

The next thing I know two firefighters are in the bathroom, and one bends down to take the baby from me. Squatting to my level, the other clamps the umbilical cord with something that resembles a clip I use to close my tortilla chip bags. He snips the cord above the clamp with strange-looking scissors.

"Here, take him and put him on the bag if needed, but he might just need the blow-by oxygen," the firefighter says, handing the baby to one of the paramedics who appears in my bathroom doorway.

"Is he okay?" I cry, "Is my baby going to be okay?"

The paramedic who has taken the baby assures me, "He's small, obviously moderately premature, but he has good color and muscle tone." He leaves the bathroom carrying the baby.

The partner of the firefighter aiding me asks me how old I am before pressing a button on his collar radio. "A viable preterm infant and his eighteen-year-old mother will be transported by EMS in less than five."

Mother.

"My name is Josh, and I'm going to help you until one of the EMS paramedics comes back in. They'll take good care of your baby. He'll probably need some help breathing. What's your name?"

"Cara," I rasp.

"Cara, I need to get some medical history from you. Are you allergic to any medications?" he asks while placing a blood pressure cuff around my arm.

"No, not that I know of," I reply, my unsteady voice barely above a whisper.

He places some type of monitor on the end of my index finger.

The other firefighter-paramedic removes the towel from between my legs, and I instinctively try to close my legs and adjust my nightshirt down over my thighs.

"Stay still, you're okay, we've got you. Hand me a trauma dressing," he asks Josh. He places it between my legs where the now-blood-soaked towel was.

"Vitals are good," Josh says to no one in particular. "Is this your first live birth?" he asks, and I nod. "No other pregnancies?" I shake my head no, still feeling as though I'm watching a scene from a movie, all happening to someone else.

This reality has no space in my brain to breathe. I open a new box located too closely to my heart called *Complete and Utter Devastation* and dump every emotion I'm feeling into it. I go completely numb.

"Do you need to call someone?" When he sees what must be a stricken look on my face, he asks, "Can I call someone for you?"

"Yes, please call my dad." I reach to take my phone from the floor and hand it to him. "It should say 'Dad' in my 'Recents.' His name is Chris," I croak out, not recognizing the sound of the voice coming out of my mouth as my own.

Imagining and anticipating the blow my poor father is about to receive, I can't bear to listen. I want to cover my ears and sing loudly like I did as a child to block out whatever it was I didn't want to hear.

"Chris, this is Josh, a paramedic with the Fort Worth Fire Department. We're responding to a call at your home from your daughter, Cara... No, sir, no fire, a medical call. Your daughter is going to be just fine, but she delivered a baby boy prematurely a few minutes ago, and they're both going to be transported to Fort Worth General Hospital for treatment. Yes, sir... No, I can't tell you that, sir... No, not a miscarriage, the baby is alive and was doing well before EMS took him out for treatment. Yes, sir; you can meet her there... yes, you're welcome."

He turns to me and says, "Your father is headed to the hospital and will meet the ambulance. How far along in your pregnancy were you?"

I look at the bloody towels littering the bathroom floor and still can't grasp the reality of the situation. In snippets, a picture begins to form from all the crumpled facts scattered across the floor of my brain.

Somehow, I find my voice.

"I didn't know I was pregnant," I say.

Josh and his partner look at one another, and I don't even attempt to tell him the reason I didn't know I was pregnant is that I freaking didn't know Jamie and I had even had sex. Which is a moot point now.

Since I know the exact date of the only time I could have conceived a baby, I say, "Since Halloween, I think."

You know! my mind screams.

"Ken, will you let the hospital know the gestation of the neonate about to arrive?"

After a pause of counting, Ken says, "Seven months, approximately thirty weeks or so," and calls it in over his radio.

Josh says, "Okay, well, Cara, he's very early, but thirty weeks is good. He's got a good chance."

A good chance, a good chance.

Rather than reassure me, as I'm sure was Josh's intent, his comment strikes terror in my heart. My mind processes his comment as a dawning realization there's a chance the baby, *my* baby, *won't* make it, and I begin to cry.

The numbness leaves and everything hits at once—the pain, the shock of finding out I was pregnant at the exact time I gave birth, trying to process how I could have been pregnant, and now grappling with the fact that my baby, *Jamie's* and my baby, could die.

It's too much.

Not only am I crying, but I begin to shake all over, my teeth chattering.

An EMS paramedic appears in the bathroom doorway with a stretcher, and Josh looks at Ken. "Let's get her up onto the stretcher and warm her up. She's experiencing some shock."

Josh speaks to me now, "We're going to try and get you more comfortable, Cara. We will help you up onto the gurney here."

Josh lifts me up with his forearms under my armpits while Ken lifts my lower body. A jab of sharp pain grips me. I cry out, my legs shaking uncontrollably.

Josh looks at the EMS paramedic and says, "The placenta still needs to come out," and then turns back to me. "You're in good hands now, Cara. We are going to leave you to EMS who will take you to the hospital. Good luck to you, and congratulations on your baby boy."

Baby boy, baby boy. Please brain, please process that, please accept it and help it to make sense.

"Thank you, thank you," I say through sobs.

The paramedic covers me with a warm, heavy blanket folded in half before he and Josh wheel me from my bathroom out into the front yard. They lift and place me into the back of a waiting ambulance. Through the fog of disorientation, I can make out figures standing outside watching, and the intrusive thought that everyone will know about this registers.

"I'm going to start an IV and give you something for pain. It will help you relax, and we'll get this placenta delivered for you," the paramedic says as he places another blanket on me.

I can hear the whimpering sounds of my baby coming from the arms of the other paramedic. He's not crying loudly like the babies do on TV when they're born. What does that mean?

Detached, I watch the paramedic who is tending to me take my hand and turn it palm up to quickly insert a needle into the vein inside my elbow. Once the needle is in, he tapes down the needle and the tube extending from it. It's reminiscent of when I was given an IV before having my wisdom teeth removed last year.

Needles normally freak me out. In the past, receiving a shot or an IV has felt like a nurse holding a snake to my arm, saying, "Just sit still while this snake bites you; it will be over in a jiffy," and I marvel at how uneventful having a needle inserted is right now compared to everything else that has just happened to me.

The paramedic takes a syringe and shoots something into the tube of the IV. In less than a second, everything goes darker, warmer, quieter.

The drug immediately helps my legs stop shaking. My eyelids droop and want to close, but the paramedic uncovers my legs and says, "I am going to palpate your tummy. It will hurt a little, but we're going to deliver the placenta. When I tell you to, I need you to push down a bit to help expel it, okay?"

I can do no more than nod once. I want him to leave me alone and let me sleep, let me slip into the land of oblivion where none of this has happened, where I can dream none of this is real.

"All right, push," he says, and I do, feeling a ball of warmth leave my body. "Good girl, good girl," he says as though I am a puppy about to receive a pat.

And then I fully drift off to that quiet, dark place I long to be.

◆◆◆

A flurry of activity surrounds me. *Where am I?* Before my eyes even open, I'm drawn back into reality, a reality that seems more implausible than my dreams. Medical personnel are hovering over me, calling my name. I try to speak, but the words are stuck in my throat.

"Baby," I say. I can't hear my own voice.

"Cara, you're at the hospital now. What do you need?" a woman in blue scrubs asks.

I clear my throat and say as loudly as I can, "Where's my baby?"

"He's in the NICU being well taken care of. As soon as we get you cleaned up and changed, the doctor will come in to examine you, and someone from the NICU will come to talk to you."

"My dad?" I whisper.

"He's outside in the waiting room. We'll call him in after we get you set up here."

She's putting something thick under me. Warm, wet cloths scrub me down my thighs to just above my knees and around my backside. The smell of antiseptic soap is strong. The resulting feel of a towel drying me makes me feel better, cleaner. The nurse pulls some type of scratchy underwear on me.

"Let's get this off you and put a clean gown on," she says, handing me a hospital gown that opens in the back. "Can you sit up a little?"

"Yes," I answer, my voice somewhat stronger now.

I pull the blood-stained nightshirt over my head with no thought that I have nothing on underneath. When the nurse reaches for a bag to place it in, I ask her to please just throw it in the trash, and she complies. She helps me get into the gown that ties in the back and then helps me put on little fuzzy socks with grippers on the bottoms.

She raises the top of my bed, and I sink back against the pillow, weak with the effort of simply changing into the gown.

The nurse connects my IV to a pole next to my bed while another nurse turns on monitors and places a blood pressure cuff around my arm.

I'm still sleepy and in pain—so much cramping.

She must read my grimace. "As soon as you use the restroom and we get you back into the bed, I'll give you some stronger pain medicine in your IV."

"Restroom? I have to get up and walk?" I ask.

"It will be hard at first, but it will loosen you up and help you recover faster. We need to make sure you can urinate on your own. Come on, I'll help you."

I scoot to the edge of the bed and place both feet flat on the floor. She lifts under my arm to help me stand. My legs are wobbly to the point of collapse, and I have to stand in place a second before I can take the first step.

When I do, the nurse grips me tighter with one arm, and with her other, she wheels my IV pole, allowing me to set the pace. I am slow. Every muscle in my stomach screams at me in protest. The pain between my legs is a throbbing taunt with every heartbeat, but I make it to the bathroom.

She stands outside the door and closes it a fraction to allow me some privacy. The hospital-issued underwear and diaper-sized pad are horrendous. I'll have to remember to ask my dad to bring me some of my own. Oh, God, how long will I have to stay here? How long will the baby have to stay here? Will I ever wake up from this unimaginable nightmare? I use the toilet, and even that causes pain.

It's much easier to walk back to the bed than it was to the bathroom. The nurse was right about it loosening me up. She helps me back into the bed and covers me with warm blankets the other nurse brought fresh from a warmer.

"That feels good," I say, "thank you."

She squirts something from a syringe into my IV that has much the same effect as the one I received in the ambulance.

"This pain medication is oxycodone, longer-lasting than the one you received earlier. You can have more every six hours, as needed."

"Thank you," I say again and suddenly feel exponentially more comfortable.

"Here is the call button if you need anything, and there on the other side of your bed is the remote for the TV."

Tears sting my eyes, a result of my gratitude for the relief I feel, both physically and emotionally. The pain medicine seems to dull my senses as well as the physical pain, which softens my stark reality—a welcome respite.

While the nurse types into the computer near my bed, I let the waves of relief wash over me. I replay the events of the morning, trying to allow them to become a part of me, to assimilate them into the new identity that has been thrust upon me so harshly. It's as if my very existence has been popped out of joint—dislocated from its socket.

My eyes begin to close of their own volition when there's a light tapping outside the door. "Come in," I call groggily.

The door swings open slowly, but when my dad sees me, he bounds to the bed in only a couple of strides.

"Daddy," I whisper like a prayer before the floodgates open and my tears fall in earnest. He sits on the edge of the bed beside me and gathers me to him, holding me in a tight embrace. I bawl like a baby into his neck, very much like I did when I learned the news of my mother's death. I can't stop.

Without saying a word, he holds me and allows me to cry. I feel his own warm tears on the side of my face. We stay like this for several minutes until my tears subside and turn to sniffles. I blow my nose with a tissue from the box on the bedside tray and push my hair back from my face.

"Cara?" He says as a question.

I tell him everything.

Jamie

've hardly made it into the hall after leaving my first-period class when my cell vibrates in my pocket. It takes me aback for a second because the phone screen says *Mr. Dawson*. He has never called me before, and I never changed the name to "Chris" after putting his number in my phone on Cara's and my first date.

Why is Cara's dad calling me at school?

I step out of the crowded hallway and into an alcove under a stairwell.

"Hello," I answer.

"Jamie, this is Chris. I'm calling about Cara."

"Is she okay?" My heart begins hammering in my ears. "Has something happened to her?" *Oh, God, please no!*

"She's been transported by ambulance to the hospital. Did you know about her condition?"

Her condition? I'm in a total panic now. "Yes, she texted me this morning and said she was having a bad flare-up of IBS and was going to stay home today. It had to have gotten bad for her to call an ambulance!"

"You don't know." Chris exhales through his teeth.

"Sir?"

"Listen, Jamie, I don't understand what all is going on, but I need you to call your parents, and you three need to meet me outside the hospital near the front entrance. She's at Fort Worth General."

"My parents? Chris, is Cara going to be okay? You're terrifying me here."

"Yes, I just left her room; she'll be fine. I'll explain when you get here."

She'll be fine, she'll be fine. I allow the words to echo in my ears, willing my heart to calm down, for my fear to recede.

What happened that required Cara to call an ambulance? Is she having some sort of mental breakdown from the stress she's been under? Is there something more seriously wrong with her that Chris needs to share with me and my parents? Cancer? *Oh, God, no, no, no.*

I call my dad, and thankfully, he answers on the first ring. "Hello."

"Dad, listen, I just got a call from Chris. Cara was sick this morning and didn't come to school. He said she was taken by ambulance to the hospital and is there now."

"Man, Jamie, what in the world is going on?"

"I don't know exactly. Chris wants you, Mom, and me to meet him at the hospital."

"What? Us? Is she asking for us? This doesn't sound good."

"He said she'll be fine, so I'm not sure what's going on. I'm coming home to hop in with you and Mom."

"I'm not at the house, but I can be there in about ten minutes. I'll reschedule this meeting with a client I was on my way to. I'm turning around now."

"Will you call Mom and fill her in on what's happening? I'll see you at the house."

"Okay, drive carefully." He pauses for half a beat. "Jamie, Chris said she was going to be okay. Just believe that."

"Thanks, Dad. I'm trying."

I end the call and run as fast as I can down the hall into the parking lot. Students have to jump aside to allow me through.

The drive to the hospital is a confusing haze. A feeling of dread like I've never known fills me, like waiting for a judge to pronounce my death sentence. When Dad, Mom, and I pull up to the hospital entrance and park, I spot Chris pacing along the sidewalk leading to the hospital entrance. He sees us and walks briskly in our direction before we can even exit the car.

Chris approaches our car, and with no greeting whatsoever says tersely, "Let's stay by the car in case one of you needs to sit down after what I'm about to tell you."

I feel the blood drain fully from my face at the seriousness of his tone. I assume Chris only told us Cara would be okay until we got here, and I brace myself for the news that she is dying or has just died. I can't breathe.

"What, what has happened?" I shout on a breathless sob.

"Cara had a preterm baby boy this morning in the bathroom at home."

I fully expect Chris to start laughing at his own joke, for cameramen to jump out at us from behind parked cars to let us know we've been pranked. I couldn't be more shocked if he told me an alien popped out of Cara's chest after her visit to Mars this morning. The pause of silence and the look on Chris's face let me know he's dead serious.

The news tries to enter headspace I have no room for. My brain struggles to pull a logical explanation together and fails.

"That's impossible," are the first words out of my mouth.

My dad takes one giant leap toward me, grabs me by the scruff of my T-shirt with both hands, and yells, "You son of a bitch, Jamie! You got Cara pregnant and didn't have the decency to tell us?"

He rears back, his hand fisted, about to pop me in the face. But Chris is on him in an instant, pulling him off of me and grabbing Dad's hands.

"Brent, stop," Chris demands. "Jamie didn't know! Cara didn't even know."

"What?" Dad looks at me, puzzled. After a beat, he says, "Whether he knew she was pregnant or not, he still got her knocked up, Chris. I should be the one holding Jamie for you to have a go at him." He spits the words like venom, crushing me.

My mom silently watches the exchanges in horror—pale and completely shocked into silence.

"Brent, listen, believe me, when I first heard from the paramedic who called me while treating Cara, I was in shock and having the same kinds of thoughts you are, but there's more to it."

"Cara and I have never had sex, so I don't understand what's going on here." I let out a whimper, sounding like a dying animal. I *feel* like a dying animal. I start to think of the possibilities.

Cheating?

No way.

Rape?

She would have told me; we share everything.

And suddenly two words begin wailing in my head like a siren—*Halloween night, Halloween night?* Could we have had sex when we were blacked out? Wouldn't at least one of us know and remember? My next thought is, *I have a son. Oh my God, I have a son*—Cara *and I have a son.*

"The baby, how's the baby?" I ask, my voice sounding pathetically desperate.

"He's holding his own; a strong one, they're saying. Let's all go inside and talk in the waiting room. I just finished speaking to Cara and the NICU doctor. The doctor who is treating Cara is in with her now."

Without anyone speaking a word, we all follow Chris into the hospital and up the elevator to the maternity floor. How my legs carry me, I don't know. How my heart doesn't beat out of my chest, I'll never know.

I'm bombarded with questions and thoughts assaulting me from all angles. My dad's fists couldn't have hurt worse had he used them on me. *How is Cara? Does she think I took advantage of her and didn't tell her? She was all alone having a baby! How much did she suffer? How can she even deal? How can I deal? Is our baby going to be okay? Can I see him? How will we ever be able to handle this? Does Cara hate me?*

Does Cara hate me?

We sit down in a small private waiting room adjacent to a larger one. As soon as we sit, my dad asks, "So was Cara raped? Do we know for certain who the father is? Christ, if Jamie's the father, is he going to be charged with rape?"

He looks at my mom, presumably asking her to draw on her criminal justice background for an answer. But Mom looks confused. Dad must also be thinking about Mark's party and what I told him about Cara and me getting drunk. He's obviously trying to put two and two together as much as I am.

He leans over and says to her, "Remember I told you about Jamie and Cara drinking too much and passing out at Mark's Halloween party?"

A fresh realization washes over Mom's features, mingled with a look of horror. I shoot Dad a look that says, *I told you that in confidence, son to father.*

Chris looks wholly devastated about the question of rape and holds up his hand. "Listen to what I know, what Cara has told me, and we can process this together and try to make some sense of it."

But my dad's words scream in my ears, *was she raped? RAPED?* Did I do that to her? Rape her? But how can that be if I don't remember? The next thought hits me as hard as landing on asphalt after a two-story fall—*Could someone have gotten to Cara the night of the party when we were both passed out?*

The thought of it produces a ringing in my ears and such a sick feeling in my gut, I look around to see where the nearest restroom is in case I need a toilet to puke in. It was my job to protect her that night, and I failed... miserably. Only one name comes to mind of anyone at that party who would be that sick—

Eric Baines.

My heart would be broken beyond repair if Eric's hands were on Cara, if he put himself inside her in the most intimate yet sinister of ways. Would he have done something like that for revenge against me? He thought I moved in and stole her from him, so he stole her virginity from her for revenge? Did he hurt Cara to get back at me?

I drop my head into my hands and rest my elbows on my knees, taking in big gulps of air. Chris had begun talking but stops when he and my parents notice I am in obvious distress.

"Jamie, are you okay?" my mom asks.

"Yes... no," I correct. "Give me a minute... please."

I try to take slower, steadier breaths to calm down. It suddenly makes sense that it very well might not have been me who got Cara pregnant, and the possibility enrages me, sickens me, not only for myself but especially for Cara.

Does my dad *want* the baby to be someone else's? Does he think *I* would want it to be someone else's in order to get myself "off the hook," so to speak? Someone other than me touching *my* sweet Cara in the most intimate way is a thought I can't handle. If she was passed out and didn't consent, it's rape, period; but what if that person was me and I don't remember? Will I be accused of rape? I take more gulps of air.

Calm down, calm down.

The nagging probability in my mind is that I most likely would have remembered if I was the one who got Cara pregnant, right? I want to both weep and throw up. So what if I'm accused of raping Cara? I know in my soul I didn't, would NEVER do that to her knowingly. Does that mean someone else did, though?

No-no-no-no. Oh, God, please, no.

If I'm the father, it would more than likely mean no one else touched Cara that night but me. And, it would mean it is MY baby lying here in this hospital, possibly fighting for his life.

If I'm not the father, I will be charged with murder, because I will fucking kill Eric Baines or anyone who would have taken advantage of Cara that way.

This nightmare is only getting worse as I suddenly realize I'm in some deep shit here either way.

I don't pray a lot, but I say a pleading prayer now: *PLEASE let the baby be mine and be healthy. I don't care if I have to go to prison. I will take whatever consequences there are, but please let him be mine. Cara doesn't deserve to have to live with the alternative.*

Calmer now, my brain begins to fire a little more clearly. I want this baby because he is Cara's. Regardless of whether or not he is mine biologically, I WILL be his father if Cara will allow me.

Absolutely no doubt about it.

I faintly hear my mom say, "Brent, this is all too much for him. What do we need to do? He's not well."

My head snaps up, and I scrub my palms down my face. "I'll be all right, Chris. Go ahead."

"Are you sure? We can give you a few more minutes." Chris soothes.

I shake my head no, and Chris looks at me for a couple of beats before continuing.

"As you all know, Cara didn't know she was pregnant and attributed the symptoms she was having to IBS flare-ups. In her mind, why would pregnancy even be a consideration if she'd never had sex before?" He shrugs and looks at me. I can't hold his gaze.

"Cara woke up sick this morning, in terrible pain and feeling like going to the restroom would be the only way to relieve it. By the time she realized something was horribly wrong, the baby was delivered right there in the bathroom."

My mom cries now and says, "My goodness, what terror Cara must have experienced."

Dad puts his hand over hers.

"She called 911, and one of the paramedics who was treating her called me to let me know what was going on. She and the baby were both brought here, and he's, of course, in the NICU, but both are doing very well, considering."

"How much did he weigh?" my mom asks. "Do they think he will be okay?"

"The NICU doctor came in and talked with us right before I left to meet y'all. He was born at a little more than thirty weeks gestation, so obviously early and small. The conception was Halloween, no doubt about that."

My dad looks over at me, lips pursed, and we have a stare-out that he wins.

Chris adds, "The baby is a good size for that gestation period, three pounds, eight ounces."

My mom lets out a muffled cry and exclaims, "That's still so small."

"It is, and he's a little over seventeen inches long, which the doctor says is on the long side for thirty-weeks' gestation." Chris looks directly at me when he says this, and I get what he's implying... I'm tall.

"Can we see him?" I ask.

"Yes, soon," Chris says as he takes off his glasses to massage the bridge of his nose.

"You're taking this too well, Chris. I keep thinking how I would feel if this happened to one of my own daughters," Dad hisses.

Chris says, "I've had more time to process it; you're still in shock."

I look over at Chris. "So Cara told you about the Halloween party and what happened? I told my dad about that night, but Cara was so afraid of disappointing you. She never wanted you to know," I say, looking down at my wringing hands before looking back at Chris, having a hard time meeting his eyes.

Chris nods and looks at me. "Cara told me you passed out in the bed with her and don't remember anything beyond kissing her?"

Embarrassed we have to even discuss something like this, I nod and say, "The honest-to-God truth. I promise with everything I am, Chris."

He looks deeply into my eyes and must see it's the truth. "I believe you. Obviously, Cara never knew anything of a sexual nature happened that night. Now is not the time for me to lecture you about what both of you should or should not have done that night. Cara assures me nothing like that had ever happened before or since, but... This is hard for me to ask as much as I know how hard it is for you to be asked, Jamie... Could someone else have had, uh... access to Cara when you two were placed in that room to sleep off the effects of the alcohol?"

My heart hurts for Chris, but I have to remain honest. "There were others at the party throughout the night, but there is only one person who would be sick enough, and I would like to think even *he* could never stoop that low—Eric Baines."

A memory of Cara lying on the floor beside the bed with her robe open when I woke up creates a fresh wave of nausea, but

I won't say it aloud, will not feed this possibility any more than I have to.

"I know the young man. Cara has grown up with him; they've been good friends over the years." Chris sighs through his teeth, and I notice his hands ball into fists at the possibility of his daughter having been assaulted. Like Dad said, he is handling this too well.

Mom says, "Jamie has told us the trouble Eric's caused him and Cara, all the jealousy and tension since they met and started dating."

"So, you are positive Eric would be the only one who—"

Chris doesn't finish because Cara's doctor steps into the waiting room.

"Dawson family?" the doctor asks. She is a petite, pretty woman about my parents' age.

Chris stands, and she recognizes him. "Ah, I was looking for you in the larger waiting room. Cara asked me to fill you in while she rests." Her voice is soft and calm.

"How is she?" Chris immediately asks on behalf of all of us.

"Is it okay to address Cara's medical situation with everyone present?" the doctor asks.

Chris nods. "Yes, we're all family."

The implication of his words strikes its target. Chris will never know the volumes those four words speak to me at this moment when I need it most.

"I'm Dr. Zeng. I just examined Cara and had a good long talk with her. First, let me address her physical health. Everything looks good. There were no complications with the birth besides the preterm labor, and she should be able to go home in a couple of days."

There is a collective sigh of relief from us all.

"The circumstances of the birth are, of course, very unusual in that it's one thing not to know you're pregnant until the onset of labor, which happens more often than we might think, and much more often in cases of preterm babies. However, it's another thing altogether if the main reason not to know you're pregnant is that you didn't know a sexual act had occurred. I would assume that's about the surest reason one would not consider pregnancy as a cause of symptoms. And how this even happened will need to be addressed."

Self-consciousness slaps me in the face when her eyes fall on me, and I wonder if she has any clue I am most likely the cause of this.

Dr. Zeng continues, "If she were sexually active and her family knew this, any one of you might have considered her symptoms she attributed to IBS as pregnancy."

We all nod in agreement.

"Who's to say that if Cara knew what happened to her the night in question it would have helped her realize she was pregnant?" She tilts her head to the side and lifts her shoulders. "We will never know, but if the pregnancy had progressed closer to term, my guess is she would have figured it out. As it stands, Cara shared with me how she attributed all her symptoms to the familiar IBS she has had in the past; which, by the way, exhibits many similar symptoms as pregnancy. When I asked her about feeling movement of the fetus, she attributed that to what she called her common-place stomach rumbles."

I think back on the many times I've heard her say she was having those. *And that was our baby moving inside her?*

"I feel like the worst father for not insisting she see a doctor," Chris laments.

"We are all trying to assuage our guilt for not picking up on this," Mom says. "But honestly, Chris, I also spoke with her about her stomach issues on a few occasions, and she never made a big deal out of them. It didn't slow her down much."

"Of all people, I should've known," I interject, looking at the doctor, fresh tears threatening to spill over, "but why would I ever suspect that? She just seemed to have the flare-ups only occasionally and didn't look pregnant. She had lost a lot of weight a few months ago and only recently gained a few more pounds above her normal weight. We were all just happy she was eating better and feeling better." I exhale heavily, overwhelmed. I'm tempted to drop my head into my hands and let go, but I somehow keep it together.

"Such little weight gain would only contribute to the reasons one wouldn't know they're pregnant," Dr. Zeng says. "Also, in the case of some women, the placenta sits right in front of the pregnancy, with the baby positioned farther back." She uses her hands demonstratively to explain. "In these cases, a woman just doesn't show her pregnancy."

"We don't know what caused the early labor," she continues. "The lack of prenatal care could be a factor, as well as the school stress she explained she has been under. We might not ever know, but she will need to be watched closely with any subsequent pregnancies.

"Cara has been through a lot of shock and trauma, so I think what her family needs to be most attuned to is her mental health. She will need a lot of support in the upcoming weeks and months. Caring for a preemie is hard in the best of circumstances. Regardless, she is doing well, and I must say it was a pleasure speaking with her. She is a remarkable young woman, very strong."

The doctor smiles sincerely, her eyes kind and reassuring. She has magically put us all at greater ease.

"Can we see her now?" I ask.

"Yes, and be sure to let a nurse know if she needs anything. I will be back around to see her again this time tomorrow."

We all thank her and stay seated when she leaves, aware we need to finish our earlier conversation before any of us go in to see Cara.

Chris rubs his temples and says, "We were talking about Eric and the possibility—" He stops, seemingly thinking of something else he needs to say. "Jamie, we'll let you go in to see Cara first, and you can text us when you're ready for us to come in. But I need to tell you, I don't think it has even crossed Cara's mind that someone other than you could have fathered the baby, our grandson."

Chris looks from me to my parents, and it's the first smile I've seen on any of their faces.

He continues, "She has been through enough without me or anyone planting that possible scenario in her mind, so please stay as upbeat as possible. I hope you understand, Jamie, that since no one knows exactly how Cara became pregnant and being assaulted is at least a possibility, I feel obligated to ask you for a paternity test. I don't think Cara needs to know it's being done, unless, of course, it results in the unthinkable. Then, we will need to get the police involved."

I swallow hard at the thought, but I nod in understanding.

Dad says, "We'll get the process started today if possible."

Tears shimmer in Mom's eyes, and I know for a fact that my parents will think of the baby as their grandson regardless of the outcome of paternity. No one was ready for this, but no matter what, he is Cara's baby, which makes him mine... which makes him theirs.

I'm not going anywhere, and if my parents truly know me the way I think they do, they know it, too.

"However, let me add something here," Chris says, looking thoughtfully at my parents and then back at me, "Eric is blond, even fairer than Cara, isn't he?" He looks into my eyes and says, "The baby has dark, curly hair."

Jamie

I stand outside Cara's hospital room door taking long, steadying breaths before knocking when the door unexpectedly swings open. A nurse exiting the room notices my raised hand and whispers, "You can go on in. I was making sure her water was full. She's resting."

I nod appreciatively and step into the darkened room. Cara is lying still with an IV in her arm and other cords connecting her to a monitor. Stepping closer, I can see she's asleep, her blonde hair fanned out around her pillow like a halo. She indeed looks like a sleeping angel, pale and beautiful—a real-life Sleeping Beauty. My throat constricts so tightly, a quiet sob breaks free before I can fully stifle it.

There is a chair next to the hospital bed, and I quietly scoot it closer to her. I sit down and watch Cara sleep for a few seconds before taking her smaller, fragile-looking hand in mine. Leaning down, I kiss her ring finger where her promise ring would normally be. This is the first time since Christmas that I have seen her left hand without it and the first time since we met I've seen her without her purity ring on the other.

I rub my thumb lightly over the slight tan line where the promise ring was. It was the one visible piece of identification connecting Cara to me, and the ring not being there is disorienting and unsettling.

I can't stand seeing Cara like this. I'm a boat adrift in a raging storm and the lamp on the lighthouse guiding me has suddenly been snuffed out. I'm overtaken by crashing waves of sadness and despair—everything wrong rushing in at me from all sides. The whole situation is drowning me.

Head down, the tears I've been holding in drop rapidly from my eyes, and there's no stopping them. They fall in torrents, dripping onto my faded jeans like heavy rain on a sidewalk. I weep for Cara, for our baby, for all the innocence stolen from Cara... from us.

When I think the heavy cloud has emptied, I look up, trying to refocus. I notice Cara's eyes moving beneath her eyelids as if dreaming. I lean in closer and smell her familiar scent, which causes a sharp pang deep within me, an ache to hold her in my arms. Before I can stop myself, I kiss her forehead, lingering there. As soon as my lips touch her skin, her eyes flutter open— wide, haunted eyes looking back at mine.

"Jamie," Cara rasps, the corner of one side of her mouth tilting upward in the slightest smile. My chest constricts with protectiveness and pure love for her.

"I'm so sorry I woke you," I say sincerely, while at the same time relieved she's awake so I can see her eyes, talk to her, know she's okay.

"I was dreaming about you, hoping you would come."

"You were?" My chest squeezes even tighter. "You don't hate me?"

"What? No, no." She says softer, "You've been crying. Is that what you've been thinking, that I hate you because of this?"

I drop my eyes. "Yes... well, no...," I look back at her, "afraid that you might. It's my fault this happened, but I don't know how, I promise. I can't remember us being together like that. I mean, obviously, it happened, but I just don't remember."

"Neither of us does, Jamie. We're both to blame, though, getting drunk like we did, all of our inhibitions obliterated. I wish we had known what we did so we could have been prepared for this. A lot makes sense now, the reason I felt sick so often. We were together, I know, but... I wish I could remember." She exhales heavily.

"I do, too, babe. I'll never forgive myself for allowing this to happen. I want to spend my life making it up to you."

Cara shakes her head. "Please don't say that. I've already thought about that and knew how obligated you would feel to me now, how this will trap you to me if you were to change your mind about us being together. I don't want that."

Anger surges through me, and I have to take a deep breath and remember Chris's words about staying upbeat and positive for Cara.

Yet his words fail to entirely take root, and I raise my voice in a quiet shout. "Trapped? You knew before any of this that I want to spend the rest of my life with you. Hell, if I had my way about it, I would have given you an engagement ring instead of a fucking promise ring! I'm not going anywhere, dammit!" I close my eyes to catch my breath and collect myself.

When I open them, I see Cara's startled expression. "Wait, I'm sorry, Cara. That is so *not* how I should have said that. Hey—"

Cara's lips slowly turn up at each corner to form a smile that gradually grows larger. It spreads to her entire face, and, without warning, she bursts into laughter. She doesn't stop. Holding her lower stomach, she says, "Ouch, ouch!" in between bubbles of laughter.

I stare at her in bewilderment, at her laughing at a time like this. Is it the drugs? I watch her curiously until a small laugh forms in my own throat, not only because Cara is laughing, but because of the absurdity of the entire situation. I'm sure we have both gone insane from it all and are experiencing the laughter of the deranged and demented, but neither of us can stop now.

"Oh my gosh!" Cara laughs harder, wiping her eyes. "Oh my gosh," she says again, trying to stop herself.

Finally, after several tears have rolled down her cheeks, she stops long enough to say, "I love you. If you would have reacted any other way, I wouldn't have believed you. My strong, passionate Jamie... If you left me right now or even wanted to, I would want to die." She pauses and says more seriously, "I need you."

"We've both gone mad, Cara. This has made us instantly insane, hasn't it?"

"Probably, but we've earned it. I mean, who wouldn't feel crazy after what just happened? Stranger than fiction is an understatement." She inhales deeply, her laughter finally dissipating.

She straightens and sits higher on her pillow. Smile muted now, she asks with intense interest, "Seriously, though, what did you think when my dad told you? It's all I could think about when they put me in the ambulance, 'What in the world will Jamie think when he finds out we have a baby?'"

"Your dad called me after he saw you and knew you were okay, and my parents and I came right away. He was smart not to tell us you had a baby until we got here to the hospital."

I tell her everything I was feeling, which was mostly alarm and disbelief, and about the horrible fear I felt from thinking she was dead or dying right before Chris told us she'd had a baby.

When I tell her the part about my dad almost beating my face in, it surprises her. I tell her it shouldn't surprise her at all because "like father, like son" applies to us in the temper department— something I promise her I will work on along with my language, now that I'm a father. The word *father* sounds like a foreign word to me each time it enters my mind.

Of course, I leave out the thoughts and conversations concerning the baby possibly not being mine, biologically anyway. Chris is right. It hasn't even occurred to Cara that he might not be, and my heart starts to ache again for her.

"Can you believe it?" she whispers.

"No, I honestly don't know how long it will take before I do. I'm just so relieved you're okay. And the baby will be okay?"

"The NICU doctor said babies born at thirty weeks have over a ninety percent chance of survival, and our baby is larger and stronger than most thirty-weekers. He's on oxygen and has a feeding tube and an IV, but that's all normal. He didn't have to be put on a ventilator like many preemies do to help them breathe. He will have to stay in the incubator until he's four pounds. He'll most likely get to go home at five pounds if everything else looks good."

"Thank God," I say, my shoulders slumping in relief. "Can we see him? Have you seen him since you got to the hospital?"

"I haven't seen him since the ambulance ride, but the nurse said I can walk to the NICU when I'm ready to see him. We can go together."

I nod, feeling excitement mingled with fear to see the baby. I can't seem to make myself believe he's actually real.

Cara looks thoughtful. "We need to give him a name. The nurse said the birth certificate person will come in the morning to help me fill out the information."

I say a silent prayer that my name, which will be the father's name on the birth certificate, of course, will be one hundred percent accurate.

"My parents and your dad are still in the waiting room and would like to see you. I told Chris I would text him when we're ready for them to come in."

"Yeah, text them in a minute, but I need to go to the bathroom first—all the fluid from the IV."

"Let me help you." I stand and then awkwardly ask, "What do I do?"

"Just make sure I don't fall. I'm a little slow. The nurse showed me how I have to take this oxygen and pulse monitor off my finger... and the blood pressure cuff off," she says while removing both of them and placing them on the bed. "Can you wheel my IV pole to the bathroom door for me?"

"Of course, babe, here." I help Cara stand, but she doesn't seem to need it.

"I'm much faster this time than the first time I had to get out of bed and walk."

"Does it hurt a lot?" I ask sheepishly. I realize how little I know about her situation, and it causes a rush of anxiety.

"Yes, but nothing like when he was coming out." She shakes her head as though reliving it. "Now it feels like I fell from a tree and straddled a sawhorse." She chuckles ruefully.

"Ow," is all I can say. My respect for Cara has climbed to the ladder's highest rung, and I watch her in awe as she walks.

I wait outside the door for her. The reality of the situation comes in tidal waves, and one has hit me full force again. We both haven't had time to process the repercussions of all this, but graduation is only three days from now, and this is supposed to be a fun-filled, carefree time for Cara. Will she be well enough to attend?

She should also be gearing up to start college in the fall, not preparing to care for our helpless newborn. In an instant, life has taken a drastic turn for us and has forced us to detour onto the road less traveled—more like *never* traveled—and I don't know how to walk it, much less lead Cara through it.

When Cara finishes and returns to the bed, I text Chris that we're ready for them to come in. She replaces the finger monitor and blood pressure cuff and covers herself with the blanket.

While we wait for them, I ask her, "Graduation is in three days; are you going to be—"

She knows what I'm asking and doesn't let me finish. "Oh, I'm going!" she declares. "Having a baby won't stop me from walking across that stage."

She flashes a determined smile, and it's the expression my parents are met with when they open the door and enter the room.

"My goodness, Cara, you look wonderful," my mother exclaims a little too cheerily, coming to the bed and hugging Cara. She takes Cara's face in her hands and kisses her near the corner of her mouth. My mom doesn't even kiss her own kids that way.

My father seems not to know exactly what to say, but he says, "We hear congratulations are in order."

Cara drops her gaze for a beat, her face coloring. "I know y'all didn't expect to become instant grandparents today." She shrugs lightly, seemingly not knowing how to continue.

"We are thrilled. We can't wait to see him. I won't lie; it was shocking, but your dad says he's doing well considering how early he came." The relief in Mom's expression must mirror my own.

Cara relates the NICU doctor's explanations of the baby's treatment and finishes with, "He did tell me it will be an extended stay here for him, with many ups and downs—good days and bad days—but that those are normal and to be expected."

"We are all here for you," my dad insists, "anything you or the baby needs."

Chris chimes in, and it makes me wonder if Dad asked him if he needs money to help with the expenses. "I'll talk to my insurance company and see what they will cover, but let's not worry about that now. We just need to pray for the baby to grow and thrive, so we can get him home."

Home. What will that look like? I set the thought aside for now.

"Would you all like to see him? I just need to call a nurse so they can get ready for us. My nurse told me earlier that only two are allowed to go in with me at one time."

"We got our NICU badge while Jamie visited with you," Mom says, "but you'll need one, Jamie. We can visit with Cara while you go get yours."

I leave Cara's room and head down to the nurses' desk to ask about a NICU badge. A male nurse points me in the direction of the NICU nurses' station. At that station, a friendly nurse in multi-colored scrubs looks at a list Cara has already given them earlier of who she will allow in to visit our baby, and of course, I'm on it.

"Oh, you're the proud daddy. Congratulations!" she exclaims genuinely. "He's doing very well for his gestation period. His breathing is much better than we would expect. We are having a little trouble regulating his blood sugar, but we're taking care of that through his feeding tube and regularly checking his numbers."

I begin to sweat at the thought of how fragile he is, how fragile life is, and I say another quick prayer that he will survive and be healthy. The thought of losing him, the thought of *Cara* losing him... *No,* I have to force myself not to go down that path.

I fill out a form and am overwhelmed by all the safety precautions, questions about recent illnesses, and sanitation instructions. Another wave of reality hits me, but this time, I'm caught in a riptide, desperately trying to swim out of it. There *is* no swimming out of this, though.

Just keep your head above it all, Jamie. You can do this. Be strong for Cara and for your son; be strong.

I unsteadily hand the form back to the nurse with my ID, and she types in all of my information. She acknowledges my distress and soothingly explains, "Don't be alarmed by all the monitors and tubes he's connected to when you go in—all routine. He has an IV, a feeding tube, and pronged oxygen in his nose. He will have all of these for a while, but as I said, he's doing better than most thirty-weekers."

I heard Cara use that term earlier and I can't help but think how he needs a name so they don't get used to referring to him as the thirty-weeker in the NICU. Also, if he has a real name, it will make him more real. I need to hurry and see him; then maybe all this won't feel like a bad dream anymore.

"Thank you," I say, "it's all just a little overwhelming right now."

"I know, I know. We are taking the very best care of him. If you need anything at all," she says as a little machine spits out a plastic badge, "let us know. If we aren't aware, we can't help." She looks me in the eye now. "Be your baby's advocate. That's what he needs most from you."

I nod, suddenly too choked up to speak. I take the badge, give her as much of a smile as I can muster, and head back toward Cara's room.

When I walk in, Cara is standing, talking to my mom, while Chris and my dad are deep in conversation. When Cara sees me, she smiles away my gloom—she's the sun piercing through my dark cloud, and I don't know how she does it at a time like this. She's like my own IV, infusing me with light and strength.

"Are you ready to go see our son, Jamie?"

"Yes, yes, I can't wait," I say, and mean it, but I have to confess, it's more about needing to know he's real. I hope my brain will somehow fully absorb the fact I have a son once I see him. The nurse was trying to prepare me for what to expect, which she did, but instead of putting any fear to rest, it has only made me more anxious, more worried about him.

Waiting for Cara to set the walking pace, I push her IV pole beside her, and we all head down the hall to the NICU. Of course, Cara and I will go in first. My heartbeat quickens as the nurse at the desk scans our badges and buzzes us into the large double doors leading to the nursery.

A nurse waves us ahead to a handwashing station where we must scrub our hands up to our elbows for a full three minutes. We apply a hand sanitizing gel afterward and are shown into a room that looks more like a hotel room than a hospital room, except for the incubator and equipment standing in the middle.

The nurse leads us over to the incubator, and there, lying on his back connected to the machines as the nurse described, is our tiny but perfect baby boy. Cara and I don't speak or make a sound for a small eternity, taking him all in, taking in all the attachments and monitors.

She breaks the silence, and I can hear the hitch in her voice. "He looks very different with all this equipment hooked up to him from how he looked in my arms this morning."

I grab her hand and squeeze it, not letting it go. I can't even speak.

With the nurse standing behind us, and Cara and me looking into his bed as though he's a mystery to be solved, I am reminded of the nativity scenes I've seen all my life around Christmas time. Our baby boy is just as much of a miracle to us as the Christ child must have been to his young parents.

"Can I hold him?" Cara asks the nurse timidly.

"Yes, only for a short time until he gains weight and gets stronger. Sit here, and I'll hand him to you." She points to the chair right beside the isolette. "He needs skin-to-skin contact to stay warm and bond with the feel and smell of you."

Cara sits in the chair, and the nurse helps her unsnap the shoulder of her hospital gown and fold it down to expose the top part of her chest. She carefully takes the baby from his bed and places him onto Cara while adjusting the cords and tubes.

The nurse instructs us on how to hold him and explains how tender his skin is, so no stroking for now, only light touches on his delicate skin.

She stays next to Cara for a bit longer then says, "Dad, pull up that chair there and I will leave you both to it." She returns to the far end of the room to her computer station.

I sit down and gently touch his warm back, marveling at his small size and all the fine, dark hair covering his little body. I suddenly realize how little I know about babies, especially premature newborns. I make a mental note to learn as much as possible once I get a chance to do some research.

Cara makes sweet cooing sounds to him and says, "Remember me from this morning, sweet baby? I'm your mommy and that's your daddy right there." She looks over into my eyes, causing my chest to tighten with an unfamiliar emotion I can only tentatively identify as protective pride—for my baby, for Cara, for... my *family*.

My heart feels as though it might burst, and at this moment, in spite of all the stress and uncertainty, I am incredibly thankful for this miracle of life. I don't know how it will all work out, knowing the road ahead will be long and hard, but I resolve to do everything in my power to see that it will.

"Cara, you're a natural with him." I admire her in amazement.

"My mother was the nursery director at our church. I've grown up getting to snuggle and change babies' diapers in the church nursery, so I have some experience. Of course, they were never this small, and it doesn't compare to the feelings of holding my own baby."

"He's got a full head of dark hair, doesn't he?" I remark, recalling Chris's words when we were in the waiting room: *Eric is blond, even fairer than Cara.*

"It's hard to tell yet, but he looks like you, I think. If you look at my newborn pics, my hair was almost this dark when I was born, but it lightened and turned blonde later," she says casually, not at all realizing the implications this fact holds for me, deflating me a bit.

My throat constricts, and I try not to let the thought of Eric crowd my mental space right now, but we need to get the damn paternity test done. I want to know one way or another, deal with the results—whatever they may be—and move forward with Cara. I will keep saying it for as long as I have to:

I'm not going anywhere.

Cara

Jamie watches me closely as I hold our baby for only the second time since he was born. I can read the fear in his eyes, so I figure it's best for him just to dive in headfirst.

"Now it's your turn to hold me, Daddy," I say in a baby voice, an attempt to lighten the heaviness of the entire situation. I work hard not to reveal my own anxiety, which would only make Jamie's worse.

"Me? Uh... I'm not sure—" he begins.

"Yes, of course. He needs to feel your skin, smell you, and bond with you, too." Jamie's wearing a black Henley with three buttons. "Here, either pull open your shirt at the collar like I'm doing with this gown, or raise your shirt, and I'll place him on your chest."

Jamie looks at me warily but complies. He unfastens the buttons and tests the collar of his shirt. When it doesn't give enough, he lifts his shirt toward his neck to create access for the baby. I can't help but stare at his corded abs and tapered waist—the dark trail of hair receding into the top button of his jeans. I feel my cheeks color. It's the first time I've seen Jamie bare-chested in broad daylight, and he's magnificent. The irony is not lost on me, though. We have a baby together and yet I have never seen Jamie's body, not fully.

The nurse helps me carefully transfer our little bundle to the middle of his chest, and Jamie cups the baby's back with a controlled, soft grasp. His large palm almost fully covers the baby. I take the blanket and cover his little body, which gives Jamie some covering, too—some privacy.

"He is definitely tiny, and he's breathing so fast." Jamie looks at me for reassurance.

"It's normal. Just relax and enjoy one another," I encourage.

Jamie does seem to relax a little. He looks down at the baby for so long without saying anything, I start to worry.

"Well, what do you think?" I ask, not certain what to make of his prolonged silence.

He lifts his head to look at me, and there are tears in his eyes. His gaze is fierce and penetrating. "I love him," he says unabashedly, and then again, "I love him."

Seeing father and son together like this, at this moment, is a beautiful lithograph to remain chiseled into the stone of my memory forever. Jamie's tears, in turn, cause tears to well up in my own eyes, and I assure him, "You are going to be the best daddy to our son. He's blessed to have you." I say confidently and add, "*I'm* blessed to have you."

Amid all the unpredictability, it's the one thing I have no doubt about.

Jamie takes a deep breath and looks back down at the baby, too overcome with emotion to speak, and my heart melts into a river wide enough to swallow all of his and my uncertainty put together.

"We love you back," I say simply.

After a few more minutes of holding the baby and discussing names for him, the nurse walks back over to return him to the isolette.

Jamie fixes his shirt and leaves to fetch his mom and dad. They will visit the baby next since my dad was able to see him earlier while waiting to see me. The nurse lets me know it's enough holding for now and shows me the holes in the isolette where we can place our hands inside to touch the baby.

I'm nervous about Jamie's parents coming in to see him. What must they really think of all this? Surely, they can't be happy about it. They didn't seem *unhappy* about the baby earlier in my hospital room, though; and would they even be here right now if they were too upset?

The nurse welcomes them, and they introduce themselves to her as the grandparents on the dad's side. That and the smiles on their faces enable me to calm down. It's plain at least a part of them is excited to meet their grandson despite it being forced upon them so unexpectedly.

Staying seated, I explain, "We've been holding him, but you can put your hands in the crib and touch him."

The nurse must have been about to say the same thing. She remains nearby for a second or two before retreating to her computer desk.

"He is so beautiful, Cara, and so itty-bitty. Yes, you are," Susan says in a singsong voice while placing her hand inside the isolette.

She touches him gently, not stroking him, but I fight the urge to tell her to make sure she doesn't stroke his skin because it's so thin and sensitive. I'm mentally fussing over him already with what must be the "momma bear" instinct I've heard spoken of all my life. It's protectiveness to a degree I've never known.

Jamie's dad stands back, more hesitant, but he studies the tiny creature before him as though his life depends on it. It takes a few seconds before a smile begins to spread across his face. "He's perfect. And such a little fighter," he says proudly, "isn't he?"

I nod in agreement.

The compliment has the same effect as if it were given directly to me, another unfamiliar feeling to add to my repertoire of new motherhood emotions—pride. It's only been hours, but I can already tell, becoming a mother today, especially of one who needs special care, has irrevocably changed me. It terrifies me, yes, absolutely, but I'm discovering it also brings me joy. This must be love in its purest form.

People describe life as a roller coaster with ups and downs. With the experience of two major life events—the death of my mother and now this—I see it differently. My life has been more like two paths running side by side—light and darkness—always competing for precedence.

On one path, it's all the dark stuff, the shock of what just happened to me, and the grief I'm already starting to feel for the loss of my future plans. Will I still be able to go to college while caring for a baby? The university I've been accepted to is probably out of the question now, and I will have to deal with it. I'll do everything in my power to finish college and pursue my career, however different that might look now. I've heard stories of single mothers making it work, and some probably didn't have near the support system I do.

How much will my life now be limited to caring for our baby? Fear of what my future holds is mixed with the present fear of our baby's fragile state, knowing his health can take a turn at any moment and that I'm responsible for this little fragile life. It threatens to push me over the edge thinking about it. How will I handle it when the future is now?

On the other path, there's a lot of good, a lot of light; it's where the sun shines. Right now, it's harder to see the light with this present darkness pressing in. But the light showcases love, and it's within that love that my joy is found.

My love for Jamie is stronger than ever. I can't get over what a wonderful human he is. He makes me happy. And now it's all about our baby. Holding him again and watching Jamie hold him and love him gives me hope, hope that even though we're young and I don't know how everything will work out, we can be a family.

So, on the one hand, I'm tearful and terrified, and on the other, happy and hopeful—all running side by side. I'm resigned to the fact that good and bad will always coexist, but it's up to me as to which one I choose to focus on. I'm going to try my hardest to look to the light.

***

Jamie has gone home with his parents so that he and his dad can take care of some work. He assured me he will return as soon as he can. He plans to gather some things he needs to stay here with me tonight and drive his own truck back to the hospital.

My dad now dozes in the chair beside me after returning earlier with a bag of clothes and toiletries I asked for. It feels nice to wear my own familiar gown and robe. He also brought my phone that still sat on the bathroom counter.

I hate to think of the sight he encountered on my bathroom floor when he went in—all the artifacts of the morning strewn about. I won't ask. He made it clear that he "cleaned things up a bit" so that everything is ready for me to return home. My poor, sweet daddy. I can't imagine the tornado of swirling emotions he must be experiencing. I hate more than anything that I have let him down.

I don't actually plan to stay at my house if I'm released tomorrow but haven't told him that yet. The NICU room has a fold-out, full-sized bed for the parents, a kitchenette, couch, and television. I plan to stay here with the baby as much as possible.

It's getting late, and my dad stretches and looks at his watch. He glances over at me and smiles. "How are you feeling, sweetheart?"

The nurse removed my IV a little while ago, and I don't have to constantly wear the finger oxygen monitor or the blood pressure cuff that was programmed to take my blood pressure every so often.

I return his smile. "Much better since I've been liberated from the machines."

"Will you be all right here if I head on back to the house for the night?" he asks.

"Yes, Jamie will be here in a few minutes and will stay in the recliner with me tonight."

"I guess you two have a lot to talk about and sort out, so I'm going to say goodbye." He moves to kiss me but stops. "Before I go, Cara, I should tell you that I love you today as much as I did yesterday, even more so. It seems like only days instead of years that I was in your mom's hospital room with her after she delivered you. You'll always be my little girl," he chokes up and swallows, "but obviously Jamie will be taking the role of the number-one man in your life now... well, besides your son." He smiles pensively through watery eyes.

"I want you to know that yes, some mistakes were made, some regretful choices, but I don't hold it against you or Jamie. I've grown to respect and love Jamie like a son." He looks confidently into my eyes. "You're both young, yes, but he's a good man, the one I've prayed for all these years for you, Cara, I'm sure of it. It's obvious how he loves you and will do good by you. You two will figure all this out."

How is it that he was led to stop and say these things at this very moment? Because it's exactly what I've needed to hear from him—that he's not too disappointed in me and that we'll be okay.

"Thank you, Daddy." I suddenly find it hard to take a breath. "I love you so much, and I'm really sorry for everything I've put you through."

"Love you, too, baby girl, and I hope that'll be the last time you apologize. It is what it is, and I'm happy I have a grandson who is doing well under his unique circumstances. It could have gone a different way today for you two." He uses his thumb to swipe at his eyes beneath his glasses.

"I've thought about it a million times, Dad."

I've also been thinking about the irony that my mom and dad tried years to have a baby before they got me, and yet...

"I'll see you tomorrow, then." He kisses me on the forehead before leaving.

It's not long after he's gone that I start to feel restless, so I head to the NICU to check on the baby and speak with the head nurse. While I'm walking back to my room, Jamie is coming down the opposite end of the hall. He has a backpack slung over his shoulder, a paper bag in one hand, and a large drink in the other.

We meet at the door, and he holds up the drink and bag. "Surprise! I brought you a burger and fries."

"It *is* a surprise, a good one!" I say, a tightly wound spring in my chest instantly recoiling. *Ah, Jamie...* seeing him is relief personified, like coming home after a grueling journey. I think about what my dad just said about Jamie. Yes, I have no doubt, Jamie is my person.

He pushes the door open with his hip to let me in. "You've lost your walking stick, I see."

"Yeah, they took the IV out a couple of hours ago. If I need pain medicine, I get to take pills now."

When we enter the room, Jamie looks around, setting his backpack in the recliner and the food on the table tray beside my bed. "We're alone?"

"For now." I smile.

He takes my face in his hands and plants a big kiss on my lips, staying there for a beat... then two. "I've been wanting to do that all day." He smiles mischievously, looking so handsome, my heart squeezes tightly with all kinds of unidentifiable emotions. He says, "Let's dig in."

I call the number to the nutrition services department and cancel my dinner tray. We eat our burgers and share the fries. We take turns dipping them in ketchup and feeding them to one another, finding humor in the task. Jamie always puts too much ketchup on mine, making me giggle.

The work shift changes, and my night nurse enters the room while we're eating, introducing herself as Sandra. She writes her name on the little whiteboard on the wall and takes my blood pressure. She asks what my pain level is from one to ten, and when I tell her about a four, she writes it on the board. She asks me if I want pain medicine and when I shake my head, she encourages me to take at least one tablet to stay in front of the pain and to help me sleep later.

After she leaves to retrieve the medication, Jamie says, "Our son needs a name."

"He does, yes. Do you have any more ideas?" When we discussed names earlier, none of the ones we liked seemed to fit; they just didn't feel right.

"I actually do."

I bring my hand to my heart in mock surprise because I feel like we have already exhausted all options. "You do? As long as it's not Bartholemew or Buford." I laugh.

"Nope." He smiles. "How would you feel about naming him after both our fathers?" He looks at me, hopeful.

It doesn't take long for me to think about it. "I like that idea. A lot. Their first names?" I ask.

"Yeah, Christopher Brent?"

"Christopher Brent," I say, trying it on for size. "I love it. He looks like a Christopher, and since my dad goes by Chris, it shouldn't be confusing."

"That was too easy. Did we just name our son?"

"Yes," I say breathlessly, "I think we did!"

I reach over and hug him. He's hesitant to let me go until the nurse returns with my medicine, and we break apart.

"I brought you two tablets, but it's up to you if you want one or both."

Remembering how it felt to be drunk those months ago and sedated this morning, and also recalling my laughing fit earlier that surely had to be partially caused by the drugs, I opt for only one and take it, thanking her.

When we're alone again, I tell Jamie about my visit to the NICU and my conversation with the charge nurse about breastfeeding and staying here at the hospital as much as possible.

"The nurse explained the importance of our baby... Christopher," I correct and smile, "receiving my breast milk through his feeding tube."

My breasts are beginning to feel heavy, so I'll need to start pumping soon. She explained this will stimulate my breasts to make more milk and keep my supply steady until Christopher can nurse straight from my breasts when his feeding tube is removed. She also explained how it will be a while before he'll be able to suckle and latch on to me because of his prematurity.

"The NICU room is equipped with my own electric breast pump and a refrigerator drawer in which to store the milk," I explain. "She said we can stay in the room as much as we want. Since there's a fold-out full-sized bed, large bathroom, and kitchenette, the rooms give the parents as much of the comforts of home as possible. If breast milk and my presence are what Christopher needs most, then that's what he will get," I say, determined to follow through.

Jamie listens as though he'll be quizzed later over the information. When I've finished, he offers, "I can take a break from work for a while, but more than ever, I need to work during the days—for the most part. I want to come in the evenings when I'm done with work and stay, too?"

"I'd like nothing more. We'll be here for some time, that's for certain."

I look at Jamie for a few seconds, recounting the day and his involvement since the shock has somewhat worn off. "You amaze me with how you've stepped up today. You've shown what a good father you already are. Some guys might have already run the other way."

Jamie looks down as if contemplating what to say to that. When he returns my gaze uncertainly, he says, "The truth is, I've been really scared; I'm still scared. I was more afraid today at different points than I've ever been in my life, and then seeing Christopher lying there so fragile and vulnerable... all those tubes coming out of him ..." his sentence hangs in the air unfinished.

"I could tell you were scared when you saw him. Heck, I was, too. It's shocking, especially when I had him this morning and saw how small he was. But you faced your fears today and did what was needed, just like I did, I guess. Thank you," I say, feeling my eyes grow heavy.

The pain medicine has begun to take effect, and I yawn. "If someone would have told me yesterday all this was about to happen, I would have told them there was no way I could cope with something like that, yet here I am. Here *we* are."

"I wouldn't even know how to react any other way. He's our son. We're responsible for him, and he needs us. More than that, I *want* to be Christopher's dad, and I *want* to be here for you. There's no place I'd rather be, Cara. I love you, and I love him," he says earnestly, holding my gaze as if needing confirmation that I believe him.

"I see that. We'll get through this, won't we?"

"If we stick together and stay open and honest about our feelings, we will, no doubt. I know it's a tough road ahead, but we can do it together."

He stops, noting my eyes drooping closed. "Now, you need to get some sleep before they come poking and prodding at you again. I'll grab the pillow and blanket from the closet and be right here if you need me. I'm tired."

"Thanks; I don't want to be alone."

He looks into my sleepy eyes and kisses my knuckles before he stands up. I'm reminded of the first time I felt his lips on my skin like that. It was outside the cafeteria in the courtyard after the first long conversation we had. I fall asleep feeling safe, knowing Jamie is right beside me in more ways than one.

***

I watch Jamie come awake this morning. He's so tall, the recliner must have been uncomfortable. His bed hair, sleepy eyes, and dark stubble create about the sexiest picture I've ever seen.

"Hey, baby," he smiles, "how are you feeling?"

"Very sore, but much better than yesterday morning, that's for sure. I can't imagine how women who have large babies, or even normal-sized babies, must feel."

"Do you honestly think you'll be up for our graduation ceremony tomorrow?"

"I think so, as long as I don't stand around too much and can find a place to sit before it begins. At least we'll be sitting throughout the actual ceremony."

Jamie seems reassured. He stands and grabs his backpack. "Do you need the bathroom? I'll clean up, change clothes, and go get some Starbucks and breakfast for us."

"No, you go ahead," I say, "I'll take a shower and get dressed while you're gone. Wait till you see the bathroom in the NICU room. It's like a real bathroom, granite countertops and everything."

"When I first saw the room, I thought it looked more like a hotel than a hospital room," Jamie says. "It's amazing how they accommodate the families of the NICU babies. I've been nothing but impressed."

While Jamie's in the bathroom, I receive a text from Jessica.

Jessica: *You're not here again today?? Where are you, and why is Jamie out, too? Y'all just decided to skip the last two days of school? Not like you, Cara!!*

I knew this was coming and already planned to tell Jessica only enough of the truth to placate her for now. We have collectively decided to wait to tell anyone other than immediate family about the baby until after graduation, which is a relief.

C: *Jess, I was so sick yesterday, I had to go to the hospital. My phone was at home until my dad brought it up. I'm going to be released today, so I will definitely be at graduation.*

Jessica: *Cara!!! In the hospital??? What's wrong? I'm glad you're okay!*

C: *I'm fine, stomach issues again, but worse this time. Since we're basically done with school, Jamie left school yesterday to be here with me.*

Not a lie, just a buttload of omission. As we finish texting, I silently pray Jessica will forgive me after I tell her the entire story. I think about Dad's congregation and the neighbors who saw the ambulance at our house. There will be many questions and even judgment from those who don't know, will never know, the entire story.

My morning shift nurse enters while I wait in the recliner beside the hospital bed for Jamie to return. I'm showered, dressed, and feeling pretty good this morning. She tells me I'll be released if Dr. Zeng permits it when she makes her rounds in a few minutes. I've only been here a day and a half-ish, but since I am doing well and only moving down the hall to our NICU room, the nurse says the doctor will probably release me.

Jamie arrives with coffee and a bag. He has been gone a long time and surprises me by saying he visited Christopher alone before going out for the late breakfast.

"Wanted some Daddy-and-son bonding time?" I ask. He smiles big and hands me my coffee and breakfast. I'm impressed that Jamie went in and held Christopher on his own initiative.

"When the doctor comes by in a while," I say, "she will probably release me to move on down to our NICU room. How is he?"

"He's doing great, according to the nurse on duty. She reminded me that it will be a slow waiting game. He just needs to grow." Jamie shrugs while taking a bite of his breakfast sandwich.

"My dad called while you were gone and asked for my consent to tell Rachel about Christopher, and I said yes, of course, knowing she will honor anything Dad asks her to keep to herself. He said they plan to visit us later." I pause. "I didn't tell you before you left, but Jessica texted me asking where we both are."

Jamie stops chewing and asks, "What did you tell her?"

"Just enough to satisfy her. She'll find out soon enough, but not until after graduation. Can you get your mom and dad to come up later when my dad is here so we can tell them the name we chose? I'm sure they'll both be thrilled."

"I think so, too. I can't wait to tell them." Jamie looks off at nothing and sighs. "Christopher Brent. It sure sounds better than 'the thirty-weeker,' doesn't it?"

"Yes," I laugh, "it does."

Jamie

My dad was able to talk to a lab yesterday and use his influence, and probably money, to have a DNA paternity testing kit overnighted. He texted me this morning to tell me it was delivered and met me in the hospital parking lot on his way to a meeting to give it to me.

I study the instructions while sitting inside my truck, swab the inside of my cheek, and place it into the little test tube provided.

Afterward, before going to fetch breakfast, I go back into the hospital straight up to the NICU and scrub in. Since I am listed as the father of record, I can give my permission for Christopher to get swabbed. Part of me is glad Cara won't know about it, but

I also hate that she won't, only because I'm keeping something from her... something we promised not to do.

However, I am complying with Chris's wishes for her not to know we're doing the test. At the same time, I'm protecting Cara from having to even consider the horrifying possibility that someone could have taken advantage of her without either of us knowing. And didn't Dr. Zeng tell us to be mindful of Cara's mental state right now?

The helpful nurse on duty swabs the inside of Christopher's cheek for cells used to determine paternity. She asks no questions, and although I feel the need to explain the story behind the reason we need a paternity test, I hold back. I hate that she must think it's because Cara has slept with more than just me. It looks bad.

It feels worse.

She doesn't make a big deal out of it, and while I'm here, she helps me take Christopher from the isolette to hold him. Feeling his body, so warm and small, wiggling on my chest is just as miraculous today as it was yesterday.

I study his minuscule fingers and toes. The pad of his largest toe is about the size of a lentil. I take in his amazing little face with its tiny button features, and I don't want to leave him. I have a feeling I'll never tire of looking into the face of our little miracle and marveling at God's creation—the fact that we as humans are allowed a hand in it.

Christopher is my son, and I love him no matter what. Acknowledging this with just the two of us together in this moment causes the backs of my eyes to sting, and I whisper to him, "Your daddy loves you, little buddy. So, so much."

The package now sits in my truck, waiting to be overnighted back to the lab. At some point today when I have more time, I'll let Cara know I have to take care of an errand, and I'll get the completed kit on its way back to the lab for analysis. The instructions promise the results via email in two to three days. It can't come soon enough. I'm tired of the "not knowing" consuming too many of my thoughts.

After Cara and I eat breakfast, the doctor comes by to examine her. I step out into the hall while she's with Cara and read a text from my sister, Megan.

Megan: *What the freak is going on? You just made me an aunt? Can I call you?*

J: *Yeah, crazy, huh? I'm at the hospital with Cara and need to just text right now.*

My parents decided to tell my sisters everything except the circumstances surrounding the mysterious conception. They were both told Cara didn't know she was pregnant and had the baby at home, adding no other details. Megan is already flying in for my graduation, so she'll be able to see Christopher while she's here.

I think about Matt back in Cali and wonder what he will think when I call to tell him about Christopher. I figure he'll be shocked yet supportive, and I would love to see him about now. If he wants to visit, I'm certain my parents will buy him a plane ticket. It'll have to wait for now, though.

Thankfully, we have all decided not to tell anyone besides family until graduation. I would hate for there to be unwanted negative attention focused on Cara at a ceremony where the students and parents of a whole community will be at one time— a gossip haven.

I don't give a rip about what people think of me, but I don't have the history here that Cara does. I already know some are going to look at me like I ruined Cara—*just a thuggy California* guy who moved right in and sweet-talked the preacher's daughter into having sex with him. I can hear it now.

I already have to talk myself down off that ledge of self-derision multiple times a day. Chris plans to tell his church congregation Sunday. How Cara plans to keep this from Jessica until after graduation is over Thursday, I don't know. Jessica is pretty good at reading Cara.

Megan: *Dude, my little bro actually dabbled in the taboo? Shame, shame! You broke a Gallagher cardinal rule, Jamie—Thou shalt not have sex if someone is going to find out about it lol!*

Megan pisses me off. Even more so now, it's evident how childish she still is, how unthoughtful. She might be older, but she's not wiser. When I don't answer, she texts again:

Megan: *Sorry, bro, I can't wait to see my nephew. I'm glad he's going to be okay.*

J: *Thanks, he's perfect. We'll talk when you get here. Are you flying into Love Field or DFW?*

Megan: *DFW. Dad said he'd pick me up. I can only stay two nights. I have to get back to my own sex partner, you know haha!*

At this point, I'm tempted to tell her to eff off and don't see how I actually keep from it.

Megan: *I hope to see you later today or this evening at the hospital. We have a lot to talk about. Mom said you're handling it well considering the shock. She said you need to put me on a visitor list.*

J: *I'll do that.*

Purposely curt in my reply.

Megan: *And I thought I was only coming to see my little bro graduate. I'm excited to meet our little guy. Congratulations!*

With that, she redeemed herself just a fraction.

J: *Thank you, Meg. We love him. So will you.*

When I returned to the hospital room with breakfast earlier, Cara was dressed in regular clothes with her hair freshly washed and dried, even had on makeup. She looks like she never had a baby, which only adds to the disorientation of whether or not all of this is real. I hope Dr. Zeng will release Cara because she's itching to get down to the NICU to see Christopher and stay there.

I also plan on staying in our NICU room as much as possible while I work for Dad during the weekdays now that school is over. More than ever, I have to know the business and earn as much as possible to support my family.

My family.

The two words have the effect of an echo in my ears—knowing in my head this new normal belongs to me but feeling as if it's happening outside of myself. I'm still waiting for the words to catch up to my reality.

I decided yesterday that if Cara can accept this and all the changes it will bring to her life, then I will *not* complain about what this means for me and my future. She'll have to make many more adjustments than I will, and I'll do whatever I can to ease her burden.

The doctor emerges from Cara's room with a smile and holds the door open for me to go back in. "She's doing extremely well for all she's been through. She is officially released from my care. Good luck to you both."

I shake Dr. Zeng's hand firmly and thank her.

After Cara signs discharge papers with the nurse, I help her get her things together, and we both walk down to Christopher's room. She is still slow-moving but a lot faster than yesterday, so she'll hopefully feel even better tomorrow for graduation. It's amazing how before we had Christopher, Cara couldn't wait for tomorrow to arrive. Now, she'll be glad to just get through the ceremony and return to the hospital to be with Christopher. I feel the same way.

I'm still timid about asking Cara too much about what's going on with her body as far as having had a baby come out of it and what that feels like. But I come right out and ask her, "Did the doctor, uh, like, have to check you down there, or?"

Cara doesn't think twice about answering. "No, she just had me lie down and pushed around on my lower stomach and asked me how much I'm bleeding."

"You're bleeding?" I ask stupidly.

"Yeah, not bad. The body has to kind of clean itself out during the healing process for a few weeks after giving birth, like a woman's period does." This seems to make her think, and she pauses. "Though I've never had a regular cycle. I suppose another reason I never imagined I was pregnant. Skipping periods for months was pretty common for me. Anyway, now it's just like having a heavy period." She blinks away, looking slightly embarrassed, having never talked to me much about her periods before.

"Cara, don't forget I have two sisters and a mom. So you don't have to be shy with me about stuff like that. Trust me, I've overheard plenty of conversations about periods and products over the years." I laugh and squeeze her ringless hand.

They took her rings and a small-chained necklace her mom gave her that she wears regularly and put them in a bag when she arrived here. I saw the bag in the bathroom this morning, and she must have packed it with her things. I'm not quite sure what to make of it. She always wore her rings.

When we reach the NICU and scan our badges, we scrub in as usual and prepare to unpack and settle into our home away from home.

***

The day after graduation, I am home stuffing clean clothes into my backpack to take to the hospital where I left Cara napping on the bed in the NICU. I started a load of our laundry in the washing machine provided for the families on the NICU floor before I left, so including those clothes, I'll have enough at the hospital from here on out.

I sit at my computer desk in my bedroom before heading back to the hospital when I notice I received an email ten minutes ago from a sender called Lab Services, with the word *CONFIDENTIAL* typed beside it. It takes a long second to absorb that it's the DNA paternity test results. My heart begins to hammer against my ribcage and pounds even faster and stronger when I open the email and the accompanying attachment.

Please let Christopher be my biological son, please let Christopher be my biological son, I chant as a prayer while the attachment loads.

The first part of the letter explains the name and methodology of the test used to determine paternity, yadda, yadda. There are a bunch of numbers and letters listed in a long table under the heading: *Results.* I skip the table and see the word *Conclusion* at the bottom and read it.

I have to blink and read it another time... and then another.

*Conclusion: Based on our analysis, it is practically proven that Mr. James A. Gallagher is **not** the biological father of the child Christopher B. Gallagher.*

Not?

Not?

NOT??

What the hell?

My mind and heart race. My head grows dizzy from lack of oxygen. Oh God, my head is about to explode like a chemistry experiment gone horribly wrong. Only two words come to mind—

Eric Baines.

I'm caught in a whirlpool of emotions threatening to drown me, time and space moving too fast, spinning, spinning. I can't think about anything, *anything*, except getting to Eric Baines.

I grab my keys and run full-speed out of the door to my truck.

Amber shouts behind me, "Jamie, where are you going? Did something happen?"

I don't answer.

Did something happen? Only the worst thing imaginable!

Hands shaking, I miss the ignition twice while trying to stick the key in. Cara showed me where Eric lives when we were out on one of the many drives we've taken; I just hope I can remember how to get there.

I speed, not even thinking about the consequences of getting pulled over by police, or worse. I drive as fast as I can down residential streets and skid around corners, tires squealing. It's as though my rage takes me directly to the front of Eric's house in no time flat, and I screech to a stop at the curb.

I stumble out of the truck and run to his front door, pounding on it with the side of my fisted hand—bang, bang, bang, bang. It reverberates like the ricochet of a bullet shot into a barrel.

Eric opens the door in surprise and says, "Dude, what are you doing here?"

I grasp the front of his shirt with both hands and drag him out onto his front porch. With no explanation, my fists begin to pummel him. The rage is so strong, there are no calculated hits.

I plow into his face, the sides of his head, his stomach, his chest. When he falls to the cement of the porch, I drop, too, and straddle him, drilling my knuckles into him over and over and over, creating a sickening popping sound with each blow.

I vaguely hear a female voice screaming from the doorway, "Stop! Stop, you're killing him, stop!"

But I keep on and on, again and again, until my arms and fists are spent and I can no longer even raise them.

I have nothing left.

Eric lies unmoving, unconscious. Blood oozes from every orifice in his face and head, forming two scarlet streams of regret trailing upward from beneath him like devil horns.

Still kneeling over him, I look down at my bloody knuckles and more clearly hear who I presume to be Eric's mother heaving for breath and saying over and over, "You've killed him!"

"You've killed him."

Fainter now, I still hear her repeating, "You've killed him, you've killed him."

And now only a whisper echoing in my head, "You've killed my son!"

My son...

My son...

I sit straight up, gasping for breath as though I've been submerged underwater and have come within a millisecond of drowning, a cold sweat dampening my face and chest.

Cara is beside me and sits up just as quickly, reaching for me. "Jamie, what's wrong?" she gasps. "You're having a nightmare."

I look around and realize where I am. We moved into the NICU room earlier, and after holding Christopher, I pulled out the bed for Cara to take a nap. I must have fallen asleep, too, but I never take naps, and it has messed with my mind.

"It was awful," I say, still wheezing.

She rubs my back soothingly, whispering reassurance as she would to a child after a bad dream, "It's okay now; it was just a dream. Do you want to tell me about it?"

I shake my head. "No, I don't want to repeat it, but it was about Christopher."

I look over at his crib, and she says, "He's fine, though, see?"

"Yes, yes," I say, although not pacified because his well-being was not at all what the dream was about. "Sorry, Cara, go back to sleep. I'm sorry I woke you."

"She looks at the clock on the wall and says, "No, we've been asleep for over an hour, and it's past lunchtime. Do you want to go get something to eat? It will make you feel better. I can actually leave the hospital legally now."

She smiles, and it's pure light, as innocent as a sunrise, again piercing through the darkness of my personal thunderhead. I should be the one continually cheering her up instead of the other way around.

"That sounds good," I say, dropping my legs over the side of the bed.

Even when a nurse isn't in our room, Christopher is constantly monitored on camera from the little webcam set up on every incubator in the NICU. I still walk over to his crib to see if he's okay—to touch him, make sure he is breathing.

I've become a helpless protector.

"You're worried about him, of course. We both are. It's coming out in your subconscious dreams. Maybe you need to voice your fears more—aloud—so you won't have any more dreams like that."

But this is a fear I can't talk to you about, Cara. It would be too difficult for you to even fathom. None of us wants to intrude on the innocence of your unquestioning faith that Christopher is my biological son, that no one other than me touched you.

"I'm sure you're right," I say, leaving it at that.

We both put on our shoes, and I adjust the fold-out bed to put it in its proper place. Finally, I leave the room and walk around the hospital to get my bearings while Cara uses the breast pump. I was regaining at least some measure of humor before I left when I refrained from making any comparison of the contraption to a dairy-cow milking machine. Yet I can't seem to shake the dream.

I return after the twenty minutes Cara said it would take her, and I scrub back in. When I open the door to our room, Cara is in the bathroom scrubbing her own hands before placing them inside the isolette to tell Christopher goodbye, that we will return soon. I chuckle at the way she speaks to him as though he understands every word, but I have a feeling it's very good for him.

I leave Cara in the hospital lobby to get my truck and drive up to the entrance so she won't have to walk more than necessary. When I open her door, she climbs in slowly and buckles in, making sure the seat belt stays loose across her pelvic area. She wants to go out for pizza.

"I know it's not the healthiest choice, especially after coming out of the burger-and-fries coma from last night, but pizza sounds good and has a significant meaning."

"Oh?" I ask. "What's that?"

"It's what we had on our first date," she says, rolling her eyes as though I should know.

"No, our first date was Tex-Mex; how could you forget that?" I pretend to be offended.

"Okay, you're right in a way. That was our first *official* date," she says, sketching air quotes, "but our first true lunch date was in the courtyard at school, the day after I met you, and we had pizza."

"Of course, yeah, I was too focused on you that day to even care if I was eating cardboard." I laugh. "I will never forget it. Your lips, *damn*, I couldn't stop looking at them and imagining kissing them. I was lovestruck. And the way you were looking at me that day... You had stars in your eyes for me. It drove me wild."

"I did," she says, smiling, "and still do... more than ever."

I turn into the next parking lot, which happens to be some type of dental clinic, and put the truck in park. Cara opens her mouth to ask what I'm doing, and I say, "Come here." I lean across the seat and thoroughly kiss her as though I've been parched.

"Mmm," she murmurs against my mouth, causing too much of an ache in my gut.

I break the kiss and say, "I have to remember you just had our baby and need to control myself."

"But I love your spontaneity." She sighs and giggles.

I pull back onto the street, and we drive outside our immediate area so as not to run into anyone we know or who knows us. We decide on a little Italian restaurant where Cara says she's eaten before. I ask her again if she's sure she is up to eating at a restaurant, and she assures me she took a pain reliever and feels up to it. It's like I'm the one who has to keep reminding her she just had a baby.

Our lunch together is a nice respite from the hospital scene. Sometimes I forget there is a lot I still don't know about Cara, and we talk mostly about our families.

After we finish our pizza, Cara asks, "Have I told you the story about when my great-grandmother gave birth to my grandmother?"

"No, what happened?" I ask, reaching for the crust she left on her plate.

"She was outside doing chores the entire time she was in labor. She went into the house, delivered my grandmother, cleaned up, and made a sling out of a bedsheet across her chest for her newborn. The story goes that she went right back outside to finish hanging the wash on the line."

"If that story is true," I say skeptically, "you get your strength from your great-grandmother. It sounds similar to my own grandma's story—my dad's mom—of walking five miles in the snow to school uphill both ways." I laugh.

When we walk back to the truck, I open Cara's door for her and help her climb in. She reaches down for something sticking out on the floorboard. It must have slid from under the seat where I put it earlier.

I cringe as I walk around to the driver's side of my truck. When I open my door to get in, she holds up a parcel addressed to DNA Paternity Testing, Inc. with my return address. With a confused look on her face, she asks, "What's this?"

Cara

"Jamie, I asked you what this is," I say, demanding an answer, the truth. His complexion has gone pale, and at first, I don't understand; it doesn't compute. But as possible meanings take shape, it feels as though my heart of glass is hit with a sledgehammer. It explodes into a million tiny pieces, all falling onto the floorboard where I found the package.

Jamie must read the dawning awareness on my face. "Let me explain, Cara," he implores.

He has gone behind my back and had a paternity test done? It's so out of character for Jamie that I am totally disoriented. Do I even know this person sitting next to me? He's distrusted me in the past when he thought there was something between Eric and me, so why not again, why not now? Only this time there's a lot more at stake than jealous pride—our baby's identity!

Who does Jamie think I would have messed around with seven months ago? Could he really be revisiting the notion that I had something going on with Eric despite my denial and protests?

Some part of my brain tells me my conclusion isn't plausible, but the irrational part of me blurts in a choked voice, "You, you think Christopher is... is not your son? You know when I got pregnant, Jamie! You have the gall to think I would ever cheat on you?" I say in disbelief as Jamie repeatedly shakes his head. "This, this is so disrespectful to me, to our son. It's your turn to see *my* temper, Jamie Gallagher!"

"Listen to me, dammit!" Jamie's volume matches my own, loud enough to hurt my ears inside the cab of his pickup. Then in a quieter voice of resignation, he says, "I didn't want you to have to worry about this, about the reason we needed to have a test done."

"What? We? *We* needed to have a test done? Who else knows about this?" My volume has not come down.

Jamie reaches for my hands in an effort to calm me, and I recoil. "Don't touch me!" I slap his hands away.

He places them on the steering wheel, staring ahead, his jaw set.

After several seconds, he begins in a steadier voice, "It's a possibility, Cara, only a possibility, that since you and I were both passed out, someone could have... could have gotten to you. We were crashed, dead to the world for over six hours."

My world abruptly stops as though I've jumped from a plane with a failed parachute. I clasp both of my hands over my mouth. "Wait; what? Who? You think I was *raped*?"

"No! I mean... no, I don't, Cara. But even if there is a one percent chance, your dad asked me to have the test done. He didn't want me to tell you, and I was respecting his wishes."

"My dad?" I whisper in disbelief.

As I begin to think of the possibility of something like rape happening to me—it's hard for me to even form the word—my mind jumps to "who," and every ounce of blood drains from my face. "Eric?" I ask, breathing erratically at the thought.

Jamie's knuckles completely lose color, gripping the wheel as though he's trying to crush it with his bare hands. "Yes," is all he manages in a whisper.

Now my breaths simply won't come at all. I'm gasping, picturing Eric sneaking into that room with me passed out and... *Could he be that cruel, that psycho? Please, God, no.*

"No, you would have woken up, I would have woken up," I say, faltering, not so sure, because obviously I *hadn't* woken up, or if awake, don't remember anything. That logic doesn't mesh or help me feel any better.

His thick eyebrows drawn down, Jamie's expression is a combination of anguish and concern. He reaches for me again; and again, I brush his hand away.

"Regardless of my dad not wanting me to know, you should have told me. We promised not to keep anything from one another. I'm not a child, and this very much involves me. This is a game-changer. Wasn't it you who just told me we would get through this whole ordeal only if we remain open and honest with each other?" I accuse.

"How is it a game-changer; what are you talking about? It doesn't change anything as far as me being Christopher's father and raising him with you. It means Eric would most likely be going to prison for a long time."

"And what would it mean for me, Jamie, *ME*?" I'm shouting again. "It would mean I have been violated in the most awful way a woman can imagine. I... oh God... I just don't think I could deal with it!" I break out into an angry, heart-wrenching cry, covering my face again. "I can't bear the thought of Christopher being Eric's son. I just can't."

"I know, babe, I know," he whispers.

I can tell the thought of Eric makes Jamie angry, but when I look back at him, there are tears brimming in his own eyes.

Jamie draws a deep breath. "I'm going to say this again, and one last time; *our* son will never be Eric's son, *ever*, no matter what the results of the test. As for you having possibly been violated, I can't even begin to tell you how sick I felt when this possibility first slammed into me. Thinking of Eric... anyone doing that to you, the effect it would have on you..."

My heart is suddenly a sieve, and every ounce of happiness and hope I had from thinking our little family was just that—*our little family*—hemorrhages out. It's easy for Jamie to say now that he will be Christopher's dad no matter what; it's easy to say it won't change anything between us, but it already has. Just the possibility has.

And what will life be like if the results definitively prove Christopher isn't Jamie's? He would have to deal with that, and I will have to deal with the fact that I've been assaulted—water so hot, I can't even allow my big toe to test it right now.

A mental box is too small to fit all the emotions I must shove them into. I need a closet, and there's no way to stamp it with a simple label. What would I even name it? *Betrayal? Hopelessness? Catastrophe?* Feeling numbness spread through me, a wall snaps into place in the space separating us, a safeguard to my sanity. "I need to go back to the hospital," I say, devoid of expression.

Jamie's head abruptly whips toward me. He looks terrified for me, so I clarify, "I need to see Christopher and try to sort all this out in my jumbled brain."

He begins to speak again, "Cara—"

I raise my hand to stop him. Then, feeling deflated and defeated, I interrupt, "Just take me back, Jamie, please."

He blinks hard and keeps his eyes closed for several beats before saying, "Okay."

He starts the truck to return to the hospital, and we ride in silence. He drops me off at the lobby entrance when we arrive. I lumber up to the room without waiting for him, but he doesn't follow.

Just as I was beginning to get my feet on the ground after delivering a baby I didn't know I was even carrying, my life has been turned upside down yet again. This time it's equivalent to the tornado that dumped Dorothy into a foreign world. The territory I've landed in is more unbelievable to me than Oz. Will I ever be able to find my way back home, back to anything remotely safe and familiar? Or has home been wiped out—not even an option for me anymore? I want so badly to be able to just click my heels together, but I need a lot more than a pair of magic slippers here.

I'm holding Christopher when Jamie comes in an hour later. He stands away from me, leaning against the wall, arms and feet crossed, watching me for the longest time before speaking.

"I talked to my dad. He and Mom are bringing Megan straight from the airport to the hospital. They should be here in about thirty minutes."

"Do your parents also know about the paternity test?"

"Yes," Jamie says resolutely.

A fresh torrent of anger hits me. I feel thoroughly demeaned and conspired against, like a little girl who has to be protected from the news that her bunny died. Her parents replace it with a new one, only for her to discover later that the markings are different.

"No time was wasted, was it? Megan, too?" I ask.

"No."

"Would she still want to see the baby if she knew he might not be yours?" I correct, "Your *biological* son."

Jamie's expression changes from blank to completely pained, "Cara..."

"Forget it, Jamie. Please don't tell any of them I know. I'll call my dad and ask him to come on to the hospital so we can bring them in together to announce the name."

Jamie nods, but the prospect has none of the joy it had when we named our son together last night.

●●●

Graduation is over, and it's still early since the ceremony began at 5:00. I have already gone to eat afterward with my dad and grandparents, to whom we broke the news about Christopher over dinner. They took it pretty well. All they know is that the baby was early and is in the hospital, nothing else; and out of decency, no questions were asked, thank goodness. They plan to visit Christopher tomorrow.

It will be another week before I am released to drive, so Dad dropped me off just a little while ago. I miss my independence—driving my own car.

I miss a lot of things.

Graduation brought little joy. In fact, the only happiness I've felt recently was yesterday, watching Jamie's and my dad's expressions when we announced Christopher's name to them. We let the nurses know what we were doing, and they allowed all four of us to be in the room together with Christopher.

Jamie took charge and said, "Well, granddads, Cara and I want to honor you as being two of the most important people in our lives and now two of the most important people in our son's life." When he looked at me, I had to look away and remind myself I was angry with him, with all of them. "So, we have decided to give our first-born son your first names—Christopher Brent."

Saying they were thrilled is a total understatement; they were both beaming. Brent took me into a tight embrace, the first hug he's ever given me, and said, "Thank you, Cara. This means more than you'll ever know. We love you and Christopher very much," which made me cry, of course. He even held Christopher for the first time afterward. It was evident that having half his name served to bond Brent and Christopher in a way nothing else could have. It was a good decision.

I tried to be as cheerful as possible when the visitors were here, but when it was only Jamie and me again, he asked if it was okay if he stayed with me and Christopher tonight.

I gave him a simple, "No."

I wouldn't tell Jamie outright yet, but I have already decided the best thing for us is to separate for a while. There might be hope for us in the future, but even that feels impossible right now.

He then pleaded, "I'll give you your space, and you won't even know I'm here. I belong with you and Christopher now. Christopher needs both of us, and I *want* to be here."

"But I don't want you here," I said with finality. "I want to be left alone."

Dejected, he took his things and left, and I didn't see or hear from him until graduation. It stung when, by the time I needed to leave the hospital room for the ceremony, he hadn't called or come to the hospital, but what did I expect? Isn't that exactly what I asked of Jamie, to leave me alone?

And now, I'm alone in the NICU room, while my friends and even Jamie are all celebrating elsewhere. In their defense, they all asked me to join them, but I declined. Ashley Barrio is having an after-graduation party that even Mark Shelton would say will be "epic," and the gang will be there after they celebrate with their respective families. It will probably go all night, and I'm sure every one of them is celebrating right now without a care in their perfect little worlds.

This is how I felt after my mother died, when so much had changed for me but everyone else around me carried on as usual. *I am lost.* I tell Jessica I'm not feeling well after having been so sick. I'm definitely not ready to tell her about Christopher. I can't deal with the emotions that telling her would release from their tightly closed compartments inside of me.

As my dad, my grandparents, and I were leaving the ceremony together, Susan repeatedly asked me to celebrate with them at their house. Jamie took my hand to pull me aside, calling to his family over his shoulder that he would catch up with them. He was still holding my left hand, rubbing his thumb over the spot where my promise ring used to sit while looking down as if to make certain it really wasn't there.

It wasn't.

He looked at me with the look he'd been giving me that bordered on pity and said, "I don't want to go with them, not without you, Cara, please. I need to be with *you*."

I responded flatly, "My grandparents are here. I'm going to eat with them and celebrate my graduation. And oh," I added in my most sarcastic tone, "tell them that as of a couple of days ago, surprise, they're now great-grandparents... although we're not quite sure who the father is yet."

Jamie's expression had remained stoic, dismissing my tone. "Can your dad drive you over after you eat dinner? Then I'll drive you back to the hospital afterward?"

I shook my head no. "I'm not going. I'll have my dad take me back to the hospital after dinner. Enjoy your family tonight. Your sister is in town for you, to celebrate *you*."

His face contorted into a grimace of pain.

When I turned to meet up with my dad at the car, Jamie called after me, "But I'm not even *me* without you." And then louder, "Cara, wait, please!"

I kept walking.

I'm now lying on the fold-out bed contemplating my future, trying to picture my life without Jamie, without his sisters or Brent... without Susan. I remember her kind words the night she asked to be a mother figure in my life, the night she took me in her arms and made me feel what it was like to have a mother's love again: *Even if you and Jamie at some point decide to part ways...*

Were her words prophetic? Did she have a mother's intuition that Jamie's and my relationship wouldn't last? Was my father right all the times he told me, *If it seems too good to be true, Cara, it probably is?*

I let go and sob into my pillow, weeping for all I have desperately been trying to hold onto but what the cruel fingers of fate are prying from my fisted hands—stability, faith in those I love, hope—all being snatched away like breadcrumbs from a windowsill.

The depression I feel is bone-deep; it's nothing I've experienced before, and I recognize it's more complicated than my circumstances. Something is going on inside of me, too, at the cellular level... the chemical part of me. I can't stop crying, and it's similar to how I feel when I'm on my period but exponentially worse.

If I thought my hormones were out of whack with all my irregular periods, they were nothing compared to this. When the nurse comes in, I hide my head under the pillow, willing myself not to sob aloud, and pretend to be asleep until she leaves.

When I think of how I've also been robbed of my mom being here to help me through this, my carefully tended-to *A Daughter's Sadness* box is ripped wide open, and every tidily folded emotion is yanked out and strewn across the surface of my heart.

Sobs wrack my entire body like tiny fists punching through every inch of my skin's surface. I long to feel her arms around me, feel her warm lips on my cheek, to hear the song she sang to me in her soft voice almost every day of my life until I thought I was too old for it and made her stop—a beautiful song about sunshine. What I wouldn't give to hear her voice one more time, to hear her sing that song to me *now*.

God, why did I ever ask her to stop singing to me?

If I don't have her to help me with Christopher and I won't have Susan's help when he's released from the hospital, what am I going to do? My own dad has a new family to look after now, so I no longer have him, either.

"I can't do this!" I shout into my pillow, crying and crying for what seems like hours until my eyes run out of tears and feel as though rubbing alcohol has been dropped directly into them.

Pull it together, Cara. Christopher is right over there and needs you. He can hear you. He needs you to be sane if not strong. I imagine the words as my mom's in that sweet, soothing voice she had, and it gives me enough strength to move. I painstakingly pull myself from the bed and go to the bathroom to splash cold water into my stinging eyes and onto my burning face. It helps only a little.

As I trudge back to the bed, I hear my father's words again, this time a calming echo in my head—another one of his sayings, *"Cara, sometimes the bridge from despair to hope is simply a good night's sleep."* More than at any other time in my life, I pray his words will ring true.

✦✦✦

I must have needed sleep because even the nurses coming in and out during the night didn't wake me. My breasts are sore and engorged with milk, leaking through the nursing pads inside my bra and covering the entire front of my nightshirt. I pumped right before going to sleep, but my milk must be coming in full force.

There are two nurses and a flurry of activity around Christopher's crib. One of the nurses is the very young and cute one I've seen checking out Jamie when she comes into the room and he's here.

"What's wrong?" I croak out in my scratchy morning voice.

I shakily grab my robe and pad over with bare feet to the isolette, trying to peer around them to see what they're doing.

"We're treating his jaundice. He needs to be under the bili-lights for a few days," the cute nurse explains while placing what looks like a white sleep mask around his head to cover his eyes. "It's technically called phototherapy, and it's very common for newborns to need it. The lights help rid his body of the built-up bilirubin he is having trouble metabolizing."

"Okay," I say, feeling helpless, which only adds to the pressure I feel in my chest this morning. "Will I still be able to hold him?"

"Yes, of course; he can be held about how long it would take to feed him if he were nursing, but not any longer. He needs to go straight back under the lights afterward. We will test him regularly with a light meter that flashes on his forehead until the amount of bilirubin is at acceptable levels. Then he won't need the light anymore."

Her smile is reassuring, but seeing Christopher's little body under the ultraviolet-looking light with his eyes fully covered is disconcerting. *My poor baby.* Something else to research. For now, I go into the nursing alcove and use the breast pump to relieve my swollen breasts. If only there was a machine to mend my aching heart.

Afterward, I clean up and put on a little makeup, which always makes me feel somewhat better—that and caffeine. After I hold Christopher and sing him the sunshine song my mom used to sing to me, I decide to head to the cafeteria to grab some coffee and food. It's already late morning, so I hurry down and barely make it before they stop serving breakfast.

Sipping my coffee, I grieve that Jamie isn't here with me and Christopher. I don't want to do this alone, unlike what I told him. I *can't* do this alone. Tears fill my eyes when I think about how I pushed Jamie away, how I treated him last night after graduation.

Why? Why?

Jamie, his parents, and my dad meant well by keeping the paternity testing from me. Am I projecting all my anger on them? It dawns on me that I'm handling what has happened like I did when my mom died. It's easier to push all my emotions down and try not to feel anything.

For whatever reason, it is also easier for me to be angry than sad or scared.

It's more than the fear of having been raped. There are women who have been violently assaulted and who had to very consciously endure every second of it and relive the horrible memories. My heart aches, *aches*, for them with a new understanding.

Worst case scenario, if Eric assaulted me, I don't have those aspects to contend with, and I have my beautiful Christopher as a result... It's as far as I will allow my brain to explore the possibility of assault.

Let's be honest, Cara, you're afraid Jamie won't want you anymore if he learns Christopher isn't his birth son. Two tears fall from my eyes down onto the table, plop, plop, narrowly missing my coffee cup.

Jamie practically hates Eric. He *would* hate him if he found out he assaulted me and fathered my son. Would he see Eric's face every time he looked at Christopher? At me? I couldn't bear it. Am I pushing Jamie away first so he won't have the chance to reject me? So he can't abandon me the way my mother did?

But would he? Would Jamie love me less if Eric assaulted me, or love Christopher less if he is Eric's birth son? If I know Jamie the way I think I do, he wouldn't. He said he wants to be his father no matter what. Not giving us the chance to find out is taking the coward's way out. *You are NOT a coward, Cara Ann,* I picture my mom saying to me. *You are not being fair to Jamie. Listen to him, believe him, love him the way you did before any of this happened.*

I don't know if I can.

I sit this way long enough for the bottom half of my coffee to get cold, so I walk over to get more. When I return to the small table, my phone chimes with an incoming text, and I reach for it, hoping it's Jamie. But it's *Mark Shelton.*

Why is Mark texting me? Not too long ago it wouldn't have been unusual to occasionally receive a text from him or one of the others in our gang's group texts, but not so much anymore. Not since Jamie and I, and then Mark and Jessica have paired off, and not since Eric has completely separated himself from us.

Mark: *Cara, they're calling people into the police station for questioning. I texted Jessica. She was here earlier. She said it's about something that happened at the Halloween party and a possible sexual assault? WTF? I'm about to go in. What am I supposed to say about that night? Y'all were wasted. Did Jamie do something to you? What am I supposed to say? Hurry!!*

My heart is racing, and my mind whirs. No one should know I had a baby, so why would anyone think I have been assaulted? What's going on? Has my dad betrayed me and called the police?

Did someone here, maybe a doctor, a nurse, tip them off that Jamie or someone else might have assaulted me since I didn't know I was pregnant, and we submitted a paternity test? At least one nurse knows about the paternity test. Has Jamie talked to someone who leaked information to the police? *When will this nightmare end?*

C: *OMG, Mark, I don't know what's going on with that. Just answer their questions, tell them the truth.*

Mark: *Jamie didn't hurt you that night, did he? Y'all are cool, right?*

C: *No, he didn't. It's complicated. You will find out soon enough. Thank you for wanting to help me, but just tell the truth.*

Mark: *Okay. Hey, Jamie is here. The police are leading him back now. His dad is with him.*

My phone is ringing now. It's *my* dad.

"Cara, get ready. I'll be there in a few minutes to pick you up. The police called looking for you. They want to question you. Be waiting out front."

What's left of my heart drops with a thud to the hospital cafeteria floor.

Jamie

My mom and Amber have gone to take Megan to catch her flight back to California, back to her "sex partner" as she so crudely referred to Decker. It's getting close to lunchtime, and I'm helping my dad in the home office when the entrance gate alarm chimes—the sensors and cameras detecting a vehicle entering.

Dad switches his monitor at his desk to camera three and says under his breath, "What the hell?"

I amble over to look. There is a police car at the gate, and I hear myself groan, "Shit," before my dad enables the gate and intercom.

"Drive on through," he hisses through clenched teeth and turns to me. "I was afraid it might come to this."

My blood runs cold as the underlying fear I've had for days now materializes before my eyes. My dad and I stand outside the front door, under the porte-cochère, waiting for the car to pull through the long driveway. There are two officers in the car, and they both step out and walk toward us.

"Good morning," one of the officers says, friendly enough, "we are looking for James Gallagher."

"That's me," I say, fear and dread gripping me, strangling me like a pair of invisible hands around my throat. I try to take in an adequate amount of air so I can remain standing.

"We're here on behalf of Detective Cook with the Fort Worth PD. He would like you to come into the station for questioning regarding an alleged crime."

I set my jaw and ask, "Am I under arrest?"

The officers both look surprised at my question. "No, nothing like that. This is to answer a few questions, to get a statement. You can drive your own vehicle and tell the clerk you're there to speak to Detective Cook."

"Does he need a lawyer? Can we have some time to contact a lawyer before he goes in to be questioned?" Dad asks.

"I don't think that's necessary, Mr. Gallagher," he looks at me, "but that's entirely up to you."

"I've got nothing to hide. My dad and I will head there now." I look at Dad and say, "I want to go now and get this over with."

He nods, sighs. "Okay, Jamie, I'll drive you."

We drive to the police station in silence, neither of us voicing our thoughts or fears. We walk into the reception area and let the clerk know why we're there. It's only seconds before an officer in dress clothes with a badge on his belt emerges from a hallway lined with doors to rooms and offices.

It's then I notice Mark Shelton sitting in a chair in the reception area looking down at his phone. He looks up, lifts his chin at me, and shrugs as if to say, *I don't know what's going on.* He returns his attention to his phone.

The officer introduces himself with a smile and shakes our hands.

"Can my dad come back with me?" I ask.

The detective nods and says, "That's fine, as long as you're the one who does the talking." He motions for us to follow him.

As we walk behind him, Dad whispers to me, "Answer the questions as briefly as you can. No fluff. Only speak to answer exactly what is asked." I nod, and we are led to a small office with the nameplate *Detective Jon Cook* posted outside the door.

"Have a seat, please, gentlemen. Would you like something to drink?"

We both shake our heads, and I say, "No, thank you."

I was hungry while working in the office with Dad and now, even the thought of food or drink makes me more nauseated than I already am.

"All right, James." He's looking only at me. "We are investigating an alleged crime that took place this last Halloween, and I will fill you in on all the allegations and possible charges in a bit, but this does involve you and Cara Dawson."

I give him a small nod of acknowledgment, and he continues, "I understand you were both there that evening, and we just want to invite you to give a statement, your version of exactly what you remember went on that night." When I nod again, he says, "And Cara will be giving her statement as well."

I snap to full attention. "She's here, now?"

"If she's not, she will be shortly; she's been called in."

My heart takes a steep dive. My sweet Cara. All I can think about is how much she's been through, how much she has endured these last few days, and now this?

"With your permission, I'll turn on the recorder and let you make your statement. It will be placed through digital software for transcription. Then, I'll print it, and if you like what you see, we'll have you sign it as a sworn statement, sound good?"

"Yeah, sure," I agree.

He switches on a recorder, and says, "This is Detective Jon T. Cook taking a witness statement for a crime allegedly occurring at the home of ..."

My ears are buzzing. I attempt to steady my breathing before I begin to speak but find it too difficult to accomplish...

"Go ahead."

I shake my head and say, "I'm sorry, what?"

"Please state your full name for the record and recount your version of the events as best you can of the evening of October thirty-first."

"James Alexander Gallagher, but I go by Jamie." I glance over at Dad and imagine him chiding me already, saying, *Just the facts.*

With an unsteady voice, I recount everything I can remember about the events of that night—when Cara and I arrived, how we stood around the first hour talking to some of her friends, the beer and punch we drank, and how we danced for quite a while.

I admit that we were feeling pretty tipsy, how Eric offered a seeming truce by asking me to play pool with him, and how Cara watched us for a while before going out back with Jessica. I convey how we didn't realize the strength of the punch before drinking way too much because we both started having trouble talking and walking.

I describe how Cara fell into the pool and that I was alerted by Mark that she had—how Jessica helped Cara change into a robe so her clothes could dry. I recount that Jessica helped Cara into the bed in Mark's brother's empty bedroom to sleep off the effects of the alcohol and that Mark helped me to the bed.

I explain that my last conscious memory of that night was falling asleep while kissing Cara who was lying beside me on the bed. I add that she was lying on the floor when I woke up six hours later.

My dad's head swivels sideways to look at me when I say this part.

I describe waking up with a horrible hangover and then waking up Cara; how we went out for breakfast and drove around for a long time before going back to Mark's to drop off Cara so she could help clean up.

I look up and say, "Then I went home. That's pretty much it."

The detective turns off the recording and smiles politely. "Okay, thank you, Jamie. I'm going to run this through transcription, print it, and let you look it over and sign it."

"Yes, sir," I say, looking quizzically over at Dad.

"Is he free to go?" Dad asks.

"Yes, of course, he always was. I'll go get this printed."

He's gone for a small eternity, and we sit in silence, both still too afraid to voice our fears. I imagine him coming back in and placing me in handcuffs to lead me to a cell. The adrenaline hums through my veins making it hard to sit still. I watch my knee vibrate above my bouncing heel.

When the detective returns, he hands me the statement. I read over it and sign it.

He then says, "I want to further explain to you both, and also to Cara, about the allegations, the evidence, and exactly what we are doing to help prosecute this case. She just finished up her statement, too. The best way to do this is to actually show you, rather than tell you. If you both would follow me into the video conferencing room..."

My heart beats out an irregular rhythm of fear. Show us? What does this mean? Was something captured on video that night we didn't know about? I think about all the security cameras in and around our own house.

When we enter the room, Cara and her dad are sitting at a long table facing a television mounted on the wall. My dad sits down next to Chris, and they both exchange puzzled looks. Cara's head is down, but I'm sure she saw me come in through her peripheral vision. I sit next to Dad, willing Cara to look over at me, but she doesn't.

Detective Cook says to us all, "After taking Jamie's statement and Officer Burgess taking Cara's statement," he nods over to a female officer sitting at a computer whom I presume to be Officer Burgess, "we want to give you all the same information at the same time and answer any questions you might have."

He turns on the TV, and when Officer Burgess clicks the computer mouse, a video of an interview begins playing.

Detective: *I am Investigative Officer Jon T. Cook of the Fort Worth PD. Let it be known this is a sworn video statement of an eyewitness in the criminal investigation of an alleged crime that took place seven months ago on the evening of October thirty-first. For the record, please state your full name.*

Jessica: *Jessica Renae Ramos.*

I look up and over at Cara, and she looks back at me now, totally baffled. Why the hell is Jessica giving a statement against me? I thought Jessica was my friend, Cara's expression reads. Betrayal doesn't even come close to the feeling I know we're both experiencing.

Detective: *Let's start with the night in question that this alleged crime took place. You were at the party where this occurred, correct?*

Jessica: *Yes, sir.*

Detective: *Can you please state the date and location—time if you remember?*

Jessica: *It was Halloween night, uh, October thirty-first. The party was held at Mark Shelton's house. It started at around 8:00 p.m. that evening. Sorry, I don't have his house address memorized.*

Detective: *That's okay, we've got that. Go ahead and describe the events leading up to the incident as you can best recall, and then we will pick up where you left off in your description of your conversation with the accused.*

Conversation with the accused... I've had lots of conversations with Jessica. What conversation are they talking about? The one we had on November 1, the morning Cara and I returned to Mark's to apologize for what happened at the party? I rack my brain trying to remember conversations I had with Jessica where I said something that might have incriminated myself.

Jessica: *Okay, well, everything was going well at the party. Everyone seemed to be getting along fine. We were eating, drinking, dancing, those kinds of things.*

Detective: *When you say drinking, Ms. Ramos, what were you all drinking at the party?*

Jessica: *Mostly beer, some bottles of water were available, and a fruit punch had hard liquor mixed in with it.*

Detective: *Do you know exactly what type of hard liquor it was?*

Jessica: *No, I don't know exactly, but almost everyone there was drinking it.*

Detective: *All right, go on.*

Jessica: *Like I said, everything was going fine. We were all a little tipsy, but no one was too bad... until later. Eric Baines asked Jamie Gallagher to play pool. Cara Dawson and I watched for a while, and then I took Cara out to the pool area with me.*

Detective: *Previously, you told us this is where, how did you put it, things started going downhill?*

Jessica: *Yes. Cara was obviously impaired, staggering as she walked, and then she fell into the pool. Mark Shelton and I grabbed her arms and pulled her out, but she clearly seemed drunk. Jamie came out of the house then, and he tried to help with Cara, but he was also having a lot of trouble walking and talking.*

I took Cara into the bathroom and helped her out of her wet clothes into a robe. Jamie needed help to walk, so Mark helped him. We led them to Mark's brother's room to lie down for a while and try to sleep it off.

Detective: *All right, so you said you talked to the accused last night and learned quite a few new facts about what went on* *behind the scenes at this party on October thirty-first, is that correct?*

I try to remember what I said to Jessica last night at graduation. *"Hi, how's it going?" "What is everyone doing after graduation tonight?"* That is hardly a conversation and definitely not anything about Mark's party. What the hell is she talking about?

Jessica: *Yes, last night there was a house party at Ashley Barrio's, and Eric Baines, well, he was pretty drunk and since my boyfriend had to leave early, Eric asked me to go talk with him out on the upstairs balcony where we could be alone. It seemed like something was bothering him and he needed to talk, so I went with him. And this is where Eric, in his drunken state, poured out his confession to me of what he did that night at the Halloween party.*

The accused? Eric Baines is the accused, not me? *Confession of what he did?* My mind and heart are in a race against each other. Forget waiting for paternity test results. Are we about to find out Eric assaulted Cara? I glance over at her. She is still watching Jessica on the TV, but her face has lost all color, as I'm sure mine has.

Jessica: *He seemed to only want to ask me about Jamie and Cara at first. He was drunk and angry and asked me where the freak the prince and princess were tonight, uh, meaning Jamie and Cara... though he used the worse word for "freak." When I told him I didn't know, he went on a rant about hating Jamie, how he wanted to get back at him for stealing Cara from him and* embarrassing him in the hallway at school one day. I don't know why he would tell me all this and think I wouldn't tell someone. Cara is one of my best friends, but I guess he was just too drunk to think about that or care.

He explained his plan to get back at Jamie on Halloween night and win Cara back. When I found out late last night, after Eric's confession, that Cara had a baby, I knew I had to call the police to tell them what Eric did to them. It's Eric's fault that it happened, that, uh, Cara had a baby.

Detective: *Okay, let's back up to exactly what Eric confessed to doing the night of the Halloween party.*

Jessica: *He said he put GHB in Jamie's drink he handed him when he asked Jamie to play pool, and he laughed about doing it. His plan was to get Jamie out of the picture, make it look like Jamie was drunk so he would go to sleep, pass out, or whatever, and then Eric could be with Cara... I guess to make his move on her. But Eric's plan backfired when Jamie didn't drink the entire drink.*

I remember all this because when Cara saw that Jamie was slurring while they were playing pool, she took the cup from him and drank the rest. That's when we went outside and she began staggering and stumbled into the pool. A couple of us had said that night that it didn't seem like Jamie and Cara drank any more than the rest of us.

After Jamie started feeling drunk, he asked Mark what was so strong in the punch, but we had all been drinking it and no one else was drunk like Jamie and Cara were. I now know it was because they were drugged. I researched the drug and learned it's used as a date rape drug to make people do what they wouldn't normally do, and it's an amnesiac, which means people who are using it don't remember what they did. So I realized it caused Jamie and Cara to... well, not know or remember what they did that night. Jamie and Cara are in love. I don't think Jamie should be in any trouble for what happened. I know Cara would have told me, and I know Jamie would have told Cara, if either knew something like that happened between them.

Detective: *No, you're correct, it would not be considered assault if there was a sexual act between Jamie and Cara; however, if Eric took advantage of the situation—obviously no consent from Cara—and it can be proven, he will be charged.*

And we all know, damn it, the only way it could be proven is if the paternity test comes back negative for me as the father, and then a DNA test would have to be ordered. I can't believe this is happening. What must Cara be thinking? She still won't look at me.

Jessica: *I asked Eric where he got that kind of drug and he gave me the website name of some type of black-market drug company. When he told me he had it hidden in the glove compartment of his car, that's when I snuck from the party later and videoed myself walking to his car and finding it. It's the little bottle I brought here this morning. And I found one of Cara's gloves from her costume laying in there, too. I don't know why he had that.*

What the hell? *So Eric drugged us and also had one of Cara's gloves?* I'm beyond weirded out and have to think to even breathe at this point. All I can think about is what I wouldn't give to be in a room alone with that sicko right now.

Jessica: *Eric should pay for what he did to them. He could have killed them. I hate to think what would have happened to Jamie or Cara if one of them had gulped down that whole drink on top of the alcohol they had already consumed. It was bad enough with each of them only having a part of the drink.*

Detective: *Thank you for coming forward with this information, Ms. Ramos. This concludes Jessica Renae Ramos's sworn witness statement. For the record, we do plan to release this information to the district attorney's office and do our part here in the Fort Worth PD to get a conviction on the charges we're filing against Mr. Baines.*

The detective shuts off the television and addresses us, "As I said, we do plan to send this case to the DA, even if you all decide not to press charges. This is a serious crime that could have ended tragically. We are available to answer any questions you might have."

Chris speaks first. He puts his arm around Cara and brings her shoulder into his in a comforting side-hug. I should be the one sitting beside her comforting her. My hands and arms ache not to be able to go to her and hold her, but she said she wanted me to leave her alone, and that's what I'm doing—giving her space.

Though it's killing me.

"This explains a lot," Chris says and looks over at me.

We all have some measure of relief in our eyes, knowing I am not here to be accused of rape like I'm sure we all expected.

I nod, still too stunned to speak.

My dad says, "It sure does. What will happen to Eric, Detective?"

"We have a judge signing a warrant for his arrest now. Several charges are possible. Possession of a controlled substance and infliction of bodily harm through gross negligence for sure, or we might be able to upgrade that to second-degree assault. Rape on the possibility he went that far, though we have no proof of that, yet."

Cara drops her head, and more than ever, I want to go to her.

The detective continues, "We are questioning a lot of kids who were at that Halloween party and other parties Mr. Baines has been to. Someone who purchases and knows how to use Rohypnol or GHB on someone usually has very evil motives and has used it before, and/or intends to use it again. We can never stress enough how both kids and adults should never take an open drink from someone or turn their heads from their drink even for a minute.

"We are also testing the contents of a drink Jessica saved last night that she said Mr. Baines gave her when they went to talk but that she didn't drink. Since she brought the drug she found in his car to us and had it in her possession, we wouldn't be able to charge Mr. Baines for that one. If it tests positive, we all can more than assume it was because Eric added the drug to the drink, not Jessica."

Chris shakes his head over and over and asks, "So do you suppose that if Cara had not accidentally consumed some of that drink, Eric would have tried to give her the drug anyway when he got her alone, away from Jamie? You think that was his plan?"

"Who's to say?" the disgust clear in the detective's voice, "but based on what he did and his knowledge of this drug, my guess would be yes. Why wouldn't he give it to her, make her a little more pliable, a little more receptive to his advances? An easy way for a guy with evil intent to create cause for the boyfriend to leave her."

"You all are talking about me as though I'm not here," Cara says loudly, and all eyes dart to her. "Can I talk to Eric myself after you bring him in? Instead of all this speculation, I want to hear from him, hear what *he* has to say about all this."

Her expression is remote, the same invisible wall stands intact, put firmly in place when she discovered the paternity test. However, behind that wall is pain—sheer, raw pain with which Cara is not dealing well. I know her well enough to see the wall about to crumble.

My jaw tightens and my face grows hot with the thought of her talking to Eric, especially now that we know just how malicious he is. I don't want Cara anywhere near that psycho.

The detective answers Cara's question, "We can arrange a meeting with the offender if that's what you decide to do, although it will be up to him whether or not he agrees to it." He adds, "In the meantime, I will keep you all informed and updated on the case. Here's my card." He pulls a small stack of business cards from his wallet and hands one to each of us. "Call me any time with concerns or questions."

Everyone stands to make their way from the small conference room. My dad and I begin to walk toward the door of the room, and I assume Cara is following Chris out as well. But when I turn to glance back, Cara is still sitting in the chair, head in her hands, shoulders shaking.

It crushes me to see her silently crying... Alone.

"Cara?" is all I can croak out through my own tightening throat.

She looks up and sees me in the doorway, leaves her chair, and runs straight into my arms. She whispers onto my neck, "Oh, God, don't leave me, Jamie, please don't leave me."

Her voice sounds desperate, conjuring an echo of a memory of that Halloween night, lying in bed with her while she chanted the same words through her fear of me leaving her alone in that dark bedroom.

"Never," I whisper back, holding her close, and kissing her temple, "never, baby."

Her arms wrap completely around me, crossed at the back of my neck. She's holding on for dear life as though I am dangling from a rope while being airlifted with her from a raging river. Both of her palms are resting on her arms, and I turn my head enough to see her left hand.

She is wearing her promise ring.

Cara

Jamie's arms wrapped around me are a shield of solace and security. Why I ever thought my heart would be safer if I took it back from him, I don't know. He's the stabilizer and rudder of this wayward ship I'm trying so desperately to navigate. I can't steer it alone. I just can't.

"I'm so sorry. I lied to you, Jamie; I never wanted you to go. I want to stay with you," I whimper through my tears into his neck, enjoying his strength and the familiar comfort of his clean scent.

"That's all I've ever wanted, Cara. It's been killing me to stay away from you. I rode with Dad, but I'll have him drop us off at home to get my truck. Here, babe." Jamie spots a box of tissues on a side table and hands me one. "This has all been too much for you, for everyone."

"These are tears for you and what *you* have gone through. They're mostly tears of relief. I'm so relieved that today wasn't about you being accused and arrested for something you didn't do. I was terrified of that for you. But Eric drugging us?"

I'd like to say more, but we're still standing in the doorway of the conference room. "I'm ready to get out of here." I exhale heavily, suddenly very weary.

I look over to see my dad and Brent talking in the hallway, both of them smiling slightly as though at least some of the weight they've been carrying has been lifted. Since our families spent Christmas together and we went on our subsequent outing to the football game, they have become fast friends. We are all sharing the same relief that Jamie isn't in any trouble.

Hope has once again declared us friends.

"Let's tell them we're ready to go. I'm having Christopher withdrawals, and we have a lot to talk about, some catching up to do," Jamie says.

Jamie climbs into the backseat with me as though Brent is our chauffeur and laces his fingers with mine. The connection is pure relief. He strokes his thumb lightly over mine the way he does when he holds my hand, making me feel halfway complete again.

Jamie says, "I knew there was something creepy about Eric from day one, the way he watched us walk out into the courtyard at lunch the day after I met you, Cara. Then his crazy possessiveness over you for something that never existed between the two of you. Hell, he almost had *me* convinced there was. I had no idea he would turn out to be such a sick son of a bitch." Jamie checks his language, looking sheepish. "Sorry, Dad."

"Where that guy is concerned, you can use any cuss word you want, and you won't hear a complaint from me. I kept worrying they would bring him through those doors while we were still there. They'd have had to wipe him up off the floor, and I can't say who out of the four of us there today would've thrown the first punch." Brent releases a mirthless laugh.

"Oh, I guaran-damn-tee it would have been me," Jamie concedes. "Consequences be damned, I've wanted to smash his face in since before any of this happened. Dad, I didn't tell you, but Cara knows that we're waiting on the results of paternity testing."

Brent looks into the rearview mirror at me. "You do? I'm so sorry. The police would be ordering one now if we hadn't already. It's not fair that it has to even be considered. Eric is going to be spending some time behind bars for what we know he's already done."

I stay quiet, still not allowing myself to fully open up to all the possibilities negative test results would bring. Whenever the thought of being assaulted enters my mind, I mentally cover it with noise-canceling headphones and force other thoughts to drown them out. Being tied to Eric and his family is something I can't fathom.

I say only, "I can't believe he drugged us and betrayed me like he has when I believed we were such good friends. So much about that night makes sense now."

"Explains why we blacked out." Jamie's jaw, with its dark, unshaven scruff, tics, and I follow the movement of his throat. It's as though he's also trying to swallow this new information and having as much trouble as I am. "All this time, we thought

Mark had spiked that punch. No wonder no one else was falling-down drunk. We're lucky it didn't do any real damage." He makes a disgusted sound through his teeth and looks out the car window with a hard look on his face.

I'm secretly glad we didn't see Eric. Jamie might have really gotten arrested today if he'd gotten his hands on him.

"Right?" I agree with Jamie, "and to think he might have even tried to use it on Jessica." I shake my head, still not able to fully believe it.

"Probably feels it's justified in his sick head. Since Jessica rejected him for Mark a few months back, she and Mark both should've been watching their backs, especially if he was pulling that you've-stolen-my-girl bullshit," Jamie spits out with no apology for the cussing this time.

We pull through the gate to Jamie's house, and I ask, "Can I go in and see Susan before we head to the hospital?" I realize how much I want to see her and hug her... how much I *love* her.

"She's not here," Brent replies. "She and Amber went shopping after taking Megan to the airport. She also let me know in the text that we're all going up to see Christopher tonight or in the morning if that works?"

My heart sinks a little at not being able to see her, but I say, "Of course. He's being treated for jaundice right now."

So no one will be shocked when they see him, I describe his little eye protection and the lights he must stay under.

The news puts an anguished look on Jamie's face, but he doesn't say much except, "I need to get there to see him."

As soon as we climb into Jamie's truck and head toward the hospital, he admonishes me, "You didn't think I would want to know about a change in Christopher's condition, Cara? It's not like I would be able to know otherwise since you banished me for two days."

He's upset, and I'm caught off guard. I stammer, "No, I mean, yes, I... I'm sorry. I was not in a good place. I should have called—"

Jamie's face turns from hard to compassionate in an instant, "No, no, I'm sorry. I'm projecting my worry for Christopher onto you." He reaches over and squeezes my arm.

I decide to shake off his accusation and say, "Unfortunately, Christopher will have some good days and not-so-good days. Jaundice in newborns is common, especially in preemies. He's doing extremely well otherwise."

"And I'm thankful, trust me. But from now on, we share everything," he repeats with emphasis, "*everything*. No more of me keeping things from you in an effort to protect you, or you keeping things from me because you're pissed off, and vice-versa, okay?"

"I promise," I say, appreciating his take-charge attitude. I find it incredibly attractive and what I need right now during this emotional bankruptcy I've been experiencing.

"So do I," he says sternly. "Speaking of promises, I first noticed you had your promise ring back on when we hugged at the police station."

"Yes," I say, admiring it in the sunlight coming in through the truck window.

"I thought maybe it was symbolic," Jamie's lips tighten, and he sighs sadly, "like you had changed your mind about us being forever, then changed it back today and put the ring back on."

I think, not for the first time, how perceptive Jamie is. "Maybe that was part of it," I say, chagrined. "Wearing the ring today was definitely a reflection of how I was feeling about you, about us. I thought a lot about how I pushed you away, and it was unfair. I had a pretty bad pity party afterward, but I was missing you terribly. I'm really sorry."

Jamie's eyes seem to say, *I'm glad you finally came to your senses.* "I missed you so bad it physically hurt, but I understood you needed time to work out some things. What about your purity ring?" he asks.

My left hand automatically flits down to fiddle with my purity ring that is no longer there, and I look up at Jamie as though it not being there startles me.

He leans over, amused, and says, "You know you always used to do that when we, uh, you know?"

"What?" I ask.

"Back before we got more disciplined—while we were trying to cool off after we would get close." He gives me a handsome side-eye look, a feather teasing my heart.

"Well, in good conscience, I can't wear it anymore, can I? I'm definitely not a virgin any longer," I say with finality—an oversized period at the end of my sentence.

We pull into the entrance of the hospital.

"Do you want me to drop you off at the lobby?" Jamie asks.

"No, I can walk. It's been four days, and I'm fine. I want to walk with you."

Jamie parks and cuts the engine. As soon as he does, I already miss the air conditioner. It's a blistering Texas day, and it won't officially be summer for several more days.

Jamie asks, "Will you do something for me? When we get to the room, if it's still important to you, will you put the purity ring back on your finger? As far as I'm concerned, it's still yours to wear if you want. Intent has everything to do with our unique circumstances. That, and not being able to remember a damn thing. It's not fair; it doesn't count, especially if, if..." The unfinished sentence dangles over us like a menacing rain cloud, the implication clear.

"It's the way I was raised, Jamie. I thought I truly wanted to give myself fully only to the man I married *after* we were married, but when I met you... I've been so confused about it. I guess my intentions were good, anyway." I pause in thought for a beat. "But *you* really might still be a true virgin."

He doesn't say anything at first and then, "I sure as hell don't want to be," and we both understand too well the implications if he learns he is.

He comes around to open my door for me. I know by now to stay put and wait for him to open it. It's important to him, and it's, well... it's sweet. I allow him to help me from the truck, although I don't need it, and he takes my hand in his.

Jamie finally speaks again as we walk, "I'm so ready to get the effing test results back. You do realize, we will probably know by this time tomorrow?"

My heart skips a few anxious beats. If there's ever been anything in my life I have not wanted to face more, it's the dreaded paternity test result—if it's negative. Yet if there's ever been anything I would be happier about right now than a positive result, I can't name it.

"I'll deal with whatever we find out when the time comes," I say. *How many times can I actually die again after I've already been killed?*

Jamie stops and faces me just inside the lobby of the hospital. "*We* will deal with it together. If you put that damn impenetrable wall back up between us again, I swear—"

"Don't get your feathers ruffled; I won't." I pause. "I'll try not to."

Softly, he says, "Look at me, Cara."

I look up into his ocean blue gaze that has the power to hypnotize me and allow it to now.

"You won't," he says fiercely.

I nod, and we continue walking to the elevators. Jamie hits the button for *up* and says, "Man, especially after thinking I might get arrested today, I can't wait to see Christopher and hold him."

"And I can't wait to get to the breast pump." I grin as Jamie looks down at my breasts, lingering there. His eyes go dark as though he's remembering touching me, making me flush.

He then meets my eyes. "Thank you," he says, kissing me quickly on the mouth.

"For what?" I ask.

"Doing what it takes to give our baby the best, and for being an amazing mom already."

His compliment surges through me like a shot of good espresso, and then is abruptly squelched by the intrusive buzz-kill. *Would you have still said that if you knew the baby was Eric's biological child?*

Jamie and I scrub in, and while we both go straight to Christopher's incubator, my breasts are aching to be relieved. Since Jamie wants to hold Christopher, and the nurse is at her computer typing, I say, "I'll leave him to you, Daddy," and nestle in the little nursing alcove. I pull the privacy curtain and get started.

"Keep that breast milk coming, Momma," the nurse calls out. "I weighed Little Guy earlier, and he is at three pounds, eleven ounces. That's wonderful, considering he lost a couple of ounces the first day or two."

Three ounces above Christopher's birth weight doesn't seem like a lot to me, but I'll take every little victory I can get. Jamie is about to lift Christopher from his isolette, when he says, "Uh oh, some of that weight might need to be deducted after I change this diaper."

"Give me a few more minutes, and I'll change him," I tell him.

"No, no, I've got it. I've watched you and the nurses do it and heard a nurse explain the instructions and precautions. It's about time I change my own son's poopy diaper."

I peek around the curtain. Watching this 6'3" young man with large, clumsy fingers struggle to change his preemie son's diaper is almost as cute as Christopher himself.

When Jamie is finished, he asks the nurse, "Can I take off his little blinders while I hold him, and I'll put them back on before he goes back under the light?"

The nurse steps over to help Jamie take off the eye protection and show him how to put it back on correctly. My heart swells, and I make a mental note to tell him again when we're alone what a wonderful dad he has already proven to be.

Jamie is humming to Christopher, who is lying peaceably in the center of his chest. I imagine my own head lying there and the deep rumble of Jamie's voice. I think of the comforting feeling it has given me before and is now giving to our son. I feel as though the sun is once again shining, at least somewhat, into my life.

When I finish pumping my breast milk, label it with the date, and put it in the refrigerator drawer, I check my phone. It's been turned on silent, and I have several missed calls and texts from Jessica.

"I'm going to give Jessica a call," I say, and stay in the little nursing alcove to dial her.

"Cara!" Jessica answers on the first ring.

"Yeah, it's me," I say without inflection.

"Oh my gosh, how are you? How could you not have told me you had a freakin' baby?!" Jessica exclaims loudly without preamble, and I have to pull the phone away from my ear.

"I'm okay, Jess." My voice sounds tired to my own ears. "You know the circumstances, and now you know I didn't know I was pregnant, didn't remember anything about Halloween night after Eric drugged us. We just returned from the police station and watched your testimony. How did you find out about the baby, anyway?"

"I found out at Ashley's party from Madison. Her mom works at the hospital, and one of the nurses told her. She told Madison, who told me. How is the baby? Is it a boy or a girl? Madison didn't know."

Madison's mom or the nurse who told her could be in some big trouble for violating patient confidentiality laws. I should probably be upset, but it's actually a relief that I no longer have to be the one to break the news.

"It's a boy. He's doing great, considering how early and small he is. He's had some blood sugar and jaundice problems, but he's perfect. He has to stay on oxygen and has a feeding tube for now. His name is Christopher Brent, named after my dad and Jamie's dad." I summarize my son's entire life as though having a premature baby is something I do every day.

"Cara, how are you even coping with all this? Can I come to the hospital to see you and the baby?"

How am *I coping with this? Well? Not well? Somewhere in between?* I shrug off that particular question.

"I would love that. I'll add you to our NICU visitors list. I need to thank you in person for doing the right thing and telling the police what Eric confessed to you. If he hadn't confessed, and if you hadn't come forward, we would be none the wiser—that asshole," I say with disgust.

"That, he is! Oh, but Mark texted me from his car, right after he walked out of the police station, and he saw two cops taking Eric in handcuffs through the side entrance. He's so busted!"

My shoulders slump forward in relief at the news, and I place my hand over the phone to tell Jamie. He purses his lips tightly, closes his eyes, and lets out a heavy breath toward the ceiling.

"Thank God," I say. "Like you said in your statement, he deserves to be punished for what he's done. Big time."

I rethink going to see Eric. Maybe I should wait until we receive the paternity results and go from there. Of course, I only knew the side of Eric he chose to reveal to me, and I don't know if I could bear to look into his deceptive eyes.

"Mark would be kicking Eric's ass if Eric wasn't in jail. Honestly, I knew he had a bit of an eccentric, jealous side, but I never imagined he would stoop to the evil he has. I shudder to think that he was trying to drug me and have his way with me last night, ewwww!" Jessica sounds like a kid who just picked up a wriggling worm.

"Hey, Jess, I need to ask you something. Try to remember. Did you check on Jamie and me throughout the six hours we were passed out in that room? Do you think it's possible Eric could have snuck in there and, and, well, you know?"

"Oh, my freakin' word. I don't want to even think he would have gone in there and had his way with you while Jamie was in there. I know it's possible because the police brought that up with me, but man, would he have done that?" Jessica stops and starts as though the realization dawns on her. "He would do something like that, wouldn't he? Wasn't that his plan? That would mean Christopher is Eric's baby, not Jamie's?"

"Yes, well, no; I mean, we hope and pray that didn't happen, but unfortunately, it's a real possibility," I say. "We're waiting on the results of a paternity test."

"How can you be so calm?" Jessica asks in a whispered gasp.

"We've had some time to process this over the last few days. After what happened to me Monday morning, nothing is a huge shock anymore."

"I'm going to be honest with you, and I feel bad about this now, but I never checked on you two. Mark probably did, though. We can ask him. I intended to check on you, but then just got so busy with the party and... I'm sorry, Cara."

I feel darkness on stealthy little paws try to creep back into my brain again, and I have to fight the urge to let it wash over me like I allowed it to last night.

"No, it's okay. I mean, we were the ultimate party poopers, right? Out of sight, out of mind, I guess, when you're at a party trying to have fun. No matter the outcome, I don't want you to feel like it's your fault. You helped me that night and again today," I say.

Jessica rushes to add, "However, still being transparent here, there was a long stretch of time after you and Jamie crashed that I remember Mark and I couldn't find Eric."

Jamie

When I wake up, two things hit my consciousness like fists against the center of my chest: Yesterday we were let in on Eric's evil schemes and he was arrested. And today is the day we will most likely find out if Eric did something unthinkable to Cara and if Christopher is my biological son.

Cara is still sleeping beside me, and I lie here trying not to stir so she can continue to sleep. Her breaths flow through her pretty pink mouth in tiny puffs. I think how I would love to have a daughter with Cara someday who looks just like her, so lovely and perfect.

What is that Robert Browning poem I've read in English class? Cara would know the whole thing. *"God's in His heaven—All's right with the world!"* Right now, that's how I feel being with Cara and my son in the same room together again, in our little "right" world, even with all its peripheral messes.

Lying here beside Cara, I've thought about the day ahead and have come up with a couple of plans as to how I want things to go down if we get the test results back. I'll share them with Cara later.

I would lie here longer with her and let her sleep, but there are wet spots forming on the front of her—leaking out from under her nightshirt and growing larger each second, like two spilled inkblots.

"Cara," I whisper gently.

"Hmm?" She stirs.

"Hey, babe, I thought you would want to know, you're leaking."

Her eyes open wide. She looks down and forms the word "Oh" with her mouth before her lips quirk upward in a faint smile.

She sits up, brushing the hair from her face, looking adorable. "I need to pump," she rasps softly.

"What can I do to help?" I look over and see a nurse at the computer. "I'll check on Christopher while you clean up and use the pump. I'll take a shower and get dressed after you're done; sound good?"

"It does, but I need coffee. I'm allowed a couple of cups a day while nursing, but I want just one."

"Okay then, I'll shower and get dressed real quick and go down to the cafeteria to get us coffee and something to eat. Give me five minutes in the bathroom."

"Does that mean you'll keep your scruff?" she whispers.

"Do you like my scruff?" I ask, rubbing a hand along my sandpapered jaw.

"Do I like it? No," she deadpans.

I start to tell her it will take longer if I have to shave when she says, "I love it. Your morning look is really sexy, Jamie."

Cara looks away, as though she's embarrassed herself, but it puts a grin on my face. Even after all this time, she still has a tendency to be a little shy with me. I find it incredibly endearing and kiss her quickly on her cheek.

"Then I'll keep it today... only so I can get your coffee back up to you faster." I wink.

"Thanks. I would hug you," Cara looks down and laughs, "but I don't want to get you wet."

When I finish showering, Cara has the breast pump ready and is retrieving the clothes she'll wear for the day from the small bureau in the corner.

"I'll be back in about fifteen minutes," I say, pulling on my running shoes.

Cara walks over to me and runs her fingers through my still-damp hair and gives me a quick kiss. "I like your just-showered look, too," she flirts.

Down in the hospital cafeteria, I order two omelets at the counter where food is freshly prepared. I pour two cups of coffee and put them in a drink holder. While I wait at a small table for our breakfast, I pull up my email and check to see if the paternity test results are posted yet.

Each time I check, which has been more times than I care to tell Cara, my heart races, and my palms grow sweaty.

Conceivably, the report could have been posted yesterday, but no such luck, and it's still not posted this morning.

When I return to the room, Cara's hair is damp, and she has put on a little makeup, which she doesn't need in order to look her beautiful self, but she looks fresh. The little nursing privacy curtain is not pulled, so I try not to look at her and, instead, go straight to the small table to set down the food.

"Sorry that it took so long, but I had fresh omelets cooked for us."

"Nice. I can smell them, yum!"

"Want me to bring you your coffee?" I ask without looking directly over at her.

"Just a second," she says as she fiddles with the pump. "I pumped some before I got in the shower but realized I had more." She chuckles.

I stay busy taking the food from the bag. Out of the corner of my eye, I can see when she's finished and has pulled her clean shirt back down.

I can't help but think how ridiculous it is that we have a son together, yet I feel I have to avert my eyes when she uses the breast pump. I never told her I've already kind of seen her before—when she was lying on the floor with her robe open on Halloween night, although it was dark and I quickly closed it for her. *But, damn, she's beautiful.*

Soon she will nurse Christopher directly at her breast. How can I be a part of that experience if Cara is so private? I'm going to have a heart-to-heart with her about this and see how she feels because I don't know if I'm setting these boundaries or she is.

I wait until she's finished eating and we're sipping our coffee to bring up that I checked my email but that the paternity report hasn't been posted yet.

"When it is, I want you and me to open it and read it together, whether that's today or whenever it posts, okay?"

She nods, but the thought of reading the results causes her to fidget, so I change the subject. "You look thinner. Are you eating enough with all the breastfeeding, or I should say breast *pumping* you've been doing? You haven't really been eating much." She ate only half her omelet.

"Although he's small, I did have a whole baby a few days ago," she laughs, "and even though I'm having some stress IBS symptoms, I'm not feeling as bloated anymore." She looks down at her chest. "Well, maybe some in the boob department."

"Speaking of which," I say as Cara lowers her chin and lifts her brows, curious as to what I might have to say about her breasts, "I have a weird request."

"What kind of request? About my boobs?" She grins.

"I know it's still a way off, but when it happens for the first time, I want to watch you feed our son, you know, nurse him. Will that embarrass you at all?" I hurry to include, "Because if it would, I'll understand."

I'm trying hard to keep my thoughts about her breasts strictly in the realm of feeding our son, but I'm reminded of how she felt under my palms, how that night and so many other times, I've wanted to be the one to put my mouth... *Stop, Jamie,* I scold myself and continue, "I want to be there for all of his firsts, to be a part of them."

"And I love that about you. Yes, of course, you can. Those are things parents should share together. The only weird thing is that we seem to be doing things kind of backward."

"What do you mean?" I ask, taking a sip of coffee.

"Isn't it normally boy sees girl and vice-versa, boy and girl like what they see, so boy and girl have sex? Everything with us is backward is all." She shrugs and takes a drink of her own coffee.

I can't help but laugh. "You're right. Our situation is certainly unique, to say the least. My mom said she nursed all of us, though, and that she wants to help you any way she can. I heard the nurse tell you how difficult it will be at first, and I've thought a lot about how it must feel for a woman to have a baby and not have her mom to help her and answer personal questions."

I see the sadness appear in Cara's eyes, and I hurt for her. I knew she was strong as soon as I met her, and I can't imagine anyone else going through all she has and coming out on the other side the way Cara has.

"The nurses have been helpful, but when the time comes to actually nurse, I'll probably need your mom's support and help. She's like a mother to me." Cara sighs wistfully. "She and your dad have helped create the good man you are. I wanted to tell you again last night, while you changed Christopher, how incredible you're being. It's not just the acts you do, but the way you love him, worry about him, and want to be a part of his care... even though it's all so new and scary for both of us. Man, how did I get so lucky?"

"I ask myself that same question constantly—how did Cara get so lucky?"

"Smooth," she says, playfully punching my arm.

Cara and I decide to spend the day out to keep our minds on other things besides the dreaded test results. We stop by my house to visit with Mom and Dad. We spend a lot of time researching the top-rated car seats to bring Christopher home in when it's time, and Cara orders some preemie onesies and socks online for him.

Afterward, we sit outside by the pool, dangling our feet in the cool water and enjoying the June sun until Cara has to get back to the hospital to use the breast pump.

I check my email while she's pumping, and it's there. The report is sitting in my inbox holding answers, whether good or bad, that will determine the trajectory of our future. My hands begin to tremble, and I try to calm down and prepare what I have planned to say. I wait for Cara to finish and for the nurse checking on Christopher to complete her report on the computer and leave.

"Cara," I say when we're alone. Her head snaps up because she recognizes something different in my tone. I hold up my phone with my email account opened, and all color drains from her face. Her eyes have grown wide in dread. "Before we open this, bear with me, I need to make a short speech."

We both instinctively move to the sofa to sit as though our legs would collapse under us otherwise.

"Jamie, this is not the time to be making speeches. I can't handle the suspense. Please just open it, and let's get this over with." She looks over at my phone, squinting to see the screen.

"I will, but give me two minutes. I wouldn't ask at a time like this unless it was important."

Relenting, she lets loose an exasperated sigh and holds her palms out in surrender. "You've got the floor, but hurry."

"Okay," I clear my throat and swallow the large lump lodged there, "as I've told you before, the results of this test won't change the fact that I am Christopher's father, will raise him with you, and will love him exactly the same, period. Will you promise me that no matter the results, from this day forward, you will never *EVER* question that?" I choke back tears.

Cara's own eyes cloud over, and she nods. I sense she truly means it, so I forge ahead.

"There is something very important that I need to ask you. You can take as long as you need to answer it, but there's a condition. If the answer to my question is no, we look at these results and move forward. If the answer is yes, we look at the results and move forward. *But,* we do not look at the results without an answer first. I have to have a solid answer. The results can wait a few days until you're sure, either way, agree?"

"It depends; I need at least a hint of what the question is first," she says, her face etched with uncertainty.

"No, that's not how it works. Please, trust me. This is important."

She looks at me as though I've just yelled up to her from the bottom of a mountain to jump, that I'll be sure to catch her. She hesitates, then exhales a pent-up breath, "I do trust you; you know I do. Let's hear it."

I go hot all over and become more nervous than a California surfer about to ride the most epic wave of his career.

"I'm asking you to marry me. Not in a year, not even in a few months. I mean now, like as soon as we can get our license and get to the courthouse. We can have a big ceremony and celebration later; that's not what I'm talking about here. But the actual act of legally becoming husband and wife now. We don't *have* to, of course, I know that, but I also know both of us, and marriage fits us."

Cara eyes me warily, but she's listening.

"You and I both know we are meant to be together, so why not now? This is what I want regardless of the outcome of the test. I want to prove it to you by asking you now, before we know the results, okay?"

Conflicted emotions flit and change shape across Cara's face like the twist of a kaleidoscope—fear, doubt, restlessness, worry—all reflected into my own heart through her gaze. My heart hammers in my chest, waiting for her to turn me down, or to hear a "Not now, Jamie, maybe in the future."

Then almost imperceptibly, a light begins to shine through the uncertainty in Cara's eyes. It takes only an instant for me to recognize that light—*hope*. *Yes!* For a few beats, hope stands alone until *trust* reluctantly raises its head as if to try out the possibility of this happening, of this actually working out.

And finally, all the emotions swirl together behind Cara's eyes and give birth to belief. I recognize it as soon as it happens.

Silence hangs in the space between us until she says breathlessly, "I can't believe this is happening, but yes, yes, I'll marry you no matter the results. I love you, Jamie, and I make a commitment to you right now that I won't change my mind, no matter the test result."

I move to take her in my arms, and she adds, "But you can't either. If you mean it now, you have to mean it forever."

"Absolutely, and although this isn't the type of proposal you've probably dreamed of, it's *our* proposal, and it will always be our special story. I took your promise ring from the little dish you had it in, so here goes." I dig inside my pocket and take her left hand, placing the ring there. "This will have to do until I can get you a real ring."

"This ring is sufficient. I love this ring."

"I want to buy you an engagement ring, and you can wear this one on the other hand when you lose the purity ring. It will be a while before we can be together intimately, even after we're married, and I'm okay with that. I'll wait for as long as it takes knowing the sweet carrot dangling from the end of that stick. Christopher will be able to come home with us about that same time, and I want to take you on a honeymoon we will never forget—pun intended." I smile as much as I can at a time like this.

I go on quickly, "As for the purity ring, I remember you said it's supposed to be given to your husband on your wedding night. When you're ready, when your body and heart are ready for me in that way, I am counting on receiving that ring from you, all right?"

Cara's cheeks color, and when she says, "I can't wait until that day," my heart melts into a river of pure love for her.

I rest my forehead against hers, trying to summon the courage to do what has to be done. The dream I had about getting a negative paternity test result flashes behind my eyes, and I begin to sweat. *At least Eric's in jail, so I can't go to his house and beat him to death if the results are not what we hope.* My little quip to myself does nothing to make me feel lighter.

"Are you ready?" I ask.

Cara looks pale and terrified but keeps it under control and whispers, "Yes."

I take her hand in a firm grip, open the email, and tap on the attachment. We lean in to read it together, and I read the last part aloud:

Conclusion: *"Based on our analysis, it is practically proven that Mr. James A. Gallagher is the biological father of the child, Christopher B. Gallagher, with the probability of >99.9%."*

I reread it silently, looking for the word "not," but it is *NOT* there. Two little letters form the one word, the only word, I see and care to see:

Is

Is.

Is!

I look at Cara, and we both stare at one another wide-eyed without blinking for a full three seconds. I try not to shout too loudly because Christopher is only a few feet away, but I do shout, "Yes!" And then again louder, "*YES!*" pumping my fist into the air.

Cara begins laughing and sobbing simultaneously, saying over and over like a prayer of thanksgiving, "Oh, God, thank you, thank you, thank you!"

"Cara, I want to shout it from the rooftop of the hospital, Christopher was conceived in love, through *our* love. He is us; Christopher is *US!*"

I take her face in my hands and give her the biggest celebratory kiss I can. "This is a pretty promising sign that Eric didn't touch you, that we were left to ourselves in that room, thank God."

"Yes, I have no doubt now," she says, wiping her eyes with the back of her hand. "Oh, I was so sure the test would show—" Her voice breaks off on a sob, and she reaches for me, all the suppressed emotions pouring out of her.

I take her in my arms, holding her tightly in relief and sheer love for her, my own tears running down my face.

"Shhh, Cara, it's all right now. Everything's okay, babe. It will all be all right now." I hold her for a few beats longer before taking her face in my hands to look into her eyes. "You okay?" I wait until she nods.

We wordlessly hold each other for a couple more minutes, absorbing the good news and everything it means for our future.

I break the silence. "We have a lot to discuss, but for now, as soon as possible, my focus is to make the mother of my son— *MY SON*—my wife."

Cara sniffles and sits up straighter. Her eyes are lit with hope. "I'm ready. I want it as much as you do now." She pauses, and says, "Cara Dawson-Gallagher," trying out the name and smiling at me through her tears. "I love it, but where will we live? How will—"

I interrupt, "Time out. We had only a snack for lunch, and after the good news, I've got my appetite back. I say we order delivery and have a relaxing evening of celebration together, just you and me... And, well, the nurses who come in and out." I chuckle. "We can talk about everything, make some plans, and we'll share the good news with everyone else in the morning."

"Some much-needed time together alone sounds wonderful. I haven't heard from anyone saying they're visiting tonight, have you?"

"Nope. Let's go hold our son, and then I'll call and order food. I'm starving now."

After spending time with Christopher, eating dinner, and preparing for bed, Cara and I lie side by side in the pull-out bed. I relish how momentous this day is, not only because we've learned Christopher is my birth son, but because it means it's highly unlikely Cara was harmed by Eric in any other way but being drugged.

It's our first night together since Christopher was born that we have the answer we need to move forward. Knowing we will be true husband and wife in a few days only makes it better.

"You were wondering earlier what home will look like when we're done here, and I have a proposition for you," I offer.

"What's that?" She comes up onto her bent elbow, cupping her cheek in her hand.

"When Christopher is released, I would like to bring you both home to my house to live until Christopher gets a little older and we get our own place. My mom can help out a lot while I'm at work. You can start your college classes when you're ready. I know how important that is to you, and I'll help in every way I can with that. It will all work out, it will." I kiss Cara's nose. "We'll be married with a baby and will need our space. There's a whole upstairs quarter we can have practically to ourselves."

"I like that plan... a lot actually, but we need to see how your parents feel about it first."

"Done, and they are thrilled, hoping you will be, too. Mom really wants to help out," I say.

"Oh, so you've already spoken to them?" She stops and smiles. "They knew you were going to ask me to marry you, didn't they?"

"Of course. I wouldn't have asked you to live in our house before talking with them first. They were only a little older than we are when they married, so they have full faith in us."

"And my dad? You talked with him, too?" Cara asks.

"Yep, he's one hundred percent on board. I had to ask him for his blessing to marry his daughter, even though it *was* over the phone this morning while waiting for our breakfast to cook," I say. "I wouldn't have asked you that, either, if I hadn't checked with him first. He's excited for us; says he knows we're meant to be together."

"What if he would have said no?" Cara asks with a playful smirk.

"Ah, man, don't make me answer that." I pause for only a beat and say, "Okay, I'll be honest. I would have had to defy him on this one and ask you anyway. It would have zapped a lot of the joy out of asking you, though. It's nice to have his blessing. Also, I have a feeling it won't be long before he and Rachel marry, and she and her boys move into your house."

"How do you know? What makes you think that?"

"Just a guess." I shrug, but I can't hide my telling grin.

"Jamie, he shared that with you, didn't he?"

I can feel my face flush with the uncertainty of whether or not to fib. I decide not to. "I'm not supposed to tell you, but we promised to share everything. Yes, he shared that he's planning to ask her soon. He wanted to be the one to tell you, kind of ask for your permission. You'll have to act surprised when he does. I presumed on my own about her moving into your house when they marry, based on her and her kids living in a small apartment and all."

"That news makes me very happy that I'm not leaving him all alone. It lets me be excited about making our temporary home at your house. Seems like the ideal timing for him and Rachel to have met and fallen in love. Now, we just hope *she* says yes." Cara laughs.

Still lying face to face, we soak up the silence and relax in it, staring deeply into one another's eyes, both sets lit with anticipation and longing for what our future holds.

"I feel like we've been somewhat vindicated the last couple of days, do you?" Cara asks.

I'm not sure what she means. "Vindicated how?"

"From people who would judge us for having a baby 'out of wedlock' as some would say, especially some people from Dad's church." Cara yawns.

I smile, still not seeing the logic. "But we did."

"Yeah, but honestly, we wouldn't have gone all the way if it weren't for that drug. We had a pact. People will know that Eric drugging us caused us to do what we normally wouldn't have."

I lift a brow to communicate that I'm not quite as convinced of that as she is. "Let's just say I'm glad everything worked out the way it did because we have Christopher, and you will soon be my wife. I don't know that I could have gone on much longer with that pact in place. Do you know how hard it's been for me not to show the woman I love how much I love her in the most instinctual way there is?"

I pause, thinking about us being together, and say, "I'm going to take you on a honeymoon when it's time, when you say it's time. My parents and your dad can help with Christopher. I want a do-over. I can't stop thinking about what it will be like when we're both together with no barriers, no boundaries or rules, nothing at all between us—nothing to stop us," I say with a heavy sigh.

She scoots closer, with her lips almost on mine, and says, "Do you know how many times I've pictured it? How many nights I've lain in bed wishing you were with me, and I mean *with* me?" Her eyes are a perfect reflection of my own longing.

"Okay, sounds like we're being brutally honest here, so I'm just going to say it and embarrass you."

"What?" she asks, her mouth even closer.

I can feel her sweet breath fan my lips like the soft touch of a feather, and I want so badly to cover her mouth with mine, but I don't just yet.

"I can't help but imagine pushing into you for the first time."

Cara's eyes close for a second, and she swallows as though picturing it, too.

I say, "Man, just the thought of it... Well, the first time I will have conscious awareness of it, that is. I'm sorry, I can't help thinking about it," I feel compelled to add, "a lot. Do you ever think about us like that?" I ask sheepishly.

"I do, yes. I do more than I care to admit. There have been times I felt I might go crazy with all this waiting, all this *wanting* and not having. I think about the times we came close. I replay those memories all the time."

Her lips touch mine, then, ever so lightly; the only part of our bodies touching, besides our gazes connected by an invisible thread of sheer love.

Our lips stay resting together, not moving, with our eyes communicating every wish, every longing, every dream we have for one another. And when I open my lips over hers and kiss her deeply, urgently, she returns my kiss with all the love and tenderness that is simply Cara.

I break my mouth from hers only enough to whisper, "It's still such a mystery for us, but I don't want us doing anything sexual together until we can be together fully, okay? I know how beautiful you will be, how beautiful that moment will be." I kiss her again more gently.

Being like this with Cara, this close to her, and talking about making love to her is too much—making me physically uncomfortable. I have to shift positions, and her eyes tell me she understands.

"I've got to stop talking about it or go take a cold shower. It has been and will be hard to wait." I realize what I said and grin. "The pun was unintended, yet apropos. Of course, we have to wait until you heal, and I'll wait until we can, but—"

"I totally get it, Jamie. I love you more than I can show you right now. Six weeks. That's how long the doctor said to wait, so that's only five more. And then I will show you... and it *will* be good." She smiles, still looking into my eyes, her own drunk with drowsiness and longing.

"Man, don't I know it? I'm excited to dive into the next chapter of our lives; and tonight... tonight we can sleep knowing our son, *our* son, Cara, was conceived through our love, regardless of us not remembering."

"Mmm, yes." She can barely keep her eyes open and is starting to drift.

"Do you think there was a plan for Christopher to be here, and even through the mistakes and the detours... whatever went wrong, it all still happened the way it was supposed to in the end?"

Cara's eyes briefly flit open. "Hmm. That's part of having faith, I guess, and maybe I have a little more of it now than I did before. I believe you just described *us* and described how Christopher got here. I see him as no less than a miracle."

I kiss Cara one final time for the night and whisper, "Sweet dreams, baby."

Already half-asleep, she replies, "Only if they're about you, Jamie," a faint smile remaining on her lips.

The Browning poem comes to my mind again. Much more than even this morning, the words ring true as I also drift off into the sweet land of dreams where Cara is waiting for me—*All's right with the world!*

Epilogue

"Put me down!" I laugh when Jamie insists on carrying me over the threshold of our brand-new home. It's not as though it's the first time we've been through the front door, or probably even the hundredth, but we did finally get the last of our things moved from his parents' house.

He carries me effortlessly. I'm a lot lighter and Jamie even more buff since we've been working out a few times a week together in his parents' home gym.

"If our bed was set up," Jamie says near my ear before settling me to my feet, "I would carry you straight to our bedroom... maybe have a repeat of last night?" He waggles his brows. "Or, hey, there's carpet in the bedroom." He shrugs and grins, melting my heart all over again.

"Mmm, sounds a lot better than trying to put this house together." I think about our last time together and practically feel Jamie's kisses and skillful hands on me again. "But our time is limited if we want to set things up enough to go get Christopher from your parents and spend our first night here."

Jamie and I drew our own house plans seven months ago and watched the house take shape from the foundation up. Seven months—the same amount of time it took to build our home was the same amount of time it took to grow Christopher inside my body. It's hard to believe he's a year old now.

Jamie's parents graciously deeded two acres of their property on the far end of their acreage to us. "I'll help you with the land you'll need to get you started," Brent had told Jamie, "but the house part is up to you."

This motivated Jamie to learn everything he could about the family business as quickly as possible in order to help it grow and to further secure our future. He's worked hard, long hours over the last year while still tirelessly helping with Christopher.

Recently, Brent has given Jamie more and more responsibility, even allowing him to meet with important clients and broker account deals. Jamie has learned to wear a designer suit well, and when he's all dressed up, ready to go meet with a client, my heart throbs like it did that day over eighteen months ago when we first locked eyes in the school cafeteria. Yes, he still looks into my eyes the same way.

The house we built is not huge like Jamie's parents' house, but it's nice—all state-of-the-art appliances, beautiful beams running across the vaulted ceiling in the main room, and a home office for me to do my college work and for Jamie to work from home when he can.

It's been a year since the shocking day that changed our lives. As Christopher gained weight and was able to leave the incubator at the hospital, Jamie and I almost solely took care of him ourselves outside of his medical checks and monitoring through the nights.

Yet I was still terrified the first night we brought our baby to our temporary home at Jamie's parents' house. It took a few days to relax and let down our guards enough to enjoy him outside of the hospital and to have faith that he was going to be okay.

Our lives might have been turned upside down for a time—they were—but they have since been turned right. Eric is not just in jail; he's in prison. Not only did he drug Jamie and me, and yes, even Jessica—the test results of the drink Eric gave her at Ashley's party came back positive for GHB—but apparently the investigation also uncovered that Eric was supplying the drug to other classmates at school, four of whom were members of the football team. I don't know how long he will be incarcerated and don't ask. I've tried to put everything about Eric behind me.

I attended counseling sessions twice a week for four months after Jamie and I married. I battled a bit of postpartum depression, but the counselor and I were able to work through it with therapy and a low-dose antidepressant safe for nursing mothers, which I no longer need to take. The counselor brought Jamie in on our last several sessions, and she helped us process all that had happened to us.

After our sessions, we both felt more confident and better equipped to step into the future as a family unit of three. It's a true saying that what doesn't kill you makes you stronger, and our little family is proof. We have richer, sweeter lives because of our experiences, and Christopher is our cherry on top.

I weaned Christopher from breastfeeding a few weeks ago, and it was bittersweet. Jamie was beside me for his first feeding and his last, always encouraging and supporting me when I felt like giving up on nursing. Christopher and I finally both got the hang of it, and I will always cherish the memory of the sentimental look in Jamie's eyes as he watched me feed our son.

The advantage now is that Jamie can feed Christopher a bottle any time, and I can gauge better how many ounces he receives, but I miss the bond between Christopher and me that nursing brought. It also means time is marching forward faster than the wind-up toy soldier sitting on the shelf in his nursery.

He's a beautiful baby, and he looks nearly identical to Jamie's baby pictures, with the same cleft in his chin and same dark, curly hair. His eyes have lightened to almost the color of Jamie's, and I see the same blue sky every time I look into them.

Christopher lights up the most when Jamie looks at him and smiles, giggling and babbling more for his daddy than for anyone.

"He said 'da-da;' I know he did!" Jamie's been exclaiming lately every time he gets Christopher to chatter the way only he can.

"Of course he did." I roll my eyes sarcastically, which only makes Jamie all the more try to convince me he did.

The truth is, I do believe Christopher is saying it, I just love to see Jamie fight for the right to claim his is the first name to be spoken on our son's lips.

After much thought, I went in a little different direction for college. I scored high enough on all of my AP exams for each one to count as a class, so I had several hours credited before starting college. I'm pursuing a Bachelor of Arts degree in child and family studies at a local university. It's an online program, and I'll add teaching certification when I'm finished. The certification program isn't online, but Christopher will be older when that time comes, and it will be easier to take in-person classes while Jamie starts his basics online. I've got two full semesters under my belt, but I'm taking the summer off so I can set up our new home and enjoy it.

Dad and Rachel married three months ago, and I want to say they love one another as much as Jamie and I do, but I'm afraid that's too tall an order. With Susan's help, Jamie and I watched Rachel's boys when they went on their short honeymoon, not that they needed much supervision. They're good boys, and it's beautiful to see the way they're so grateful for my dad—now their dad, too.

The boys seem in awe of Dad and their new life and home. I can only imagine how they must feel now after having lost their father so tragically to war and after watching their mom struggle to raise them alone for the last six years. I was happy to pass the baton of my old room to Rachel's oldest son and help them all get settled. My dad loves the boys and treats them as his own— the very thing Jamie would have done with Christopher had things turned out differently for us.

Jamie and I never had the large wedding or reception he thought I might want when he asked me to marry him. I've always wanted to get married someday, but I wasn't one of those girls who, from a young age, dreamed of having a big, fancy wedding and reception; that's never been me. We decided we were happy with the way things were—no hoopla or pomp.

Just happiness.

We were married at the big downtown Fort Worth courthouse when Christopher was two weeks old, and I marveled at the tears that streamed down Jamie's face as he looked into my eyes and repeated his vows. It was only one of the many ways I've been completely convinced of Jamie's undying love for me.

When Christopher was a little less than eight weeks old, Jamie and I took a road trip down the Texas Gulf Coast, like he's wanted to do since moving to Texas, for a wonderful fun-in-the-sun honeymoon. But it wasn't the first time Jamie and I were together—intimately together. That happened one night after Christopher had been home for about a week, six weeks after he was born, and almost four weeks after we were married.

Jamie's parents and Amber had left that morning to visit old friends in SoCal and then take the long drive up to see Megan while she was still on summer break. Jamie had just rocked Christopher to sleep and placed him in his crib. He shut the door quietly, placing a finger over his lips when he saw me in the hallway, and tiptoed back to our room.

"Did you remember to turn on the monitor?" I whispered.

"Yup."

Jamie lay down on his stomach across our bed and resumed a recorded TV episode we had both been watching the night before.

He had no idea what I had up my sleeve for the evening. Since Jamie and I married, I've wanted to do certain things that would... well, please him, even if it wasn't time for me yet, but he wouldn't have it.

"No, I told you, when we do anything together, it will be when we can both be together fully; that's what I want, okay? I also told you I'll wait for as long as it takes."

Little did he know the wait was about to be over.

I had only worn tame pajamas to bed leading up to that night. Knowing Jamie was waiting patiently for us to be together, I didn't want to torture him, right? That night, I put on something new and sexy I had bought at the mall and was saving for the occasion. It was soft pink and lacy with tiny black bows, leaving little to the imagination, but just enough.

I put my familiar robe over it and called out from the bathroom, "Jamie, can you pause that for a sec? I have something to give you."

"Give me?" he asked as he pushed pause on the remote.

"Yes." I opened the door to the bathroom with my hand fisted and walked over to the bed. "Here you go."

I held out my fist for him to open his hand, and he looked up at me warily as though I was about to hand him a live insect.

When he opened his hand and held it out to me, I dropped my purity ring into the center of his outstretched palm. He stared at it as though looking away might cause it to disappear. Head still down, Jamie's eyes slowly moved up to look at me under his thick lashes the way he does that sends tingles and shivers straight to my core.

"Babe," he said into my eyes before looking back at the ring again as if I'd just given him the key to unlock the greatest mystery of all time—maybe I had.

His gaze remained locked on mine. "Really?"

"Really," I whispered as I undid the belt of my robe and let it fall to the floor next to the bed where I was standing.

"Oh wow... wow," Jamie whispered, "am I dreaming here?" His heated gaze roamed across my body long enough to make me feel self-conscious. He looked back up into my eyes, swallowed, and said softly, "You're the most beautiful thing I've ever seen, Cara Gallagher. Come here." He placed his hands on my hips and pulled me onto the bed with him.

The TV set on pause was the only light in our bedroom, and it bathed our bodies in its warm glow, adding to the ethereal feel of our first time together—our first *conscious* time together.

Seeing Jamie, all of Jamie, was like admiring a sculpture carved by a celestial being's own hand. His breath hitched as my fingertips lightly traced the trail of hair along his flat abdomen that I have wanted to follow for so long.

"Damn, Cara, I think this is going to be more than I can bear. I can't believe this is finally happening. I love you, my sweet, beautiful wife."

We feasted on one another, worshiped and explored each other with our eyes, our hands, our mouths—saying the things we have wanted to say for so long but couldn't express in words or in any other way but this.

We unhurriedly took our time, reminding me of the night Jamie climbed in through my bedroom window, but knowing this time we would get to finish what we started. *Finally.* We savored every second of expressing our love until it was sheer torture to continue without fitting ourselves together.

"I can't wait any longer," Jamie gasped when I touched him again, "I want you, babe, more than anything."

The feeling of knowing there were no boundaries, nothing to stop us, and no hurry for anything—until that second—was indescribable.

"Same, Jamie," I said with the same breathless urgency as though our coming together would finally give us both the sustenance we needed to live this day forward.

After waiting for what felt like half an eternity, we were finally at the precipice of that moment, the very second we both had only imagined and dreamed of.

It happened.

When it did, it was good—*so good.*

Everything is good with Jamie.

My Jamie.

THE END

We hope you enjoyed this romance.

If you liked this book, please remember to review it on Goodreads, social media, and/or wherever you got it from.

Thank you for reading!

*FOR MORE BOOKS
PLEASE GO TO 5310PUBLISHING.COM*

You might also like...

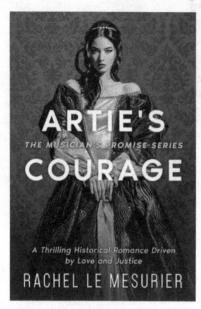

A courageous farm girl's life is changed forever when she falls in love with a charming street musician, opening her eyes to the cruel mistreatment of Mexico's mine workers and compelling her to stand with them against their oppressor — the man she is marrying.

Esperanza lives a charmed life. The daughter of a wealthy landowner, her family is thrilled when she attracts the attentions of the handsome and mysterious Don Raúl, opening the door to a glittering life of opulence for them all.

However, a chance encounter with a charming street musician forces Esperanza to open her eyes to the cruel underworld of Mexico's mistreated working classes, and she begins to doubt everything she ever thought she wanted.

As the people begin to rise up in a bloodthirsty revolution against their oppressors, Esperanza is forced to make choices that she hoped never to face. Esperanza's decisions threaten to tear apart her family, her heart, and the country she loves.

In this brutal world where a few careless words can cost lives, will the price of freedom prove to be more than what she is willing to pay?

Led by strong female characters, *ARTIE'S COURAGE* turns the common damsel in distress trope on its head. Based on real historical events, this thrilling page-turner story of love and courage in the face of adversity follows characters on an emotional journey through laughter, tears, passion, and heartbreak.

You might also like...

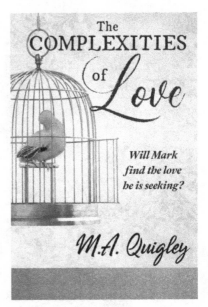

An Australian teen learns about life, hidden love, and family secrets. Mark Cooney grows up aware that there is something different about him and hopes that his parents will never find out.

Mark's best friend Dave disappeared when he was thirteen and returned ten years later. Mark became more and more vulnerable as they got closer. It came with a price.

Tormented by his inner demons and refusing to be controlled by anyone, Dave reveals a secret that he has kept since childhood, which leads to grave consequences for Mark and his family.

The Complexities of Love **is a coming-of-age story about Mark as he confronts the truth about his family and his identity.**

All he yearns for is for Dave to return his love, but will that happen, or will he find someone else?

FOR MORE BOOKS, PLEASE GO TO 5310PUBLISHING.COM

You might also like...

She had always loved being used as the weapon, being both the arrow and the target. But when Eleri learns the truth about the impact of their pasts and all the chaos that they have created, they are tasked with the impossible: to undo the damage they have caused.

Fyodor and Eleri know that they are strong and influential, but **will their power be enough to alter the course of history forever?**

A young woman with a larger-than-life legacy and an incredible sense of self truly believed that what she was doing was right. With all of her being, she thought that she was helping to serve a long-overdue justice.

When Eleri learns that she had been used as a pawn in a larger, evil plot, she has to find it in herself to right her wrongs - even if it means going against everything and everyone she ever loved. The war had been raging since she was a young child, and she had never thought to question it.

When Eleri and her best friend Fyodor discover that their leaders have been doctoring and altering history and are planning to disintegrate an entire population, they realize that they may be the only two who can prevent this atrocity.

In a race against time, power, and their own morals, they can only hope that their willpower and strength are enough to overturn a war that has already begun.

FOR MORE BOOKS, PLEASE GO TO 5310PUBLISHING.COM

You might also like...

After the suicide of her only child, Alice is committed to finding out why her son took his own life.

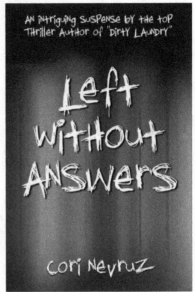

With no warning signs or even a letter, Alice searches for answers regarding her son Hank's death. She turns to Hank's best and only friend, Arnold, for answers.

But Arnold, like Alice's husband, has moved on from the tragedy and pleads her to do the same. **Arnold is confident that revealing Hank's big secret will help Alice grieve.**

But when Alice starts finding sticky notes that could only be from her dead son, her desire for revenge intensifies along with her desperate search for the truth. Alice becomes more detached from her friends, husband, and reality after each note. Eventually, a letter from Arnold provides her with insight and a target: Hank's ruthless bully.

Can Hank's notes provide the answers Alice is seeking before she completely unravels? When she is left with no one and nothing except sticky notes from her dead son, will Alice accept the truth, or will her need for closure endanger the life of yet another child?

Hank, Alice's only child, is dead. Unbeknownst to her, Hank had been bullied for years. Alice is on a mission to find the person responsible for driving Hank to take his own life. Certainly, someone was to blame. Be it one of the bullies who tortured Hank day in and day out, or was it his overshadowed best friend, Arnold, who must have seen more than he lets on.

As Alice searches for answers and closure, the more she learns about Hank's secret life, the more she feels *Left Without Answers.*

You might also like...

In a land destroyed by war, at a time that mirrored the excitements and dangers of the Old West, at a place where both magic and machine collide... a hero will rise from the darkest depths to the glory of freedom and honour.

This hero is Honey Beaumont.

The Adventurer's Guild stands for justice and serves the common man, provided they can pay. With newfound skills and friends in tow, only one hero can find the strength and courage to return to the man who tried to destroy him and make things right for his people.

Embarking on a journey of a lifetime, being a hero is harder than he could have ever imagined, but at least he has his friends by his side to help him save the day.

"**A great read.** This is a book written with several well-developed characters set in a world that has changed dramatically. This book will keep you turning pages. I can't wait to see if there is a following book. **Highly recommend to people who like action.**" — Starred Review 5/5

"**An exciting tale in a unique world featuring Honey Beaumont's magical journey from who he was when he was born to the hero he was meant to be. A fast and exciting read. I couldn't put it down!**" — Starred Review 5/5

FOR MORE BOOKS, PLEASE GO TO 5310PUBLISHING.COM